Praise for *Curse of the Night Witch*

★ "Tightly paced...worthy of every magical ounce... What sets this series opener apart is the author's exquisite use of real Latin American folktales to broaden her fiction, bolstering the particulars of the world she creates here."

—*Kirkus Reviews,* Starred Review

★ "Debut author Aster takes inspiration from Colombian folklore to craft a rousing series opener that's both fast-paced and thrilling. As her protagonists face off against a host of horrors, they learn the value of friendship and explore the possibility of changing one's fate in a world where destiny is predetermined."

—*Publishers Weekly*, Starred Review

"Aster balances a fast-paced plot rife with hair-raising action and snippets of Emblem Island folklore, offering a story about sacrifice and risk-taking that's great for young mythology fans."

—*Booklist*

"A fast-paced island adventure with enough quirks to entice most young fantasy readers."

—*School Library Journal*

"A great fast-paced, high-stakes adventure."

—*MG Book Village*

CURSE OF THE FORGOTTEN CITY

ALSO BY ALEX ASTER

The Emblem Island series

Curse of the Night Witch

EMBLEM ISLAND

CURSE OF THE FORGOTTEN CITY

BOOK 2

ALEX ASTER

Published by Sourcebooks Young Readers, an imprint of Sourcebooks Kids
P.O. Box 4410, Naperville, Illinois 60567-4410
(630) 961-3900
sourcebookskids.com

Library of Congress Cataloging-in-Publication data is on file with the publisher.

Source of Production: Sheridan Books, Chelsea, Michigan, United States
Date of Production: April 2021
Run Number: 5021113

Printed and bound in the United States of America.
SB 10 9 8 7 6 5 4 3 2 1

For my twin sister, Daniella, my first reader and forever friend.

CURSE OF THE FORGOTTEN CITY

1

THE WATERBREATHER

Tor Luna looked down at the girl in the sand and wondered if she was dead. Just moments before, she had washed ashore, like the torn plank of a shipwreck. Her peculiarly pale skin matched her silver hair, and neither was as strange as the marking on her wrist. A rare symbol that matched Tor's.

A fish.

It was the emblem he had spent almost his entire life wishing for. The one he had finally gotten, under the worst of circumstances. The power to breathe underwater.

Tor stumbled to the side as his friend Melda pushed past him to get to the girl, who had surprised them all moments earlier with a warning: "They're coming."

Melda flipped the girl onto her side, revealing a deep

gash along her rib cage. Blood stained the pearls stitched onto the girl's dress. Melda looked over her shoulder, eyes wide. "Engle, get help!"

Engle took off, following her orders without hesitation. Whether he moved with such speed because he had a new respect for Melda after their deadly journey together, or because of the power of her leadership emblem, Tor wasn't sure.

"Tor, *do something*!" Melda said as she firmly pressed the wound. The girl still wasn't moving.

If anyone could save her, it was Tor. A month ago he became the most powerful being on Emblem Island after inheriting all of the Night Witch's abilities. His first new emblem had already sprouted.

And, if the Night Witch's dying words were to be believed, more would follow.

Tor knelt next to Melda on the sand. He placed a shaking hand on the girl's shoulder. It was ice cold. "I—I don't know how."

Melda ripped the hem of her long skirt off and wrapped it around the girl's torso, tying it tight. It didn't take long for the light blue fabric to stain red.

"Wake up!" Melda cried, and her voice made Tor flinch. Those with leadership emblems had especially loud voices. He would know. Before he had made a wish that had gotten him cursed, he had worn the same purple bands around his wrist, marking him as a future leader.

Without warning, Melda took off running toward the water. Tor watched, blood pooling beneath his hands, as she grabbed something buried halfway into the sand.

She was back in an instant and before Tor could cover his ears, Melda put the conch to her lips and blew.

A sound like a siren pierced the salty air, and the girl's eyes flew open.

Behind them, faraway shouts sounded. Tor recognized the three voices. They belonged to Engle, Mrs. Herida, who was the only healer in their village, and Tor's mother—Chieftess of Estrelle.

"You're going to live," Melda said steadily to the girl. "Now who did this to you? *Who* is coming?"

The girl's green eyes suddenly narrowed. One hand found her wound. She sat up, wincing, her long silvery hair caked in sand and blood.

Though her fingers shook, her voice was steady.

"Pirates."

The Vicious Sea

Wherever there is treasure, there are pirates. And wherever there are pirates, there are mermaids.

And wherever there are mermaids, there is hunger.

The sea is an endless cauldron, and pirates sit within it, simmering, accepting both the biting salt and starry beauty.

For any gift the sea gives, it takes back twofold.

Beware of songs sweet as honey that ring through the darkness.

Never make a bargain with a pirate that isn't inked in blood.

Do not trust cloudless skies, for they are almost certainly followed by a storm.

And above all, do not stare too carefully into the sea—

For the sea will begin to stare back.

2

THE CALAVERA

The healer had stopped the bleeding. Tor tried not to look at his hands, stained red right over the lifeline running through his palm. Instead, he eyed the horizon, half expecting ships to appear at any moment.

"Pirates?" Tor said, turning to watch as Mrs. Herida continued to stitch the wound. Though she had applied some numbing oil from willow bark, the girl bit down on her lip with each poke of the needle.

She nodded, face remarkably pale. "Not just any pirates." She whispered the next few words the same way Tor used to say *Night Witch*. "The Calavera."

Tor's mother, Chieftess Luna, knelt at her side. "You're sure?"

She nodded.

"What's the Calavera?" Engle said, who was also facing the sea. "I don't see anything."

Tor felt a bit better. If Engle, with a sightseeing emblem that allowed him to see incredibly far distances, couldn't spot the pirates, then they were still miles away. He wondered how long it had taken the girl with the waterbreathing marking to reach shore. Where had she come from?

Chieftess Luna shook her head. "They're a myth. A group of pirates cursed by the Night Witch to sail forever just short of shore, never to make landfall."

"But now there is no Night Witch," Melda said stormily.

Tor swallowed. "Which means their curse could have died with her."

All of her curses had probably been broken that day, not just Tor's. He remembered the Night Witch's last words.

Make no mistake, Tor Luna, darkness has already set its sights on your village.

The girl hissed as Mrs. Herida put her finger to the stitches, silently speeding their healing process. Then, she turned to Tor. "They took my grandmother. And everyone else." She eyed the fish emblem on his arm, visible. "You can help me, I know it."

Tor hurried to pull his sleeve down. Mrs. Herida was rummaging through her pack for something, distracted. He didn't think she'd seen the new marking he'd been keeping hidden, but he had to be more careful. No one other than his friends and their parents knew what had happened to his old emblem.

When he turned back to face the girl, she wore a serpentine smile, as if she had gleaned his secret and was deciding how to leverage that information.

Melda glared at her. "Who are you? Where did you come from?"

The girl leveled a cold look back at her. "I'm Vesper. And I'm from a settlement of waterbreathers called Swordscale."

Chieftess Luna stood, tanned knees caked in sand. "So, it's real, then? The forgotten city of Swordscale?"

Vesper nodded. "As real as the Night Witch and the Calavera." She gritted her teeth as Mrs. Herida applied a salve to her now scabbed-over wound. "One of our own betrayed us. He led the Calavera to our city and got them through the enchantments."

Tor massaged his temples, a massive headache taking form. "Why did they attack? What are they after?"

Vesper took a lock of her strange silver hair between her fingers. "What any good pirate is after. Control of the seas." She glanced at the ocean, foamy waves reaching toward her legs with every push, closer and closer still, as if the sea was trying to pull her back. "They seek the Pirate's Pearl."

Chieftess Luna's nostrils flared. Tor turned to his mother. "You've heard of it?" It seemed the Chieftess of Estrelle knew much more about the sea than she had ever told Tor.

Her hand formed a fist, the purple leadership emblem vibrant on her wrist. "There is a book. Passed through the family line, written long ago. It speaks of...all of this."

Vesper grimaced. "Good that someone wrote it all down. Swordscales are too superstitious to put those myths to paper. The Calavera came in search of the pearl. It had been entrusted with my people for centuries—but little did they know, it had already been stolen a long time ago."

"By who?" Tor asked.

She shook her head. "I don't know. But the Calavera won't stop until they find it. The pearl controls the sea. If they get their hands on it, they could flood all of Emblem Island, if they wish. They could drain the ocean dry." Vesper took a deep breath. "They're coming. Here. They can't be far behind me. You need to hurry. They plan to take Estrelle and make it their base as they search for the pearl. They'll burn the entire village down to get control. Or they'll burn it just because they feel like it. Now that the curse has been broken, they're desperate to step onto land—and wreak havoc."

Havoc. On Estrelle.

The healer applied a final ointment that smelled of honey and mint. With a nod signaling her work was done, she walked briskly back to the village, no doubt to warn her family of the impending danger.

Chieftess Luna straightened. Tor imagined plans were already being formed in her mind, on how to evacuate the village, where to lead its inhabitants to safety. But there might not be enough time. There were too many people, and they wouldn't be able to get far enough. Not if the pirates' appetite for pillaging was as great as Vesper claimed, and if she was right about how soon to expect them.

Tor and Melda shared a look. She closed her eyes for a moment, and Tor knew she felt the same way he did. That they had both had enough of adventure to last a lifetime. That they were both *tired*. Even Engle, always up for an adventure, looked wary.

When Melda opened those still shockingly gray eyes, a reminder of how wrong their last adventure had gone, her expression was steady. "The Night Witch cursed the Calavera. She might have had something that could stop them." Engle whirled to face her as Melda pulled a coin from her pocket and held it between her fingers.

It was the telecorp's coin, the one that had been enchanted to take them home once their journey to the Night

Witch was over. It glimmered in the sunlight, like it still held power.

Engle stared at it. "You think it can still teleport us between Estrelle and her castle?"

Melda nodded.

Tor never wanted to return to that place. It was there that he had been forced to replace the Night Witch, after she had deemed herself too sinister to fight the evil she promised had its eyes set on Emblem Island.

Tor suddenly realized that even back then she knew the Calavera would come. She had to have known what her death would mean, that curses would break and chaos would ensue. Still, she died and left it all to him, her heir.

He hated her, even more than before.

But Estrelle was in trouble. Tor saw it in the lines of his mother's face as she mentally worked out how they might escape. So, he stepped forward and put a hand over Melda's. Engle did the same.

"We'll be back soon, Mom." His mother looked like she might object, mouth widening—but then she nodded. Likely grateful her son was getting away from the coast.

But before they could spirit away, Vesper spoke. "Wait! I can help."

Melda raised an eyebrow at her, looking doubtful.

Vesper groaned as she stood. Tor's mother reached an arm out to help her up. She moved her silver hair, revealing a marking on her neck, right below her ear. That of a gem.

An emblem.

Tor gaped at her. "You have two?"

On Emblem Island, having more than one emblem was considered wicked. It was why the Night Witch was so feared and why Tor had gone to great lengths to hide his new marking. No one was meant to have more than one; it was too much power to wield responsibly.

Vesper nodded. "In Swordscale, everyone has two."

Tor's shoulders shifted slightly forward, as if some of the weight had been taken away. Maybe he wasn't so alone. So wicked.

He didn't know what the gem emblem stood for, but if she said she could help them stop the pirates from attacking Estrelle, he would trust her. Even if Melda was giving him a look that showed she clearly didn't.

Vesper placed her hand on top of Tor's. And then, the four of them were gone.

The Calavera's Curse

On a still sea, on a full moon, at midnight, it is said that a ship born of smoke and bone can be spotted on the horizon.

It never stops, not for a moment. It doesn't have an anchor. It simply sails on forever, toward villages it cannot pillage. Toward ports with no harbor. Toward land it cannot reach.

The Calavera made their ships from the bones of their victims—and there were many. Once upon another time, there had been a code of honor that ruled the waters. But the Calavera did not just want treasure, they wanted power. So they made their own rules. They sunk each vessel that dared sail their way, vowing to be the last ships on the sea. And the killings did not stop when they reached land. They docked only to wreak havoc.

They had to be stopped.

A brave young pirate offered his blood to the ocean, begging for the Calavera's reign of the seas to be ended. Far away, but always close by, the Night

Witch heard the man's plea. She decided the Calavera had become too strong, threatening even her own dark power.

So, she spun a curse as lethal and cruel as a spider's web. It trapped the Calavera on their ships, sinking them to the seafloor. Only the lead ship, the biggest vessel, named *Tiburon*, stayed afloat. And it was cursed to sail forevermore without ever reaching shore.

3

THE NIGHT WITCH'S SHIP

Wind hissed in Tor's ears as they touched down. His legs felt too stiff, like the bones had been snapped apart and glued back together in the moments it took to travel. Seconds longer than it had taken last time. Tor wondered if the coin's power was dwindling with each use.

They had landed in a small field, atop the cliff Tor had scaled a month prior. The grass was pale, no color within it, except for the occasional black spot. A thick mist smeared the sky and sun away. Tor shivered. It was cold as winter.

The Lake of the Lost stretched before them, hundreds of feet below, gray as Melda's eyes and eerily calm. Engle went still beside Tor. His eyes squeezed shut, jaw set tensely. Melda found Engle's hand. Then Tor's. And gripped them for just a second. Remembering. Vesper watched them from a few feet away.

A moment later, Engle smiled and said, "Let's hope the witch kept her fridge stocked. I haven't had breakfast."

Tor returned his grin. Then he turned and stilled.

The Night Witch's castle sprawled across the mountain, an endless stretch of silver bricks, arched windows, and dozens of towers spiraling into the sky, each topped with a different stone creature, eyes fixed on Tor as he took a step forward.

He wanted to hate it, but something at his core clicked into place, a puzzle he hadn't realized he was putting together.

Tor could almost hear, somewhere deep in his mind, the Night Witch cackling.

"We have to hurry," he said, shaking the feeling away. He made his way to the glinting front doors, made of pure metal.

They had no handle.

But Tor knew what to do. He pressed a palm against the cold iron, and the doors swung open, revealing a room so large and a ceiling of glass so clear, it was as if they were still outside.

"What are we looking for?" Engle asked, his all-seeing eyes already whirling back and forth as he took in every detail of the room.

"I...don't know," Tor said. He turned to Melda.

She shrugged. "Anything having to do with the sea, I guess."

They split up, and Tor took so many different stairs and

corridors that he would have feared getting lost in the maze that was the castle, if he didn't sense a spark of recognition within him, the tug of an invisible thread that spooled down the halls, pulling him along.

He stopped in a library. Its shelves reached the ceiling, and only the top ones held books, accessible by sliding ladder. The others held objects. Gems, scrolled maps, tiny figures. Tor was reaching toward an hourglass when the floorboards behind him creaked.

"How?" Vesper.

He whipped around to face her. "How what?"

She took a step forward. "No one beyond our people is supposed to have that emblem." She nodded toward his arm. "How?"

He splayed his arms, motioning at the castle around him. "The Night Witch. She gave me the emblem I always wanted."

Vesper lifted a brow. "The cruel villain of every kid's nightmares did it out of the kindness of her heart?"

Tor laughed without humor. "No." He wondered if he should be telling her this, a secret he had desperately protected for a month. Melda clearly didn't care for Vesper—maybe didn't trust her. But even though he hadn't made his own mind up about the waterbreather, he found himself saying, "She also gave me her other abilities. And responsibilities." Her green eyes widened and he scowled. "I don't want any of them or anything to do with it. Giving them to me was just another curse, to end the one that had made me look for her in the first place."

Vesper tilted her head at him. "A curse indeed."

She looked like she might say something else, but her gaze drifted to just above Tor's head, to a row of shelves he had looked at earlier.

A tiny anchor sat on the middle shelf, right beside a miniature silver snowflake. Both were small enough to be charms on a bracelet.

"That's what we need," Vesper said, grabbing them. She turned to leave, then spotted Tor's incredulous look over her shoulder. "Trust me," was all she said.

And, since Tor had no plan of his own, he took the hourglass he had spotted, then followed her back down through the castle.

● ☽ ◗ ☾

"Where is she going?" Melda asked with crossed arms and black brows in frustrated arches. Tor, Engle, and Melda had just rushed out of the castle, on Vesper's heels. The waterbreather kept running, toward the cliff, with no signs of slowing down.

"I have no idea," Tor said.

A few feet from the edge, Vesper stopped suddenly. Tor caught up with her, panting. Engle eyed the two charms in her palm.

He watched as Vesper took the tiny silver anchor between her fingers and threw it into the Lake of the Lost.

"Have you lost your mind?" Melda said. Vesper only smirked. She held her hand out as the tiny charm disappeared from view, Engle looking away as it sunk to the bottom.

Tor wondered what he had been thinking to trust a stranger.

Then the lake began to shake. Bubble. Tor took a step back as something broke through the gray water with a spray so large it almost reached them on the cliff.

A ship burst from the lake, bow first, before landing on its surface with another breathtaking splash. It looked huge even from hundreds of feet away—dark as night, with cobweb sails.

Engle blinked. "What did you say your second emblem did?"

Vesper folded her fingers back, stretching them each with a satisfying crack. "I can manipulate the size of things, make objects big or small." She held her hand out, and Tor watched as the ship below shrunk until it was so small he couldn't make it out, then floated up to Vesper's awaiting palm. The tiny charm anchor from before was now connected to the miniature ship, by a chain that trailed down her thumb.

"How did you know the anchor meant there was a shrunken ship in the lake?" Melda asked.

Vesper shrugged, then held up her wrist. There was a bracelet there, holding half a dozen charms. "Because of my emblem, I can sense things that have been enchanted to be small. When we arrived on the cliff, I felt something in the water, and when I saw the anchor, I knew what it was. Some enchanted objects are locked and require keys of sorts to make them larger. The anchor is a key."

"And the snowflake?" Melda asked, her voice tight.

Vesper handed the charm in question to Tor. The tiny flake glimmered once as it touched his skin, a most peculiar hello. "This contains enchantment that will ensure the Calavera don't reach shore."

It was cold in Tor's palm. "How?"

"It will freeze them in place. But not forever. And we'll have to get close enough for it to work."

Melda frowned. "Then what do we do when they thaw again? Estrelle will still be in danger."

Tor bit his back teeth together. He knew what this was—the beginning of another quest he didn't want to be a part of. But Melda was right. The snowflake charm was just a temporary solution. "The Pirate's Pearl would give them control of the seas, right?"

Vesper nodded.

He sighed. "Then we have to find it before they do. And use it to send them back where they came from."

Melda turned away from him. He watched her hands reach for the necklace she no longer had, something she always used to do when she was worried.

Engle shrugged. "I *was* saying just this morning how much I miss adventure."

At that, Melda glared at him. "I certainly don't." She faced Tor. "But I suppose we don't have a choice, do we?"

"I'm in," Vesper said, which didn't do anything to dim Melda's annoyance.

With that, they stacked their hands on the gold coin to return home. It glowed—and a breath later, they were in front of different water.

Estrelle's Sapphire Sea was just as blue as its namesake gem. Shockingly deep blue, all the way until the horizon.

Blue all the way to a dozen ships, made from swirling smoke and bones.

"The Calavera," Vesper breathed.

Tor's grip on the snowflake tightened. Its metal edges dug into his palm. He had never seen ships so big. Even in its full glory, the Night Witch's boat could have fit inside one of their hulls.

Engle swallowed, his vision seeing far past Tor's own, thanks to his emblem. "There are hundreds of them...and they're...they're..."

"Dead?" Vesper said.

"They're more bone than flesh!" he said.

Vesper nodded. "Their curse at work. They have to reach land to become whole."

They were just a mile short of shore.

"Let's go then," Melda said.

There was a voice behind them. "Tor."

His mother.

She stood there, holding something against her chest. A book.

"Mom, I have to go. We have a plan to stop the pirates, at least for a bit. And a ship." He tried his best to stand very straight, chin high, like the leader he never wanted to be, though his fingers shook at his sides. "We're going to find the Pirate's Pearl ourselves and save Estrelle." He lifted his palm, giving her a good view of the scar the Night Witch had left in the center of his palm, a vicious mark across his lifeline. "I might be the only one who can. I have to try."

A tear shot down Chieftess Luna's cheek, and Tor didn't

think he had ever seen his mother cry. "I know." Worry lines etched across her forehead. Her hair, now gray after she gave the color to a goblin in search for her son, was tied back. "I know what you are now, and what you must do," she said. She, more than anyone, knew the sacrifices necessary to protect and serve. "You will need this. Your ancestor saved a pirate who had washed onto these very shores, long ago. In gratitude, we were gifted this book. A guide to the seas. You would have read it, had..." She didn't finish her sentence, but Tor did in his head: *You would have read it, had you not made a wish that had resulted in you becoming Emblem Island's new wicked, the Night Witch's replacement. You would have read it if you had followed the rules, and become Estrelle's future leader instead.*

She handed him the book. Its cover was made of barnacles and shells, stuck together in uneven patterns. Its pages smelled of salt and brine, long yellowed and ripped in some places.

It had a name: *Book of Seas.*

"We can only hold them off for so long," Tor said, holding up the snowflake charm. His mother's eyes darted to it, then met his once more. "Estrelle needs to be evacuated...just in case." *Just in case we fail* were the words he didn't say.

Chieftess Luna swallowed. "Leave it to me," she said,

and threw her arms around her son. "I wish I could have done more to protect you. I wish I could do more now."

Not far away, he spotted Melda embracing her own mother. She must have come looking for her daughter. Engle's parents were far away, at the Alabaster Caves, where they worked as researchers.

He breathed in the cinnamon scent of his mom, of home, one last time, knowing it could be a while before he returned. "You did everything right," he said. Tor pulled away, trying to smile. "I'm the one who made a bad wish."

She took his hand and pressed a nail against his palm. Not on his lifeline, but on the scar the Night Witch had left. "The only way I can fathom letting you leave is knowing what you are. And what you now wield." Chieftess Luna shuddered. "You are strong, Tor, you always have been. Don't let this new part of you change who you are."

He hugged his mother once more. She motioned for Engle and hugged him, too.

"You three, keep eyes on each other," she said, addressing Melda, Engle, and Tor. Then she looked at Vesper and nodded, looking uncertain whether to trust her, but left with no other choice. Tor squeezed his mother's hand.

Then, he turned to the sea.

They waded into the ocean until the water reached their

knees. Vesper tossed the tiny ship into the waves. Under her directing hand, it became a boat just big enough for them to climb inside. It grew, bit by bit, the farther they sailed out. Tor held tightly onto a ledge as it slowly expanded around them. When they were deep enough that his mother was just a tiny figure in the distance, the ship bloomed in one dizzying whoosh and they all were propelled high into the sky. Tor lost his grip and rolled right into the center of the deck, its wooden planks expanding longer and longer, more ship rippling from its center, the sides growing farther and farther away. Only when the water was deep blue did the ship snap into its full form, a mermaid decorating its front.

Tor stood on wobbly legs, taking in the vessel around him. Steady as land, yet fluid as the sea. He wanted to explore its every inch but didn't have time to study the boat as he walked to its bow, salt filling his nose, wind howling in his ears and sending his hair back.

The ships of smoke and bone now sailed so close he could see their passengers. Engle had been right. The crew looked almost indistinguishable from the bone boat itself—skin covering only bits of their bodies. A man grinned at Tor with only half of his lips and a quarter of his teeth.

"Tor." Melda was by his side. Engle was at the other.

He nodded. "I know."

They drifted closer, wind whipping their hair back, salt filling their nostrils.

"*Tor.*"

"Just a little closer."

They were headed straight toward the main ship, a beast with a swirling phantom shark at its front, its jaw opened wide, rows of teeth on full display.

Tor watched the teeth, getting bigger and bigger—and closer.

"Tor!"

He threw the snowflake as hard as he could in the space between their ship and the rest.

The ocean cracked as soon as the snowflake landed, turning to ice that rippled in waves, long sheets that traveled faster than wind. Ships groaned as they came to a halt, frozen in place. And the frost did not stop at the water—it traveled with insatiable hunger, climbing up the hulls, to the decks, freezing the half-dead sailors before they could make a single move, screams hushing almost as quickly as they started. Someone managed to throw a sword, and it, too, froze before reaching the Night Witch's ship, falling with a clank onto the ice.

Frozen—a line of ships and people like a row of statues.

But not everyone stood still. Three men had somehow escaped the ice. One with a wide, black hat floating just above his head—Tor thought him to be the Calavera captain. Next to him stood a man with hair like Vesper's, silver. *The Swordscale traitor*.

Between them was someone who made a chill rush down Tor's spine. A man in a cloak, without a mouth. Just sickly pale flesh pulled too tightly across his face. His eyes were black, only a dot of bright yellow alive within them. He stared at Tor with a frightening intensity, then tilted his head under the cloak just as the ice tried again, rushing at them in full force. Before it could reach the three men, the one in the hooded cape conjured a purple flame in his palm. And with another flash of mauve, they disappeared.

"Grandma!" Vesper gripped the side of the boat, and Tor followed her gaze to a silver-haired woman on another ship, now frozen, reaching toward her granddaughter. She was surrounded by others who wore scaled outfits and had the same strange hair. Vesper's people. Apparently taken from Swordscale and now caught in the snowflake curse just like the rest of them. "It's just temporary," Melda whispered.

Vesper whipped back around. "I know," she said sharply. Then she took a breath. "This is a powerful charm... We have fourteen days before it melts. Two weeks to find the pearl."

"How do you know?" Engle asked.

She shook her head impatiently. "The enchantment

has an energy. When it spreads, or gets larger or smaller, I sense it."

Engle perked up. "Could you make *me* small?" He turned to Tor. "If I was tiny, my hut would be like a palace!" He brightened. "And one doughnut would be like a *thousand* doughnuts!"

Melda glared at him.

Tor ignored him. "Did you see that..." He didn't know what to call it. "Figure?"

"It's called a spectral," Vesper said, walking across the deck. "And if it's helping the Calavera, we have bigger worries than we thought."

"Those three got away," Melda said. "They're going to try to find the pearl by themselves, aren't they?"

Vesper nodded. "The Calavera are the cruelest pirates to sail the seas. With the Pirate's Pearl, they would be unstoppable. No ship or coastal town or even underwater settlement would be safe."

Tor wanted to go back home. He didn't want another adventure. More than anything, he wished there was someone else...someone *else* chosen by the Night Witch. But Estrelle was in trouble, so he found himself saying, "Then we really have to find it before they do."

Engle scratched at his cheek. "How are we going to do that? We don't even know where to start."

The current had moved them steadily eastward, away from the frozen ships. Away from Estrelle. From their families.

Vesper reached toward her bracelet. "This map of the sea has been in my family for generations." She unclipped a tiny charm the shape of a scalloped seashell and let it grow in her palm.

Then, she opened it.

Colors erupted in the air, spraying from the shell like magma from a volcano. They twisted and spiraled—the red of sunset, the blue of fish scales, the green of Zura, the silver of moonlight. The colors spilled down onto the ship's wide deck and puddled until they formed a new three-dimensional painting, brushed across the wooden planks. Tor took a step back as a sea appeared around his feet, followed by mountains and long strips of land.

With a howl, the hues fell into place.

"That's Emblem Island," Melda said, looking down at the strange map.

"And that's us!" Engle said, pointing. He was right. A tiny ship bobbed in the sea, near a line of frozen ships. Tor had to kneel to see it, Melda crouching next to him. It was as if they were giants, peeking over clouds at the island below.

Melda held her head high. "This is a very nice map, but we still don't know where we need to go."

"I have an idea." Vesper turned to Tor. "Can I see that book?"

The *Book of Seas* had fallen to his feet when the ship had grown. He picked it up and handed it over. Vesper flipped quickly, eyes narrowed, scanning the titles of each page.

She nodded sharply. "There. I knew she'd be in it." She closed the book before Tor could get a look at the page. "And the story's the same as the one I've heard."

"Who'd be in it?" Engle asked.

"Mora, blood queen of the sea."

Engle's all-seeing eyes went wide as dobbles. "*Blood* queen?"

"She's known for helping those at sea with acts of vengeance. And she's ancient. She might tell us where to find the Pirate's Pearl, to get revenge on the Calavera. According to lore, she doesn't want to see them gain control of the sea any more than we do."

Melda scoffed. "Sure, she might help us. But at what cost?"

Vesper shrugged. "I suppose we'll find out."

Melda whirled to face Engle and Tor, as if expecting them to disagree with Vesper's plan to seek out the blood queen.

Tor didn't want to go against Melda. He trusted his friend's judgment. But Vesper was from the sea, and they had no other leads.

He peered over his shoulder, at the line of ships frozen in place, farther than they had been before. The current had taken them deeper out to sea with every second.

Vesper had said the freezing enchantment would only hold for two weeks. Which meant the clock was ticking.

"I think it's worth a try," he said, and watched shock bloom across Melda's face, followed by a flash of hurt.

She turned to Engle. "Do you agree?"

Engle looked less sure. But he faced Tor and smiled. Though it didn't meet his eyes. "I'm in. I've never met a blood queen, but she can't be worse than Queen Aurelia, can she?"

Melda was tense as she turned to Vesper and said, "Very well. Where do we find this blood queen?"

Vesper moved her hand through the air as if strumming an invisible harp. The map narrowed to the coast, becoming more detailed as it zeroed in, until Tor saw a cave very clearly. Inside sat a woman with blue scales down her arms and across her chest. She had silver hair, wet across her back, and bright blue eyes. She blinked, and the colors scattered. The map zoomed out again, until they saw themselves on the water once more.

"Look," Vesper said. Tor focused on the ship, where a silver line began to form. It trailed away from the vessel, across the sea, beckoning them to follow. Tor, Vesper, Melda, and Engle walked slowly behind the line as it moved across the deck, up the stairs, and to the ship's upper deck, weaving itself across Emblem Island's coast. It only stopped when it reached an isle, where a miniature version of the same woman that had been projected before sat waiting.

Vesper closed the shell, and the map vanished.

"Now that we've found her on the map, it will show us the best route."

"That's lightning!" Engle said. "Do you think she has food in that cave? I really didn't have breakfast."

Melda sighed. "I find *that* hard to believe," she said. "And we have bigger problems than your endless appetite." She lifted her arms, turning for emphasis. "How in Emblem are we supposed to sail a ship?"

Tor swallowed. He hadn't thought of that. The vessel didn't even have a wheel.

Vesper's eyebrows knitted together. She turned to Tor. "You said the Night Witch gave you her powers, right?"

Melda shot Tor a look. He turned away from it, not knowing why he had shared so much with Vesper. A stranger.

But he had. And they were all on the same journey now.

Tor nodded.

"This ship belonged to her, and it looks different from the others. Look." Vesper stuck her chin toward the frozen row of boats, now tiny in their wake. "They have more ropes, and the masts are not the same. And there's no wheel."

"What are you getting at?" Melda said.

"By inheriting her abilities, this is *your* ship now. Only you can command it."

"And how do you propose he do that?" Melda snapped.

Vesper kept her eyes on Tor. "Think of where we need to go. Picture it in your mind's eye. Smell the sea, the blood queen, the isle, like it's right in front of you."

Tor closed his eyes. He remembered the blood queen from the map, her hair dripping a dark puddle. A chill crept up his spine as he remembered a different woman. A different dark puddle. One like a torn-out piece of nighttime sky. One he had almost drowned in.

There was a burst, and Tor opened his eyes just in time to see the cobweb sails puff up and out, like his father's pastries in the oven or his sheets on the clothesline, filled with a mystical wind. The cobwebs fell away, replaced by a dark midnight blue fabric, speckled with silver stars.

Then there was a snap as the ropes untied themselves from their masts. Once unmoored, they flew through the air, hurtling toward Tor.

He made a move to duck or jump away, but the ropes were quicker, tying around his wrists and ankles in a flash.

Melda gasped, but Vesper raised a hand to keep her from untying Tor.

The ropes glowed faintly gold, for just a moment.

Then the vessel turned, guided by invisible hands, and the ship began to sail.

● ☽ ◗ ☾

Tor closed his eyes against the salt. Water sprayed the deck as the ship plummeted down, right into the center of yet another swell. The ocean hissed as the ship passed roughly through it, the waves so jagged and vicious, it was as if the sea was trying to block their journey.

For an hour they had sailed, Tor tangled in the ropes.

Melda gripped the side of the ship and turned to him, lips pale. "Can you try sailing steadier?"

Engle grinned at her, looking thrilled as he was flung up and down, not bothering to hold on. "Can you try having a little fun?"

Vesper sat below on the lower deck, twirling the charms of her strange bracelet, not looking fazed in the slightest at the rising and falling of the ship. Of course not, Tor thought. She was from Swordscale. The waves were her home.

Tor tugged on the ropes around his wrist and ankles,

feeling like a prisoner. His arm jerked up in response, as if he was a puppet and the ship was his puppeteer.

He gritted his teeth, trying to imagine the Night Witch on this ship. She would never have allowed the boat to command her. No. She would have led it the same way she had led Tor, Engle, and Melda to her lair.

Angry and head pounding with nausea, Tor pulled with all of his strength against the ropes, shooting a firm message through his mind, the same way he had visualized the blood queen's location.

At once, the ropes went slack. They unraveled, landing in a heap at his feet. Slowly, the ship started to sail a bit smoother under Tor's orders, commanding the waves instead of succumbing to them.

"You tamed it," Vesper said from below.

Tor walked to where Melda and Engle now leaned against the starboard. Melda's upper lip curled into a snarl. "I don't like her," she said quietly. "And, more important than that, I don't trust her."

Engle shrugged. He bit into a strange, bumpy fruit Tor had seen Vesper give him, from a pouch of miniature foods on her bracelet that she could grow to normal size for eating. "She seems okay. She *did* warn us the Calavera were coming."

Melda rolled her eyes as Engle chewed with his mouth open. "She was also *dying*. She needed our help."

Tor lowered his gaze. "What are you saying, Melda?"

She looked out to the sea. Estrelle was long behind them, and the coast was just a line, too far away for anyone but Engle to see clearly. "I don't know." She turned back to Tor. "Just—be careful, okay?"

Tor nodded. "I have something for you, actually." He reached down to grab the hourglass he had taken from the Night Witch's castle. Dark blue sand shifted inside. It was tiny, barely bigger than his hand. "I'm not sure what it is, but I thought you might."

Melda studied it closely, tilting the glass up and down. "I think it's an arenahora... We studied them in leadership." A month ago, Tor thought, she might have added a *remember?* to the end of her sentence. But she knew him better now. "They can be attached to a task, or an event, or anything, really. They track time, depending on what you meld them to." She closed her eyes for a moment, pressing the arenahora to her emblem. The sand turned purple to match it, then multiplied, shifting almost completely to one side.

"What happened?" Engle asked. "What did you do?"

Melda opened her eyes and grinned. "I just thought of the snowflake charm that froze the Calavera. If I'm correct, the hourglass has matched with the timing of the ice melting. So we'll know exactly how much time we have, down to the second." She turned to Tor. "Thank you."

He bowed his head, then took a step closer to his friends. "Look, I'm—" He took a deep breath. "I'm sorry."

Engle raised his eyebrows at him. Melda just stared.

"It's too soon for another deadly adventure," he said, trying to keep his tone light, though dread stirred in his stomach like an elixir in a cauldron. "And again, it's my fault."

Melda opened her mouth to argue, but Tor shook his head.

"It is. The Night Witch is gone because of me, and her death is the only reason the Calavera are able to invade Estrelle in the first place." He looked down at the fish painted in silver on his arm. It glimmered in the sun, undeniably pretty. "This wish continues to haunt me...us. I regret it every day. *Every* day." He met their eyes again. "I'm just—I'm just sorry."

Engle planted a hand on his shoulder. "We know, Tor," he said. He walked past them, to the book Vesper had set against the upper deck's ledge—the *Book of Seas*. "You know, sea monsters are even more deadly than the monsters in *Cuentos*." Engle had always been fascinated with monstrous creatures, which had been useful during their last journey. He thumbed lazily through the pages, then grinned. "How about we start with the one about the blood queen?"

The Blood Queen

Once, the sea turned gray. Its creatures fled to its depths, to escape the darkness that had raged through Emblem Island and taken the ocean's blue color with it. A darkness that wished to destroy everything Emblem Island had been—and the future of what it might become.

But the mermaids suffered most of all. Unable to peek their heads up toward the clouds they once loved and soak in the colorful waters that had brought them such joy, some became sinister. Others perished.

Many magical creatures went extinct in those dark ages, unable to live in perpetual night.

When the evil finally passed, a single spark of energy remained. An ember of power, burning at Emblem Island's heart.

The leader of the mermaids, Casamara, felt that spark. She knew if she could reach a drop of that power, she could save her kind. So she volunteered to go to land, knowing that once she did, she could never go back to the water. For a mermaid that leaves the sea can never return.

Casamara found the ember of power and brought a piece of it to her people, saving them. For years she lived in a cove on land, staring longingly at everything she had once loved, before dying of a broken heart.

Once ever century after that, a mermaid is chosen to make the same honorable trek Casamara had, to bring a bit of power to the sea. Most saw the sacrifice as an honor—but one mermaid, Mora, rejected the journey.

Still, against her wishes, the sea washed her ashore. Forever bound to land, Mora swore vengeance against the mermaids. She not only refused to bring the ember of power back to the sea... She took it for herself.

Mora's lifeline extended to twice its previous length, and for two hundred years she lived in the same Cove of Casamara, bringing ruin to her former people. To keep her immortality, she made a deal with the Night Witch. In exchange for being the keeper of keys to the Night Witch's curses at sea, Mora's lifeline would lengthen for every person she killed.

So Mora became a blood queen, keeper of the ocean's secrets and curses, and the deadliest of its creatures.

4

THE COVE OF CASAMARA

The Night Witch's ship was fitted for a full crew. Below deck sat ten rooms, small, but ornately decorated, as if the witch herself had used them once. As soon as Tor entered his after a day of sailing, a candle ignited atop a richly carved nightstand. Cobwebs and dust clinging to the corners of the room fell away, the ship cleaning itself, and a fresh set of sheets appeared from thin air, unrolled themselves with a crack, then floated gently onto the bed. The ship was enchanted. Every inch of it.

Tor looked out the tiny rounded window. Waves crashed against the thick glass, then rescinded, only to return. He closed his eyes and could feel the boat—some part of him had melded with it. It was an extension of himself.

According to Vesper, they would reach the blood queen the next morning.

He swallowed, remembering her story. Just like the Night Witch, she gained power by killing others. How long had it been since travelers had happened upon her cove?

Would she kill them before they could get answers?

The ship lurched to the side, and a vase fell to the floor, shattering into a thousand sea glass pieces. Before Tor could stoop to clean them up, they vanished.

He needed to go to bed. He buried himself under the sheets, and the candle blew itself out.

With darkness came dreams.

And with Tor's dreams came the Night Witch.

He had dreamt of her almost every night since their journey. She was dead, yet immortalized in his mind. It was always the same—the Night Witch smiling as dark power billowed out of her. Still smiling as she dug her nail into his palm. Then, the nightmare ended with the Night Witch plunging off the cliff, becoming a dozen birds, half dark and half bright.

This time, however, Tor's dream was different.

This time, she spoke.

Her hair floated around her, as if she was submerged in water. They were both back in that cave on the cliff. The Night Witch looked almost the same as she had that day, yet slightly changed. Her eyes were glazed over, her skin was slightly translucent. She smiled sadly. "I hope you remember what I told you, Tor Luna," she said, voice deep as the depths of the sea. She took his hand and traced his lifeline. "He's coming. They all are."

She walked away, silk dress dragging behind her.

"Who's coming?" he asked, his voice sounding far away. "How do I stop them? Where do I find the pearl?"

The Night Witch looked over her shoulder at him, head tilted. Her toes lingered just inches from the sharp edge of the cave. She opened her mouth—but before she could speak again, a scream barreled through the air. Her eyes widened.

And she plunged off the cliff once again.

Tor sat up in bed, the candle flickering immediately on. His shadow cast against the wooden wall, long and bobbing along with the rhythm of the sea.

His heart beat fast as an Eve drum. The thin sheets stuck to him in a sweaty layer. He stepped out of bed, and that's when he heard it.

A scream through the darkness. The same one that had interrupted his dream.

Tor rushed out of the room, into the narrow hallway. Melda was already there, eyes wide. "It's Engle," she said, and a moment later, they swung his door open.

Engle thrashed across his bed, the blanket tight in his

fists as he moved violently from side to side. A prisoner trying to escape his chains.

But his eyes were closed.

Melda rushed to him, then hovered there, uncertain of what to do. She turned to Tor. “He’s still asleep.”

Engle screamed once more, and Tor took him by the shoulders. “Engle,” he said firmly. His friend kept moving, head going from side to side, eyes scrunched tightly closed.

“No,” Engle wailed. “It hurts, it hurts!” Suddenly, Engle gripped his own torso, and yelled again, then whimpered, chest concaving as if he had been wounded.

“Engle!” Tor yelled into his face, but his friend didn’t wake. “En—”

Melda grabbed the glass of water from Engle’s bedside and threw it into his face.

Engle gasped and straightened immediately, nearly knocking heads with Tor. His chest rose and fell as he panted, eyes wide, water dripping from his light brown hair, down onto his freckled cheeks.

He looked around, blinking furiously, then gaped at Melda. “Did you just *throw* that at me?”

Melda put down the glass with shaking fingers and raised her chin. “I did.”

“Why in the world did you do that?”

"You were moving like you were possessed!"

Engle pressed his palm to his forehead and winced, like it hurt. "Oh. Sorry about that. Did I wake you both?"

Melda and Tor shared a look.

"Does this...happen a lot?" Tor asked gently.

Engle scratched the back of his head. He shrugged. "Kind of. Ever since...ever since the Lake of the Lost."

A chill snaked down Tor's spine. That was the worst day of *his* life—but he hadn't even considered it was Engle's as well. His friend hadn't spoken a word about it afterward.

The image flashed in his mind—Engle being snatched away by the bonesulkers and pulled deep below the Lake of the Lost's gray waters. Engle had been a whisper away from death that day, would have died if it wasn't for Melda.

Tor blinked, and there was Melda, just inches away from Engle, gripping his hand. "I have nightmares about that, too," she said softly. "Do you...do you want to talk about it?"

Engle stared back at her intently. Squeezed her hand back.

Then, a moment later, he shook her grip away and grinned deviously. "I hope you're not trying to get me to forgive the fact that you threw a glass of water at me. Let's see if you like being awakened like that tomorrow morning!"

Melda's gaze narrowed, and she didn't say another word before leaving the room.

Engle shrugged. "No sense of humor. Goodnight, *Grim*elda!" he said loud enough for her to hear down the hall, grinning at Melda's full name. He stretched his neck to the side with a satisfying crack, and turned back to Tor. "I'm fine, don't worry about me. Go back to bed. Can't have *Captain* Tor bleary-eyed tomorrow, can we?"

Tor wanted to stay and make Engle talk about it. But he stood and smiled for his friend's benefit. Once in bed, he stayed up late, wondering how the three of them were going to succeed on another deadly quest when they hadn't even gotten over the last one.

In the morning, Vesper was gone.

"Your screaming probably scared her off," Tor said lightly, though his stomach was in knots. What if Melda had been right? What if they couldn't trust the waterbreather, and she had disappeared in the night?

They searched every room, closet, and corner of the brig.

"I hate to say I told you so," Melda said as they reached the deck. Just like below, it was empty. "But I *did* say—"

"Anyone fancy some sea-foam for breakfast?"

Tor, Melda, and Engle raced to the edge of the boat and

found a bobbing silver head in the water. Vesper. She was holding a curved oyster shell filled with something sparkling.

She seamlessly climbed up a ladder carved into the side of the boat, shrinking the bowl, and making it large again once she was seated in front of them. Her hair was plastered against her head and shoulders, her scaled dress glimmered in the early-morning sun. She produced a spoon from a tiny purse—one of the many charms of her strange bracelet—and motioned toward the sea foam. "If you get it fresh, just after sunrise, the salt hasn't gotten to it yet, and it's delightfully sweet." She offered the spoon to Engle, who took it without question.

He tried the foam, and his eyes bulged in approval. "It's like spun sugar mixed with shaved glacier ice!" He took more and offered it to Melda. "Here, try it!"

Melda regarded him with coldness. "No, thanks," she said. And whether it was because she was still upset at Engle from last night or because she didn't want to accept anything from Vesper, Tor didn't know.

"Did you go for a swim?" Tor asked.

Vesper nodded and glared up at the sky. "Wanted to find some seaweed to help with the burns."

Engle raised an eyebrow, taking a break from devouring the entirety of Vesper's sea foam. "Burns?"

"My skin isn't accustomed to the sun," she explained,

motioning toward her pale complexion. "It'll burn easily. I'll have to take precautions." She tilted her head at Tor. "You haven't used it yet, have you?"

Tor knew what she meant. The emblem on his wrist, the one he had wanted for years. The ability to breathe underwater.

She was right. He hadn't. After returning from his journey, he'd had no desire to. In a way, he hated it, the same way he hated the witch who had given it to him. It was a reminder that he was changed.

He simply shook his head no.

Vesper frowned at him. "You should come with me next time."

Tor offered a noncommittal smile back.

Engle let out a low whistle. Empty shell bowl in his hand, he stared out past the ship's bow. "That doesn't look like the stuff of nightmares, does it?"

In the distance, the coast became rocky and jagged, stone so crooked even the sea had failed to smooth it. Barnacles scaled up the black stone in swells, sharp as knives. A purple halo of light escaped from the lip of the cave, simultaneously wicked and beautiful—a warning to keep away, as well as a beckoning forward.

The perfect lair for a blood queen.

Tor felt a surge in his bones as the ship creaked to a halt, its sails deflating. The anchor plunged into the water.

"Do we swim the rest of the way?" Melda asked quietly, surveying the dozen yards to the cave, the water too shallow for the ship to pass.

Before she finished her sentence, a bridge of crushed seashells surfaced from the depths of the ocean, extending all the way to the ship's hull.

"I guess she's expecting us," Engle said nervously. And, as if to prove himself after the last night's events, he was the first off the ship, head held high. Melda rolled her eyes and followed.

Then Tor, then Vesper, who treaded more carefully. She looked afraid, Tor realized. Terrified.

After reading the blood queen's story, he was, too, he supposed. But not really, not as much as he should be. Another day, another monster to face—a piece of him still felt numb, left frozen.

Left broken.

He gave her a reassuring smile. "We've faced worse," he said, the lie filling his mouth. The tale had claimed the blood queen was the deadliest of the sea's creatures.

"Have you now?" a voice boomed, solid as a rogue wave, filling the cave. It came from a pool of water the size of a large well. Silver as the moon. The water rippled as her voice came through it.

Then, something pierced its center. The crown of a head. Slowly, bit by bit, the blood queen emerged from the water, water dripping unusually thick from her skin, opaque as liquid silver.

The blood queen looked like royalty who had spent too much time in the sea. Her hair was as stunning as smeared moonlight, her cheekbones sharp, her features delicate. Her skin was the light blue of shallow water, and she wore a dress made completely of pearls.

She walked on the water as if it were solid ground, then stood before them, immediately turning to Tor. "My friend is dead, then?"

A tiny part of Tor lurched, sadness tucked within the part of his soul that did not completely belong to him. "The Night Witch?"

Mora's eyes narrowed, and she bared teeth that did not match her beauty at all—sharp as a shark's, crowding her mouth. "She is as much a Night Witch as I am the great, feared blood queen."

Engle swallowed. "So...you haven't killed all of those people?"

She turned to him. "Of course I have. But who's to say they didn't deserve it?"

Engle blinked at her.

"You aren't going to kill us and drink the blood from our hearts, then?" Vesper said from her place right near the exit of the cave. Prepared to bolt.

Mora shot a look at her identical hair and raised an eyebrow. "Swordscale legends, I presume?" She tilted her silver head. "Though I'm not above feasting on a wicked heart, yours are all..." She looked surprised for a moment. "*Mostly* good. Pure of intentions, at least." She scrunched her face in disgust. "I have no use for that in my elixirs."

Tor realized the pool the blood queen had risen from was a giant cauldron. A bone floated up from its surfaces, then another, and Mora grinned. "Who knows, maybe I'll change my mind...supplies are a bit *scarce* lately..."

Vesper took a step toward the exit of the cave, and Mora's head fell back in a howl of laughter.

Melda stepped forward. "We're in search of the Pirate's Pearl. Do you know of it?"

The blood queen's head snapped to the side with otherworldly speed. She smiled, shark's teeth emerging once more. "The Pirate's Pearl? Now why on Emblem would you lot want something like that?"

"We want to find it before someone else does."

"Who?"

"The Calavera."

The blood queen hissed. She turned in her massive cauldron. "Of course. They've been freed now." She faced Tor. "I feel the power running through you, like high tide rushing in. She gave you so, so much." Mora took Tor's hand in her own. Her skin was slimed over, too soft, like it had permanently pruned underwater. He resisted the urge to recoil. "I'll need your blood," she said. Then, before waiting for a reply, she swiped a sword-sharp nail across his lifeline.

Tor cried out, not just because of the pain, but because of the memory of another person who had done the exact same thing. The wound reopened, and blood came spilling out. She turned his hand over, and Tor watched the pool turn crimson.

Melda lunged forward, as if she was going to push the blood queen away. Before she could, Mora dropped Tor's hand. He winced, watching the cut stitch itself back together. Melda gripped his arm protectively. "What did you need the blood for?" she asked, livid.

The blood queen shrugged. "Another potion. Something I've been working on..."

Anger flared in Melda's eyes.

"Simmer down, little leader, an exchange is an exchange... I'll help you find the pearl." She waved a hand across the pool, and the blood disappeared, replaced by an image. "There is a compass, enchanted to help one find what they have lost."

"But we never *had* the pearl. How will it help us find something we never lost?" Melda asked.

Mora turned to Vesper. The waterbreather seemed to pale even more beneath the blood queen's gaze. "The pearl used to be guarded by those in the forgotten city of Swordscale, before it was stolen from them and hidden well. *She* must hold the compass. And it will lead her to the pearl her people lost."

She stroked the waters again, and the image changed. "The compass was buried on Indigo Isle. And the only way to it is through the Devil's Mouth, a cluster of pointed rocks nearly impossible to navigate through."

Melda gritted her teeth at the image in the cauldron. The rocks formed an impenetrable maze. One wrong turn and their ship would be ripped to shreds. "How do we know you're telling the truth?"

Tor didn't dare breathe as the blood queen turned slowly toward Melda.

Engle swallowed.

But Mora simply bowed her head. "Immortals are cursed in many ways. One of them is that we must always tell the truth. It makes tricking and scheming all the more difficult."

Tor stiffened. The Night Witch was immortal. Which meant...

"You can't escape your fate, boy, as much as you wish to," the blood queen said. "None of us can."

When they left the cave, their ship bobbed before them, not having moved an inch. Mora joined them on the shell path, more barnacle-crusted land appearing beneath her feet as she made her way around the ship, to its very tip. The trail formed a small hill and she climbed it, to the mermaid carved into the ship's bow. Tor watched her place a piece of sea glass on each of the siren's eyes.

"She'll help you in the Devil's Mouth," Mora said.

Then, without looking back, she followed the trail back to her cave, water erasing the bridge at her heels.

Vesper opened her shell charm once more, revealing a path to the next location she gave it—the Devil's Mouth. From a bird's-eye view, the labyrinth of rocks looked treacherous. Tor couldn't imagine what it would look like right in front of him.

"We'll be there in a day," Vesper said.

Engle sighed, disappointed. "What are we supposed to do until then?"

Melda stared at him. "Possibly try not to get killed by a number of creatures from that *book,*" she said, arms across her chest.

"Well, I'm starving," Engle said, to the surprise of no one. "We need to stop for food."

"I'm hungry, too," Tor admitted. "Tonight was supposed to be stuffed purple peppers..."

"Purple peppers?" Engle gasped. "I love those."

"Me too. I would duel a pirate for a few right about now, with toppings—" Before he could finish his sentence, something appeared on the deck. A plate of stuffed peppers, complete with shredded cheese and sprinkled paprika.

Engle stood frozen, mouth in a perfect circle.

Tor blinked. Melda and Vesper didn't say a word.

"Do it again," his friend said quietly, not moving an inch toward the plate.

Tor remembered Vesper's words. The ship belonged to him now. He closed his eyes, then let his imagination wander, thoughts forming like fireworks. He imagined a slew of his favorite breakfast foods, each more delicious than the last, and heard Engle gasp.

Tor opened his eyes to see that a table had appeared, covered in platters holding various steaming foods—flower-stuffed empanadas, scrambled eggs with cheese and spices, maple bacon, toast with chestnut spread, emerald cream puffs, diamond-dusted croissants, fruit plates, canela tea, pink salt hot chocolate, sapphire berry smoothies, bright red cherry juice.

Engle grinned at him. "I take it all back. I'm thrilled you're the new Night Witch." He promptly dug in.

Melda reached for a blue smoothie. "Do you think you can make anything we need appear?"

Tor went through a list of things he could want, and felt, somewhere inside himself, that the ship had a limited inventory. "No. But I think the ship has the same types of things we would find at an inn. And necessities for sailing."

Engle licked his fingers clean of emerald cream. "No day-old bread this time, eh?"

Melda smiled a bit, remembering.

Vesper raised an eyebrow, then shrugged, reaching for the plate of sliced fruit and fried meat. She put a piece of pineapple in her mouth, then made a strange face as she chewed it, as if not expecting it to be tart.

Tor realized it had been almost a full day since he'd had something to eat. He hadn't even had a single pang of hunger until then. Had he gotten used to an empty stomach after so many hours without food during their last journey?

Or was it something else? Time on the sea seemed to flow differently. Every hour seemed to have the potential of passing as quickly as a sputtering ocean breeze or as endlessly as the horizon.

He ate quietly, teeth sinking into ripe, rich, tangy mango. The eggs were soft and well-seasoned, pepper and cayenne bright on the tip of his tongue, and he smiled at the sweetness of diamonds from a stuffed pastry.

It made him think of his father, a cook. What had his mother told him about Tor's absence? And Rosa—his little sister, who always kept the house full of music, thanks to her singing emblem. Did she wonder where he was?

He had left them, again. On a quest that even with a banquet spread before him, couldn't help but seem fruitless.

Tor's breath hitched as the ship suddenly shuddered—there was a sudden crack of wood so loud, it seemed to splinter the air.

The deck flipped violently to the side, sending all the food and metal plates clattering away.

He stood from where he had fallen, arms outstretched for balance, the ship still dangerously tilted to one side.

"We hit something," Engle said, seeing through the front of the ship for a split second. On good days, his sightseeing emblem allowed him to see through objects.

They walked cautiously to the bow of the ship, where the mermaid was whole, the spot next to her in splinters. As if she had narrowly avoided the hit.

Before them, something jutted from the sea, made of perfectly white marble.

Gates.

The Forgotten City of Swordscale

A sailor who nearly drowned surfaced only to claim he had seen a city beneath the water. When his captain went to investigate, it was gone. Nothing to discover.

Hundreds of years ago, waterbreathers took to the sea, fleeing the great Osteria War. Their emblems were useless in the land-based battle, so instead of choosing a side, they left to build their own settlement beneath the sea, with one goal: forever-lasting peace.

And so, the underwater city of Swordscale was created.

Record of any past wars were burned and forbidden to be put to paper—the idea of battle erased altogether. The waterbreathers sought to raise children who did not know anything but peace, convinced it would mean they would never have conflict. Inhabitants were not allowed to leave, for fear that they would see the rest of the world, where war raged on.

And to keep any potential threat out, Swordscales made a deal with the blood queen, who spun a spell that allowed the city to move in an instant. Its location is constantly changing, as it sweeps across the seafloor.

A mysterious moving city of peace, born from war.

5

THE CITY OF SANDSTONE

Vesper reached dangerously far off the ship to touch a finger against the marble gates. "I can't believe it," she said.

Engle scoffed. "Yeah, I can't believe no one's knocked down these gates yet, either. I mean, they're just sitting in the middle of the sea, waiting to sink the next ship that sails by?"

Vesper turned to him. "These gates are typically hidden far below and don't rise for just anyone. They're an invitation."

"To what?" Tor asked.

She grinned. "The hidden city of Sandstone."

There was a moment of quiet.

Engle scratched the side of his head. "The *what*?"

Vesper blinked. "You all haven't finished the book, have you?" She scoffed. "Surely Sandstone is in that book of legends."

Melda crossed her arms across her chest. "I finished it last night." Of course she had. Tor found himself once again grateful for the existence of Grimelda Alexander. "And it is. Both of the two forgotten cities are mentioned." Of course she had. Tor found himself once again grateful for the existence of Grimelda Alexander.

"So what is it?" Tor asked, glancing warily at the gates. An arch curved like a crown sat at its top. Its doors were just barely open.

"An underwater city, like Swordscale," Vesper said, a gleam in her eye. "One that fell centuries ago. Its ruins are said to contain many lost wonders." She touched the gates once more. "Only those invited may enter. It's hidden to everyone else."

Engle raised an eyebrow. "If it's so hidden and secret, how did it fall anyway?"

Melda frowned at the mess below, their breakfast smeared across the deck. "You'll have plenty of time to guess, while they explore. I'll be in my room." She turned to go, then she said over her shoulder, "Don't take long. We can't afford to lose too much time." She held the arenahora above her head for good measure.

Engle's face fell, suddenly realizing he wouldn't be able to see the city. "Fine. Bring me something nice, will you?"

He trailed Melda downstairs, grumbling about their interrupted meal.

Tor was left with Vesper by his side. Her shoulders were pink, the sun already having left its mark on her. The bridge of her nose was now golden, freckles quickly forming. She looked wistfully at the gates. "I've always dreamt of visiting Sandstone," she said. "Never, in a thousand years, did I believe I would." She offered Tor her hand.

For a moment, he considered not taking it. He had loved the sea for as long as he could remember, taking early-morning swims in the ocean before school, memorizing every bit of the seafloor off Estrelle's coast. Swimming was his passion—that was why he had risked everything by making his Eve wish.

But he hadn't swam since he had been made a wicked. He hadn't wanted to...not once.

Which meant he hadn't known what it was like to explore the ocean as a waterbreather.

Vesper looked at him knowingly. "I've spent my entire life in the seas," she said. "Now, I'm above it, air chapping my lips, sun burning my skin." She looked past him, mind somewhere else. "Change is only bad if you let it be."

Tor swallowed. The sea lapped below, reaching for him. Calling him forward with its siren call. His stomach swirled with guilt. Not only for the sacrifices that were needed for him to have gotten the emblem he had always wanted, but also for taking precious minutes out of their time-sensitive journey for something as trivial as a swim. But this wasn't just for his benefit, he reasoned—maybe they would find something useful in the underwater city. Vesper *had* said it was rumored to contain lost wonders. Perhaps one of them would help in their search for the pearl.

He took her hand.

And jumped.

Underwater, Tor saw the gates extended for miles, down to an abyss. Vesper swam through the small opening, beckoning for him to follow.

He did, diving deeper and deeper below.

Past the gates, the water looked exactly the same as it did on the other side. A few schools of fish passed him by without a glance. Vesper swam straight down, farther and farther without a thought. Tor followed, reaching forward, then back, bare feet kicking behind him. He had never been so deep before—deep enough he would have drowned before making it back to the surface.

The sea changed colors every ten or so feet, getting slighter darker. Green, to light blue, to deep blue. The sun above, a golden, fractured light, began to dim. His ears started popping at the pressure.

Something lurched in his chest. His lungs constricted painfully, and his throat ached.

Vesper turned around to face him. Then, she spoke, as easily as she had on land. It had a slight echo. "Tor, *breathe*."

He hesitated, even as his organs seemed to shrivel, eating at themselves. *What did she mean, breathe? Wouldn't the water rush into his lungs, drowning him?*

She shook him by the shoulders, bubbles escaping her lips as she said again, "Tor, BREATHE!"

Unable to take the pressure in his chest a moment longer, he gasped for air—

And found it. No, not air, something thicker. Remarkably smooth in his throat. It filled his lungs, and he took another breath. Then another.

Vesper nodded. "See? Tor, you're a waterbreather. You never have to surface."

Something clicked into place, pieces coming together. The shadow that had been haunting him, the guilt and anger at having been given the Night Witch's power, fell away in the water. Tor smiled wide, looking around as if seeing the ocean for the first time. "I'm a waterbreather," he said, his words spilling seamlessly from his mouth. He said it again, so loud a fish stopped to gape at him. "I'm a waterbreather!"

Tor dove down, bubbles erupting from his every kick. He spun, and turned to float on his back, without water rushing into his nostrils. The sun was just a golden smudge far above. Fish traveled in layers, some closer to him, some near the surface—and he saw it all. An entire world above and beneath him.

He turned back around and kept swimming toward the dark below, Vesper now following him. He swam until the darkness cleared, and then he saw it.

Sandstone stretched for miles beneath his kicking feet, rolling streets of stone carved right into the seafloor. Buildings were domed in the same blue of the sea, masking the city from above, and crafted from compacted sandreal-life versions of the sandcastles he used to make on Estrelle's shores. A palace sat at the center, made up of several smaller, circular structures, each framed by tall columns. The space between them was filled in by giant, blooming coral. Reefs of every color decorated each block of Sandstone, a rainbow trail through the city.

He had so many questions about underwater life, all of which Vesper could answer.

"What do you eat?" he asked her.

She was floating by his side. "Seafood...obviously."

"Have you never had land food? Vegetables?"

She lifted a shoulder. "Now I have," she said, and Tor remembered their breakfast.

"Do you have school?"

"We have elders, who teach us what we need to know. Practical knowledge." She sighed, bubbles escaping her mouth. "Or, at least, what *they* believe is practical."

She dived down, their conversation clearly over.

Tor made his way toward what must have been a neighborhood, once upon a time. Dozens of sandcastle houses sat side by side, the same size as his own home back in Estrelle. Shells had been pressed into some exteriors for decoration. Some had fallen to the ground.

Beyond the neighborhood was a market, a cluster of shops with empty windows. White marble statues filled the town square, giant carvings of a variety of sea creatures, most of which Tor didn't recognize. What else was hidden in the waters beyond Sapphire Sea besides this forgotten city? For the first time in a long while, a spark of excitement lit in Tor's chest. He wanted to see it all.

At the end of the road of statues stood the second-largest building in Sandstone, a swirling tower.

"It's a library," Vesper said. He tensed and whipped around, not realizing she had continued to follow him. She grabbed his hand and said, "Think heavy thoughts. Ships, marble, whales, anchors." At once, they began to lower to Sandstone's road, bubbles trailing from their mouths, as if Tor's pockets had been suddenly filled with rocks.

The moment her feet touched the street, Vesper began walking, as normally as she had on land.

Tor still floated inches above.

Vesper motioned down. "Come on, then. We don't have all day."

He thought about boulders, the hydroclops, mountains, the heaviest things he could imagine. And, a second later, he, too, had landed.

Tor followed Vesper into the library, through an archway. No door. Inside the tower was a swirling spiral of bookshelves, the center completely empty, so Tor could see all the way to the sea-glass ceiling. There had to have been millions of books inside, all neatly pressed into shelves that lined the library walls.

And it was abandoned, just like the rest of the city. "Where did everyone go?" he asked.

Vesper shrugged, making her way up the stairs that went around and around the interior of the hollow tower. "If you believe the legends, one of their own went to land, after years of hearing stories of the darkness and gloom on Emblem Island, only to find it bursting with light and color. He returned to tell the rest, and they abandoned their watery home for the great wonders of island life." She quirked an eyebrow at him. "But leave all of this?" She threw an arm up as she reached the first floor, other hand trailing along a coral-crusted balcony. "Leave this sacred, ancient knowledge behind?" She clicked her tongue against the roof of her mouth and continued, down the rows of books, seeming to be looking for something. "I don't believe that." Vesper stopped suddenly, so quickly that Tor almost bumped into her back. She turned to face him, expression serious. "I think they fled."

Tor blinked. "Fled what?"

She shrugged. "Couldn't tell you. A curse by the Night Witch? Pirates? Invaders? It happened hundreds of years ago. I don't think anyone knows. And these things aren't written down in Swordscale." Vesper bent to look at a row of books, brow scrunched. "They didn't go to Emblem Island, though, that's for sure. There would be a lot more people with water-breathing markings if that was the case, and there aren't. I'd be able to sense it."

"So where did they go?"

She looked away from the shelf to glance at him. "Another

hidden underwater world, of course. One so secret it's not written about in pirate books."

He leaned down, too. "What exactly are you looking for?"

Frustrated, Vesper straightened again, continuing around the long halls of the tower to the second floor. "Something that might not exist. Another myth."

Tor didn't quite like the sound of that. If Vesper had known exactly what to search for in Sandstone, why hadn't she told the others?

As Vesper kept walking around and around the stacks, Tor grabbed a book off the shelf, only to find blank pages inside. He reached for another—blank as well.

"It's enchanted," Vesper said from above, poking her silver head over the balcony. She rolled her eyes. "Press your emblem to the first page."

Tor did as she said, and the moment the fish on his skin came into contact with the paper, ink flooded its pages. A title appeared on the cover—*How to Catch a Gleamington and Why You Never Should.*

He slipped the book back into its place on the shelf, before grabbing another—*Low Tide Rituals for the First-time Seafloor Excavator.* Another—*A History of Mermaid Tail Colors.*

Before he could read another cover, there was a thud above, followed by an "Ow!"

Tor rushed to the fifth floor, halfway up the tower. Here the manuscripts were older. Instead of books, each shelf was packed high with tightly rolled scrolls. Vesper was still on the floor, looking like she'd fallen. She scowled at something against the wall. "Help me get that, will you?"

He followed her gaze and froze.

On a tiny shelf carved into the wall sat a skull.

Vesper scoffed. "Not afraid of it, are you? Legend says more than a thousand years ago a great oracle lived in Sandstone. And power from her fortunetelling emblem is still in her bones."

Tor took a step back. "You're not thinking of taking it, are you?"

Vesper stood, dusting herself off. "Of course not. I'm just trying to get it to work..." She stepped past Tor to reach back into the shelf, gripping the skull by its sides. "Just a little..." She fell back again with the effort, but something had changed.

The skull's jaw had opened.

Inside, where a tongue once was, a tiny, thin scroll unraveled.

"This must be it," Vesper said, reaching for the parchment. It was yellowed and blank. And there were just a few inches of it left.

"*What*, exactly, is that?"

She took the paper between her two fingers. Then, to Tor's surprise, she ripped it. "Legend says if you're able to tear a bit of her parchment tongue off, she will give you a prophecy."

Tor stared at the bit of paper in Vesper's palm. Slowly, words began to be etched on it, letter by letter.

Vesper went still.

The curling script fell into place.

Your quest will prove useless—

and one of you will perish.

Though now impossible, Tor felt very much like he was drowning.

Something groaned below. He gripped the balcony and stared down at the rest of the tower. That's when he noticed it extended underground, beneath the entrance. The hollow center of the library was pitch black like a well, so far down Tor would be surprised if even Engle could see the bottom.

Another noise echoed through it—one like a growl.

Vesper was by his side in an instant. "What was that?"

"I don't know," Tor said quietly. "But it's coming from there." He pointed down at the abyss.

From which something surfaced.

Fast as lightning, a giant squid burst from the darkness, tentacles first. Tor jumped back toward the hall, pulling Vesper down with him, just as a tentacle the size of a hydroclops struck where he had been standing. The stone balcony crumbled away, falling to the depths below.

"What is that thing?" Tor asked, back now pressed against the bottom of the wall. The squid was looping back, its long orange tentacles thrashing around—trying to find them.

"It's a capsizal, a type of squid." She looked panicked. "Some sacred places underwater have keepers, animals who protect them." Vesper shook her head. "I thought, since the city was abandoned—"

Tor tensed; Vesper screamed.

The giant squid's enormous eye took up the entire floor as it gazed directly at them.

"Go!" Vesper said, and Tor almost tripped getting to his feet. He shot down the path that lined the walls of the spiral tower, ducking behind bookshelves, trying not to look behind him.

They climbed to the next floor, then the next. Then, Vesper said, "Look out!"

Something wrapped around Tor's chest so tight he gasped. It pulled him back down in a whoosh, into the middle of the library.

"Fight it!"

The squid had him by the waist now. He punched its tentacle with all his might, but its skin was tough as leather, its suction cups stuck tightly against him.

"Can't you make it small?" Tor asked, gasping for breath.

Vesper was staring at him, wide-eyed, from a balcony. "No, I haven't—I haven't mastered large living things!"

The squid jerked its tentacle—and Tor—forward. Toward its mouth. The creature was at least three times bigger than the Night Witch's ship, its body taking up nearly the entire tower. "Can you *try*?"

Vesper squinted, hand outstretched. Focusing. A vein popped from her neck in strain. But the squid remained giant. And Tor was almost at its mouth.

Vesper suddenly brightened. She took a few steps back, then jumped over a crumbled part of the balcony, landing on another one of the monster's tentacles. It whipped her back and forth, but she gripped its skin and stayed on. Tor watched as she took a charm from her bracelet and made it big—a dagger. Then, she aimed for the soft skin in between the beast's suction cups.

It roared as the blade found its mark, and the tentacle around Tor loosened. "Think thoughts light as a feather!" Vesper yelled as Tor squirmed free.

First, he fell, right down through the tower, after the monster. But the moment he thought of hoppers—the giant red balloons that Emblemites used for travel—the strange underwater gravity stopped, and the sea took over. He swam once more, up after Vesper, toward the very top of the tower. Its stained glass ceiling had a tiny hole in its center, and Vesper made it a big one.

Before the giant squid could recover, its tentacles having smashed the library to bits on its way down, Tor and Vesper slipped through the hole and out of the underwater city.

The Pirate's Pearl

There were once two moons. One, high in the sky like a pearl, and the other, its reflection, pretty on the sea.

The moon high above fell in love with its reflection, and would do whatever it commanded. When the water moon wanted the tides to rush in, the high moon allowed it. When it wanted the tide to again be low, the high moon made it so.

A pirate discovered the influence of the second moon and devised a plan to capture it. One night, he cut the second moon from its place on the sea and folded it up until it was no more than the size of a real pearl.

Devastated, the moon above sought its vengeance, sending a torrent of storms toward the pirate's ship. But the pearl had absorbed some of the moon's powers, and, by simply lifting it above his head, the pirate stopped the water.

News of the pearl spread, and seekers from every part of the island came forward to claim it: the blood queen, the mermaids, the coastal kings, other pirates. They all descended upon the pearl like vultures. It was decided that a contest would be made, to see who was worthy to wield it.

The mermaids were decided to be too wicked.

The blood queen too grim.

The pirates too treacherous.

The kings too greedy.

At last, there was no one left to claim the pearl, and all parties were set to go to war—until a girl came forward. With hair the silver of sirens, she said, *I come from Swordscale, a community happy to be left be. We do not desire control of any sea—simply to be left alone.*

So, the pearl was given to Swordscale for safekeeping until someone worthy of the power could claim it.

6

THE DEVIL'S MOUTH

The ship creaked beneath Tor as he shivered. Melda stood in front of him, arms crossed, mouth scrunched to the side. She was biting her cheek in worry.

"Why, exactly, did the sea monster attack you? Guardians of libraries aren't supposed to do so unless their territory is threatened."

Vesper shrugged limply. "It could have seen us taking a prophecy as a threat."

Melda had the small piece of paper in her hand, its parchment somehow immune to water, droplets dripping right off its edges. "About this prophecy—how much faith can we really put in it?"

Engle was still blinking at it, wide-eyed, like his super vision was studying every curve of ink. "Prophecies don't lie, that's what they say, don't they? That's why we haven't had someone born with a fortunetelling emblem in ages! They're too valuable, only born once a century, isn't it? And when they are, they're smart enough to hide their marking—I know *I* would. Can you imagine the line at your door of people looking for their futures to be told?"

Melda rolled her eyes. "Yes. But prophecies are also riddles. Full of hidden meaning."

Engle raised an eyebrow at her. "I would say this one is pretty clear, Melda."

He was right. Tor repeated the words in his mind. According to the fortuneteller, their quest was doomed. Not only that, but one of them would die before it was over.

Melda was yelling now. "So, what? Should we go home? Let the Calavera destroy Estrelle and the rest of Emblem Island? Give up?" She shook her head. "We knew this journey would be difficult. But we set sail anyway."

Engle scoffed. "You saw the prophecy! We won't even *find* the pearl, our quest will be *useless*. And one of us will die trying. We might as well go home and try to fight."

Melda scrunched her hands into fists. "I refuse to let a skull in a forgotten city rule my destiny. The future is fluid; it can be changed."

Vesper had been very quiet, sitting a few feet away from Tor, towel wet across her shoulders.

Melda turned to her, eyes blazing. "And you? *You* sought out the oracle. *You* asked for this prophecy. Did you get the answer you wanted?"

Tor braced himself for a fight.

But Vesper simply looked up, expression blank. The fiery light in her eyes had vanished. "No. I didn't," she said, before retreating to her room.

● ☽ ◗ ☾

Melda, Engle, and Tor held a vote. They were a team. The prophecy, to be believed or not, affected them all.

"I say we keep going," Melda said.

Tor wanted to be as resolute as Melda. But deep inside, he saw the prophecy as a sign. Maybe they *should* turn back. Maybe they were in way over their heads...

But, in the end, he sided with her. Only because he couldn't bear returning to Estrelle, admitting he had given up.

Engle didn't feel the same way. "I say we turn back."

Melda studied him incredulously. "Since when are *you* afraid?"

Engle did not meet her gaze.

She took a step closer to him, hands on her hips. "Aren't you the one who jumped off the balcony in the City of Zeal first, when the lips told you to? Aren't *you* the one who adored that death trap of a zippy in the rain forest?" Engle turned away. Tor watched his jaw tense, his nostrils flare. "Didn't you say, just *yesterday*, that you missed adventure?" She shook her head. "Since when are you afraid of *anything*?"

Engle whirled to face her. "Since I almost *died*," he yelled, no sign of humor on his face.

Tor stilled. Melda just blinked at him. In the years Tor had known his best friend, he had never once seen him so serious.

"Engle, I—"

He walked away before Melda could finish her sentence. She turned slowly to face Tor, mouth ajar.

Tor wore a similar expression.

"He's not okay, is he?"

He swallowed. "No. I don't think he is."

She nodded. "I can fix this," he heard her whisper to herself, before she trailed after him.

Tor wondered if he should check on them in a few minutes, if only to make sure one hadn't pushed the other overboard. Engle had never said anything like that before, had never gotten *angry*, even. He would talk to him, he decided. Once Engle was in a better mood.

He sat on the deck, sensing the life in the wood beneath him, in the ocean all around him. Felt the breeze against his nose, as if he *was* the ship. The connection that tethered them had gotten stronger in the last day, and somehow, Tor knew he could command the ship to do whatever he wanted, as long as he was aboard.

It was a good distraction, testing this bond. Because if Tor thought really hard about Engle or the prophecy, he found he agreed with him more than Melda. And if he had it his way, he might change their course and turn around in the middle of the night...

But Engle's plan to go back and fight wouldn't work, either. They were no match for the dozens of Calavera ships, all smoke, corpse, and bone. Only with the pearl's power could they send the Calavera back across the horizon, to the bloodied waters from which they came.

And what of the Calavera captain, the Swordscale traitor, and the mysterious spectral? They had disappeared in a flash of light, not relying on the ships to travel. Were they already close to finding the pearl? Would they use its power to destroy Estrelle while Tor was miles away, unable to help?

He sighed, throwing his doubts behind him. All they did was weigh him down.

They needed to find the pearl—*without* one of them dying. He didn't care what the prophecy said. They would find a way to do both.

Tor smiled, then. Because, as impossible as that seemed, they had done it before. A month ago, their lifelines had predicted their death.

Yet there they were.

He took a deep breath. Melda was right. A long-dead fortuneteller wouldn't control their destiny.

Tor spent the afternoon reading through the *Book of Seas.* The more he knew about the obstacles they might face, the better he could prepare for them. He read until he fell asleep, the sun shining across his arms and legs, the clothes provided by the ship light and airy. Perfect for sailing.

When he awoke, the stars were above him, huddled together like gossiping old women. Watching him.

He straightened. The deck was empty. *Had they left him out here all night? Had they gone to bed without dinner?*

No, not empty.

As Tor faced the bow, he saw something that knocked the air right out of his lungs.

The Night Witch stood at the helm of the ship, watching the water. She turned, as if feeling his gaze on her back.

"He knows I am gone," she said. She walked slowly toward him, but the deck did not creak beneath her bare feet. "He knows my curses have been lifted."

Tor wanted to say something, ask a question, scream

maybe, but his body had gone rigid. He couldn't even open his mouth. All he could do was watch as the Night Witch walked closer, then closer still.

Until she was leaning before him.

"It won't be long now. You are in danger, Tor Luna." At her final word, she reached a hand forward and pressed a sharp nail to his forehead.

He awoke again with a gasp.

The sky was not night, but the bruise of late afternoon.

Only Vesper stood on the upper deck, watching him. "Are you...all right?" she said awkwardly.

Tor blinked half a dozen times in a row. He tried to stand but found that his legs were still slightly numb beneath him. His hands shook at his sides. "I'm fine," he said, breathless.

The Night Witch was visiting him, traveling through nightmares. Not to torment him...

But to warn him.

Vesper did not leave. She bent down and sat next to him. "That was a close call, right?"

Tor had to think for a moment what she was talking about, mind still filled with the image of the Night Witch.

She raised an eyebrow at him. "The creature in the library?"

"Oh. Yeah."

"What do *you* think of the prophecy?" She glanced at him sidelong, waiting intently for his reply.

Tor breathed out. Shrugged. "I hope Melda's right, that fate is fluid." Tor glanced down at his lifeline. It was a scatter of deep valleys and high peaks, too messy and complicated to accurately read or rely on. Engle's and Melda's were nearly identical. Did that mean that the three of them were safe?

Vesper followed his stare. "Those don't work out here," she said simply. She held her own palm out. Just a faint rainbow line ran across her hands. Faded almost completely. Impossible to read. "Once, we had some, just like you. But the power of Emblem Island has diminished. The farther away from its land you get, the less it affects you." She tapped against his lifeline. "As far as I've heard, these don't predict what happens on the sea. Not anymore."

Tor hoped the waterbreather was misinformed. Because if both she and the prophecy were right, then it didn't matter that their lifelines were long.

Any of them could die.

He tried to stand again and found that his body had completely thawed. As he stretched his arms over his head, wincing, he thought of something.

"How did you escape the pirates? And get to Estrelle

before them?" he asked. She had reached their shore far sooner than the Calavera. It was a fact that made him a little suspicious of Vesper. How had she escaped the pirates, when the rest of Swordscale had been captured?

She studied him. Tor had a feeling she was making a quick decision, whether or not to tell him. Finally, she shrugged. "There is an underwater portal to Swordscale, just off Estrelle's shores. When they attacked, my grandmother told me to go to it. And I did."

"What's the portal tied to?"

"A sunken ship."

Tor blinked. The bone boat—the one he had visited countless times on his swims over the years, the one he had not dared to touch, because of his town's superstitions against it. "I know that boat," he said.

She lifted a shoulder. "I know." Vesper's face reddened slightly. "I've seen you before...from a distance. Swimming."

She *saw* him. Tor wondered how he felt about that. He teetered between being angry at having been watched and grateful that even when he thought he was the only person on Emblem Island who knew what it was like to love the sea, he hadn't been alone.

"It's how I knew where to go when they attacked." She didn't drop his gaze. "It's how I knew I could trust you."

Later that night, after dinner, Tor fell asleep hoping he could trust her, too.

● ☽ ◗ ☾

Tor awoke refreshed. He had slept peacefully, without a visit from the Night Witch. He had even slept through Engle's nightmares.

He knocked on his friend's door, planning to speak to him in private before going upstairs. But there was no reply. He waited for a few moments before heading up to the deck, where he found Engle at the helm, scouting.

"Nothing yet," Engle said as he approached, grinning at him like he didn't have a care in the world. "But Vesper says we're close."

The waterbreather sat a few yards away, a miniature version of her colorful map spilled onto the deck before her.

No sign of Melda. Tor asked the ship for some quick breakfast of banana hazelnut muffins and canela tea with cream. He was at the hatch that led below, about to bring some down for Melda, when she surfaced.

"Thanks," she said curtly, taking the pastry from him, but not taking a bite.

"Melda, do you want to—" Before he could ask if she

wanted to speak to Engle further, there was a yell from the upper deck.

"You better get up here, Captain Luna!" Engle yelled, mouth clearly full.

A distant field of mountainous spikes laid out before them, like a sea monster barring its teeth from beneath the sea. Tor stared silently at the jutting rocks. They seemed to grow taller the closer they got.

And they were getting closer quickly.

The ship rushed at the Devil's Mouth at full speed, tugged toward it like the pull of a waterfall. Too fast, it would be nearly impossible to navigate through the labyrinth so quickly. Tor closed his eyes and pulled on his connection with the ship, trying to slow it down. His back teeth ground together painfully with the effort. But a current had quickly swept the ship into its hands, whisking it right toward the deadly maze.

That's what made it so dangerous, Tor thought—not only how close the sharp rocks were together, but the speed at which they would have to face them.

Steps clattered behind him, then Melda was at his side. Her expression turned grim. "Right, then. Let's prove this fortuneteller wrong." She turned to him. "Tor, you control the ship, which means you can't hesitate. Move around the rocks as quickly and accurately as you can. Consider the current, the wind, the speed, *everything.*" She turned again. "Engle, while Tor focuses on what's right in front of him, you look ahead. Make sure there aren't any surprises he needs to know about." She winced. "Since you've only been sailing a couple days, it's very possible we'll have a collision. I'll see about finding anything to treat leaks."

She disappeared below, and Tor focused ahead.

They had officially entered the Devil's Mouth. Rocks like giant swords jutted out of the water, high into the sky, mountains cut into slices and used to form a labyrinth. Crashing into just one would undoubtedly sink their ship.

And there were dozens.

An ancient shipwreck laid tangled to Tor's right, a mighty vessel now just a skeleton wedged between two rocks, its sails tattered. White birds were perched on what was left of its mast, cooing sharply.

"Tor," Engle said.

He steadied himself, both feet planted heavily against the deck, head tilted high. He hummed, fishing for the connection of the boat, and, right on cue, the ropes that had once trapped him flew through the air, then wrapped around his limbs, one by one. This time, instead of being a puppet, he felt like the puppet master.

"Ready?" Engle said.

Tor nodded.

Before he could blink, the ship lurched in the unforgiving current and all he saw was rock—thick as the helm and tall as their mast. He pulled his left arm down, the rope going taut, and the ship moved at the last moment, the rock scrapping loudly against its side.

Engle made a face. "That'll leave a mark," he said.

The vessel swayed in the path of another rock, this one thin and tall as a tower, and Tor dodged it more easily, missing it completely. Ahead, two more jutted from the sea just yards away from each other, both a hundred feet high. It was too late to go around them both, the current knocking the ship around like they had been sucked into the center of a storm. Tor gripped the ropes hard and charged forward—toward the narrow space between them.

Engle gulped. "You think we'll fit?"

Tor gritted his teeth. "We have to."

He focused, sweat dripping down his temples as the rocks neared. Closer. And closer. He steadied the ship, maneuvered it carefully, tipping it this way and that, testing the current and grip, making sure it would clear the rocks and—

A wave came out of nowhere, knocking them violently to the side, right toward one of the rocks.

Before the starboard side of the ship could shatter, the

rock simply disappeared. Except no, it was still there—just made so small, the ship went right over it with a slight bump.

Tor whirled around to see Vesper, hand outstretched, panting. “I can’t do that again, not for a while.” She slumped down to the deck. “You’re on your own now.”

Engle grabbed Tor’s shoulder. “Watch out!” He yanked Tor’s arm like it was a wheel, and they barely missed another rock, just a few feet tall, but solid and sharp enough to shred the bottom of the ship like scissors across fabric.

Tor nodded thanks to his wide-eyed friend. Then, he swallowed.

Ahead stood a wall of rocks like a row of daggers, too close together to navigate around.

And the current pulled their ship right toward its center.

“It gets worse beyond it,” Engle said. “There are too many.”

“Turn around!” Melda yelled, rushing up to the upper deck. Tor tried, yanking to the side with all of his might. But the current was stronger, and it pushed him back into the path of the rocks.

There had to be something they could do, something they could use. Tor squinted, digging deep inside himself, calling the Night Witch forward.

Help me, he pleaded.

But there was no response.

His hands turned to fists. Just a few more yards and they would be shipwrecked, tangled in the Devil's Mouth for eternity.

Where were those powers he had supposedly inherited? Where were the gifts the Night Witch had given Tor to help him fight the darkness she promised would come?

Where—

With a crack, the wooden siren carved into the front of the ship animated, its top half breaking free. She looked back at them with sea glass eyes, the ones the blood queen had gifted her. She held a sword, covered in barnacles.

With her head high, the mermaid turned to face the rocks, blade raised. And carved a path through them.

Each monstrous rock the siren struck crumbled into powder. She wielded her sword expertly, slicing through each one that dared block their way, and Tor watched as the great shards of mountain sunk back into the ocean like pieces of broken glass.

She cut each down with long slices, only to turn and slay another.

When they had cleared the wall of rocks, the siren broke completely free and slid silently into the sea. Tor spotted her glimmering tail far ahead, reflecting fractured rainbow beneath the sun, and then the mermaid leapt from the water to cut down the leftover rocks. He navigated the ship easily through the rubble, following the siren like a guiding star.

And as suddenly as the Devil's Mouth had pulled the ship in, it spit them out.

The current left them in calm, sparkling waters.

"Did she...leave?" Melda said, staring down into the sea. She jumped back with a shout as the siren leapt before her, found its place against the mast, and went still.

"Thank you," Tor said, unsure if the mermaid could hear him. He turned around, heart still a racing roar in his chest, and watched the maze get farther away. His arms felt heavy and already sore at his sides. At his command, the ropes at his wrists unraveled, and Tor winced as his knees buckled.

"Up ahead," Engle said.

Tor jerked his head around, fearing another obstacle had entered their path. But there was only a golden line smeared across the horizon. Just a tiny smudge. "Indigo Isle."

How many had died trying to get to it?

"It's ridiculously small," Melda said as they approached.

Indeed, Indigo Isle was smaller than their ship, a single palm tree in its center. Not much more than a sandbar.

They came to a stop before reaching it, the waters too shallow. The moment Tor thought they would need a rowboat, one appeared, tethered to the vessel with rope.

Shoulder to shoulder in the small dinghy, it was a short trip to the isle. The waves were smooth and frothy, and soon Tor's paddle dug into sand.

"Could they be any more literal?" Engle asked. "I mean, I know they say X marks the spot, but..."

X, did, in fact, mark the spot: a red X of colored sand, right in the palm tree's shade. Engle shrugged. "Got to love the uncomplicated," he said, then began using his hands to dig. Tor joined in, then Melda. Vesper spotted a large conch shell a few yards away, with spots along its spiral.

"These are rare and coveted in Swordscale," she told them as she picked it up.

An hour later, they had a hole almost large enough to climb into, and Vesper was resting against the tree, conch shell in her lap. Tor began to doubt the obviousness of the X, whether it was a trap—or a distraction.

Until his fingers slammed into something solid.

Vesper lifted her head at his gasp. He dug more furiously, fingers finding the edges of something hard and square. Melda and Engle leaned back as he pulled it out and dusted off a golden jewelry box, covered in an ornate seashell pattern. One that might have held a ring or necklace once.

"Well, open it," Engle said, sand caked into the sweat on his brow.

Tor did.

Vesper sighed from behind his shoulder. "That's not a compass."

He gritted his teeth. It wasn't. Seated on the cushioned bottom of the box was a ripped, yellowed piece of parchment.

So sorry to disappoint—I've taken the enchantment. Send my best regards to your very blue hair.

Signed Captain Forecastle.

Engle fell back onto the sand, eyes closing. "You've got to be joking."

"Blue hair?" Vesper said, an eyebrow raised.

Melda shrugged, undeterred. "Well, then, we have to find this *Captain Forecastle*."

Engle snorted. "And just how do you expect us to do that?"

She held her head high. "I have an idea."

Tor didn't dare ask what this idea was, in fear that the small scrap of hope he still harbored in his chest would shrivel up and burn in the unrelenting sun.

Melda took the note from the box and held it carefully. They rowed back to the ship in silence, Vesper leaping over the side to swim for a few minutes, complaining of the heat. Once aboard, Melda did not waste a moment. She strode across the deck, up the stairs, and to the helm. To the mermaid. She gripped the railing, and leaned dangerously far over it, note in her other hand. Tor watched as she pressed the parchment to the mermaid's delicate nose as if she were a hound.

Engle whispered, "She doesn't actually think that will work, does she?"

Tor watched as the mermaid's head dipped in a silent nod.

And the ship began to move.

The ship sailed quietly away from Indigo Isle, away from the coast, guided by the mermaid at its helm, who had apparently charted a course to the mysterious Captain Forecastle. For the first few hours, Tor, Melda, Engle, and Vesper stayed on the deck, watching. Waiting.

But the ship did not stop. So, when the stars came out and the sea looked like ink, they went to bed.

The next morning, Tor had just asked the ship to brew him a morning cup of cocoa when the wooden walls of his room groaned, and they came to a sudden halt.

He threw on clothes and ran up the stairs. The sharp beam of sunlight made him squint, reminding him he had been meaning to ask the ship for a hat. Melda and Engle were already on the deck, muttering to each other.

"What's wrong?"

Engle was squinting, which was unusual. "We stopped, but I don't see anything. No land in any direction."

Tor whirled around. Engle was right. They had anchored right in the middle of the sea, no coast or island anywhere to be seen.

Then how had they reached Captain Forecastle?

Melda sighed. "Maybe I was wrong."

Tor walked past them, up to where a wheel might have sat if this was a normal ship. He strode to the mermaid, to see her view.

He swallowed. "No, Melda. I think you were right."

A gaping hole the size of Estrelle's town square had been cut away from the sea and completely drained, all the way to the seafloor. Water rushed down its edges like continuous waterfalls, the rest of the ocean completely intact. Their ship sat perilously close to the edge, just a few feet away from tipping right over the watery cliff and straight down hundreds of feet.

Engle gasped. "There's a man down there!"

Melda blinked. "I guess we found Captain Forecastle."

The Moon's Revenge

After its reflection was stolen, the moon swore vengeance.

Each full moon, the sea sits still, afraid to stir. Fish escape to its depths. Pirates stay in port. Even the wind is quiet.

Tides can rise and fall in minutes.

Ships might shatter to pieces.

The dead surface from the sea's depths.

Beware a waxing moon. For when it becomes whole, chaos ensues.

And even mermaids can be drowned during a full moon.

7

CAPTAIN FORECASTLE

Tor wished for rope. It spooled at his feet, then down across the deck. Engle tied a knot around the mermaid and gave it a tug. "This should hold, I think."

Melda gave him a look. "Very reassuring."

Engle ignored her. "How do you think he got trapped down there?"

Melda sighed. "Probably not by being an upstanding seaman." She turned to Tor. "Be careful. We can't trust him."

Engle rolled his eyes, "What's with you and trust issues lately?" He threw a pointed look at Vesper, who was eating a fresh bowl of seafoam on the lower deck.

Before Melda could respond, Tor said, "She's right. He's probably a pirate."

Tor grabbed the end of the rope; Melda, Engle, and the siren held the other side. Then, he jumped.

He bit his tongue so hard tears blurred his vision as he fell, fell, fell, until Melda and Engle pulled taut on the rope, and he came to a sudden halt, its rough strands burning his palms. "Sorry!" Melda yelled down. He looked up and saw the mermaid peeking over the entrance to the hole, the ship still slightly visible through the water. He was only about twenty feet down.

The ocean was a wall in front of him. Fish swam on the other side, schools of them. Coral bloomed far away. A shark swam over, regarded him for a moment, then swam off. He dipped a hand through and pierced the wall easily, his fingers coming back wet.

Little by little, Melda and Engle released the rope, sending him farther and farther down. He watched the sea the entire way, trying to distract himself from the distance below his feet. And the man who waited there.

The sea's layers were fascinating—each different, just like the sections of the rain forest Zura. Closer to the sunny surface, the sea creatures were a rainbow of shades, like the painter who had imagined them had every color in his palette to choose from. He saw an orange clown fish, a blue wiry-legged starfish, a purple eel with golden spots that slithered like a serpent and changed its shade to green right before his eyes. A tiny lavender octopus swept gracefully by, its tentacles looking tangled together. It was followed by two others, one the pink of watermelon, and the other light blue with white smudges, as if it had decided to mimic the sky.

Farther down, it seemed as if the painter had used up all of his bright pigment. The creatures below embraced the darkness, their shades becoming more muted, just like traveling through Emblem Island.

It became harder to see into the ocean the more he traveled, and, for a moment, he wished for Engle's emblem. Just to see what lived this far down—if anything. Though Sandstone was built into the seafloor, it was not far off the coast, not nearly as deep.

Tor knew they must be in the middle of the ocean, in some of its most vicious waters. He wondered, truly wondered, what lurked this far below.

His feet pressed against sand.

Tor whirled, prepared to defend himself against what must be a crazed man, after being stranded in such a place.

But the man before him was grinning. He had long, curled hair and tanned skin leathered by the sun. Swirling tattoos trailed from beneath his long sleeves all the way down to the tips of his fingers. He took off his captain's hat, revealing a rather large bald spot with an eye tattooed in its center, then gave a bow. "Don't get many visitors down here, as ye can imagine!" he said. His brow furrowed as he surveyed his surroundings, as if seeing them for the very first time. "Might we interest ye in some...er...fermented seaweed?" He pointed at a sad lump of dark green. "Or giant tube eel jerky?"

Tor resisted the urge to gag. "Um...no thanks."

The man kept talking. "Ye sure? Caught it ourselves!" With a slicing sound, he quickly unsheathed a long curved and gleaming pirate's sword from his belt, raising it high in the air. Tor took a step back.

The pirate jabbed the blade straight through the seawall, demonstrating how he had caught the eel. He wagged a calloused finger at Tor. "Takes loads of practice, and even more patience, but the taste is worth it!" He put the sword back and Tor took a breath.

Maybe he should turn around and claim he had the wrong deep-sea prison, Tor thought to himself.

But they needed the compass to find the pearl.

"Are you Captain Forecastle?"

The man took a break from chewing on his foul-smelling jerky—which looked like it required *quite* a bit of chewing—and grinned. "Ye heard of us?"

Us? Perhaps the pirate was mad. "Er...yes. My friends and I are on a quest. And we believe you might have something we need."

Captain Forecastle brightened. "A quest? Love 'em!" He leaned in, and Tor swore something crawled through the man's long curly hair. "Especially the sea kind." He pulled an extremely thin miniature sword from his front jacket pocket and began picking his teeth with it. "Now, what is it ye need?" he asked, tongue darting dangerously close to the blade.

"The compass from Indigo Isle."

Captain Forecastle went still. He sheathed the teeth-picking blade and shook his head. "That compass was stolen from us long ago by the same pirates who got us locked in here, ye know."

Tor felt the bite of disappointment, right in his chest. They had come all this way...

But perhaps the pirate could still be of use. If he could get him to say *who* had stolen the compass...

"How *did* you end up down here?"

Captain Forecastle sat himself down on what looked like an overturned barrel, halfway dug into the sand. "That there's a long story, but we were wrongly imprisoned, swear it to our last breath! A curse doled out from the sea itself, a curse for a curse..." He poked a finger through the sea wall. "And cruel as the rushing tide. Could try to escape by swimming through here, but would drown before reaching the surface. The curse even kept us alive, to suffer in this watery tomb for eternity. Don't eat this because we need to." He winked as he took another rubbery bite of jerky. "But because it tastes so nice."

Tor nodded politely and was about to ask another question when the pirate interrupted him.

"What is it yer after, boy?"

Tor swallowed. Something told him not to say it, but the words tripped off his tongue nonetheless. "The Pirate's Pearl."

Captain Forecastle smiled again, teeth half rotted, some covered in jewels he unquestionably stole. "Now that, we can help ye find."

Tor stilled. "How?"

"Well, we know where our compass is. We'll lead ye to it, then to the pearl."

Tor remembered Melda's warning. They couldn't trust a pirate. There was something about it in the *Book of Seas*, but he couldn't remember the exact warning. "And in exchange?"

The captain grinned even wider. "Ye know, a true bargain is a scale. It must be even on both sides..." He shrugged. "All we ask is that ye free us."

That didn't seem so bad to Tor. They needed him out of the hole to help them find the compass, anyway.

"To be clear, by *us* you just mean *you*, right? It's just...the way you speak?" He didn't need to be unleashing some sort of sea spirit or demon by freeing the pirate.

Captain Forecastle frowned, then nodded.

Tor pretended to consider it, then sighed. "Fine. You have yourself a bargain."

"Grand." He put two hands on his belly, surprisingly bulbous for a man who had been subsiding on eel jerky. "Hope yer friends have strong arms."

Tor was let up first. When Engle hauled him up over the side and onto the deck, Melda nearly collapsed with relief.

Vesper stood. "Did you get it?"

Tor scratched the back of his neck and winced. "Not exactly." It took all four of them to get Captain Forecastle up. Tor was very sure they would drop him on more than one occasion, but at the end, the mermaid seemed to put in a little effort, and he made it safely aboard, flopping like a fish.

Vesper looked him over and scrunched her now-freckled nose.

Captain Forecastle didn't seem to notice as he straightened and took a step toward her. "A waterbreather, eh? Look just like a mermaid, with that hair."

Vesper stiffened, then promptly walked to the other side of the ship.

Captain Forecastle shrugged. He turned to Engle and Melda. "Now how on Emblem are ye four sailing a ship of this size?" He scratched at his beard, long, curly, and exceptionally unkept. "Where's the wheel gone?"

"*That* is none of your concern, pirate," Melda said with disdain.

Captain Forecastle gripped his middle and laughed. "Pirate? A pirate *steals* things, roams above the sea, is part of a crew, goes on quests." He shrugged. "We've been stuck in those depths for years, would reckon the title of pirate wears off if ye don't do much pirating." He tilted his head at her. "Would say *yer* more of a pirate than us."

Melda scoffed. "We haven't stolen anything!"

He raised a thick brow. "Oh? Assume you went to Indigo Isle, in search for the compass, eh? If it had been there, would ye have taken it? Would it have belonged to ye?" He laughed again. "Besides, yer sails have gone gold at the edges. Someone's stolen something."

Tor looked up—and Captain Forecastle was right. Had they always been that way? Tor couldn't exactly remember; the gold was too subtle.

Melda glared at him. "By your own logic, then, I'd *reckon* your title of captain has expired, too. Unless you had a ship and crew in that hole?"

Captain Forecastle stopped to consider that. He frowned. "All right, then, we're pirates."

Melda rolled her eyes. "Glad we got that cleared up."

The pirate puffed out his chest and walked proudly across the ship. "Suppose ye'll be wanting to know where we're headed?"

Tor sighed. "Yes."

"Grand!" He took off his hat, then reached inside, his arm going farther than was supposed to be possible, disappearing all the way up to his shoulder as he rummaged around. Finally, he pulled out a spyglass, opening it up with a flick of his wrist.

He put an eye to the telescope, and Engle looked like he was about to say something, then shrugged. "Nuttier than a cashew," he murmured to Tor, before returning to a bag of saltwater taffy Vesper had given him.

Tor watched as Captain Forecastle looked through the spyglass for a few moments, nodding and muttering to himself, before flipping it over to look through the opposite end.

Melda gave him a pointed look. "Tell me when Captain Cuckoo picks a direction." She shook her head as she retreated down below.

Tor ventured over to where Captain Forecastle stood, twisting the spyglass longer and longer in his hands until it stretched more than five feet, the weight tipping the pirate a few degrees short of falling off the boat. "Um—how is that going?"

He closed the spyglass up to a tiny stub in half a second. "Swimmingly! Now, let us think a minute on where to go."

Tor wanted to ask what on Emblem had he been doing before, but forced himself to be calm.

Captain Forecastle tipped his head this way and that while he muttered to himself. "Well, they'd have first gone to Troutsnout, to get provisions, maybe Amara if they had some gold to spare—*beautiful city, that*—then, straight-away to Scuttlepig to sell... No, that'd be too risky, too many people looking for the pearl, they'd go somewhere less seedy, somewhere with plenty of buyers. Somewhere it would be hidden, 'til talk of the pearl surfaced again." He pointed a finger at nothing in particular. "*That's* where it'd be, no question!"

"Um—and where is that?"

Captain Forecastle gripped him by the shoulders, close enough that Tor's eyes watered at his stench. "Perla, my boy! The City of Seekers."

Perla. A major fishing city, one he had always wanted to visit.

Tor nodded. He could work with that. "Great. I'll set a course," he said, trying to sound more experienced than he was. Captain Forecastle was no doubt trying to find a way to commandeer the ship—he didn't need to know how the vessel worked. Or about Vesper's bracelet, which was undoubtedly valuable. "Why don't you go find a room below and get freshened up? Everything you need should be waiting for you."

Captain Forecastle nodded, thankfully lowering his arms. He sniffed himself, then frowned. "Suppose we *could* use a bath." He smiled. "Maybe four." He planted a hand on Tor's shoulder, laughing, before walking away.

When Tor was sure the pirate was downstairs, he went over to Vesper. Soon, they were staring down at the shell charm's map, coating the deck in color. "That's us, and that's Perla," she said. "It's far. Six days' journey, if the wind's on our side. Seven if it's not."

Tor swallowed. They didn't have much time. By Vesper's own assessment, and Melda's arenahora, the ice keeping both The Calavera and Swordscale prisoners would only hold for ten days longer.

"Then we have to hurry."

Vesper nodded. She turned away, and Tor took a step forward. She had been distant the last day, avoiding them more than usual.

"Are you all right?" he said.

She raised an eyebrow, as if shocked he was asking her such a thing. "I'm fine. Worried about my people, obviously." She smirked. "It's also no secret that your friends don't like me."

"Engle does." He shrugged. "Though, honestly, it might be because you keep giving him sea snacks." Tor frowned. "Melda just...has a hard time trusting people. We all do, after..." He cleared his throat. "She *wants* to trust you. We all do." Tor held her gaze. "We *can,* right?"

For a moment, Vesper stilled. Then, she smiled. "Of course you can."

● ☽ ◗ ☾

It was afternoon before Captain Forecastle surfaced, wearing a fresh cotton shirt underneath his tattered jacket, and a new set of pants. His boots weren't caked in sand anymore, and his beard looked freshly combed through, no crawling critters in sight.

He gripped the sides of his now-gleaming hat. "This is a *fine* ship ye got yerselves." He peered sidelong at Tor. "How did ye say ye procured it?"

"None of your business, pirate," Melda said, giving him a pointed look as she passed him by.

Captain Forecastle shrugged. He turned to Tor. "So where will we be making port? Ponterey or Fort Sickim?"

"We won't be," Tor said simply.

The pirate's eyes bulged. He pointed up at the sky without looking. "What nonsense are ye spouting, boy? It's a full moon tonight!"

Tor looked up; the shadow of a full moon was already starting to show. He had read that legend in the book and didn't take it lightly. Still, he didn't have a choice. "We're on a tight timeline. We can't afford to spend an entire night docked."

Captain Forecastle sputtered, then scoffed. "Ye won't be on a tight timeline once yer in an underwater graveyard!" He muttered to himself, shaking his head as he walked the length of the deck. "A death wish! Fish below, help us. Captain Forecastle, on a ship during a full moon! We know better than that!"

Melda raised her eyebrows at him and said sweetly, "If the decision isn't to your liking, we would be more than happy to bring you back to your *hole*."

Captain Forecastle pursed his sun-cracked lips and straightened. "Unnecessary. I suppose we'll face whatever wrath the sea has in store for us."

That evening, Tor asked the ship for a feast to keep their mind off the moon, which now shined whole above them, a gleaming orb like an eye. Watching. Waiting.

A long table appeared on the deck, framed by richly crafted wooden chairs, a clean white tablecloth billowing atop it. One by one, gleaming silverware fell with tiny thuds from nowhere, before a dozen domed platters clattered into place at the table's center.

They took turns removing the domes, revealing steaming hot bacon-wrapped meats, almond-crusted fish, triple-baked pink potatoes, maple moraberry glazed chicken wings, and buttered garlic vegetables.

Everyone ate like they were famished, especially Engle, who always had food on his mind, but no one as vigorously as Captain Forecastle, who sucked on bare chicken bones and licked oil from his fingers, making Vesper look like she wanted to gag. They watched him eat in silence as he dipped his hands into the whipped fruit and salad, foregoing silverware altogether, then lifted a soup bowl to his lips and slurped enthusiastically.

He lowered the bowl only when it was empty, then bowed his head sheepishly at their stares. "It's been...a while since we had a feast this mighty."

Engle blinked. "I've never seen anyone eat more than me," he said, frowning down at his plate. He looked like he might just finish the rest of the food out of spite, but before he could lift the fork to his lips, there was a chime like a clock reaching midnight.

And the ship stilled.

Captain Forecastle hauled himself up with a groan and wiped a silk napkin roughly across his mouth, letting it drop onto his plate. "Get ready to see the sea as it truly is," he said, before chugging an entire glass of ale. It dripped down his chin, then absorbed into his beard. "Because it's not hiding its true face any longer. It's just taken off its masquerade mask."

Tor stood, along with the others. He swiped a hand through the air, and their dinner disappeared, along with the furniture.

Another chime rang through the night, echoing loudly across the water. Tor, Melda, and Engle found each other, backs pressed together, each choosing a direction to look.

"The book says even mermaids can drown on a full moon," Melda said quickly. "That means *you* can, too, Tor, even as a waterbreather." She shook her head. "The sea can't harm us if we're not in it. Our best bet is to try to stay on the boat, by whatever means necessary."

Engle swallowed. "I read the same story, Melda. The ship's no use if it's shattered into pieces."

One last chime.

Then, there was a knock. On the side of the boat, like knuckles against a door.

No one moved.

Three more knocks.

Captain Forecastle turned to them, sneering, clearly still upset at not having gotten his way. "Well, are ye going to get that?"

Tor swallowed. He, Melda, and Engle inched toward the starboard side. He peered over, to where the knocking had come from.

A young boy looked up at them. His lips were blue, his skin bloated and pale. His hair was an inky mess plastered to his head. He stood firmly on the water as if it was as solid as sand. "Would you let me in? I'm drenched. And cold. So cold."

He looked dead. Tor was pretty sure he was dead. Yet here, and solid enough to be knocking on the ship's side.

Captain Forecastle nodded. "We must be in the Tortuga Triangle," he said. "Famed for its ship-sinking storms. Those who have drowned rise to the surface under the light of the full moon here..." He shrugged at Engle's horrified look. "We told ye."

Tor looked to Melda. She had tears in her eyes as she beheld the boy. "Don't you have somewhere you need to go? A...better place?"

The boy shrugged, blue eyes turning to stare at her. "I don't know. They just left me behind. I fell in, and they kept sailing."

One by one, more figures emerged from the water, rising

until their feet were firmly on the sea. And they each turned toward the ship.

The boy looked back at the other figures and growled. "I was here first!" he yelled at them as they neared, some running. "I get first dibs!"

Melda took a step back, almost knocking into Captain Forecastle. "First dibs on what?" she asked, breathless.

"On a new body," he said.

Back in the middle of the deck, Engle gulped. "Well, they can't get *on*, can they? The ship is big and—"

Vesper's eyes bulged. "The ladder!"

Already, a woman had climbed almost to the top, her bloated face peeking up over the side. She grinned fiendishly. "Would love to have silver hair in me next life," she said, eyes fixed on Vesper.

Tor shot his hand forward, and the ship obeyed—the ladder fell away, and the woman's eyes bulged before she slipped down its side.

He peered over the railing once more, and there were dozens of them, surrounding the ship, fighting for who got to be closest, some trying to climb atop others.

"There's a man up there! Looks weathered, but he'll do!"

"I wouldn't mind being a child again."

"I'll take anything, get out of me way!"

Melda gripped Tor's wrist. "They're going to find a way on here, we need to start moving, *now.*"

Tor reached for the ship, sensing it around him. He pushed.

But the vessel did not move an inch. It felt stuck, trapped, the sea around them having gone heavy as molasses.

"Can you free it?" Melda asked, staring at his face, now twisted in effort.

"I'm trying," he wheezed out, forehead a mess of folds as he continued to push. It was like trying to move a boulder.

The ship groaned, but did not break free.

"You can ask the ship for almost anything, right? Ask for something helpful. Ask for—" Melda's eyes brightened. "As for a fishing rod and a giant turnip!"

Tor gaped at her. "What?"

She glared at him. "You didn't read all of the stories, did you?"

"Um—"

"JUST DO IT!"

He blinked, and then there they were, on the deck. Melda wasted no time, grabbing the rod and turnip and shoving them at Engle. "You're the animal expert. Care to catch a sea monster?"

Engle grinned, then ran after her, to the front of the ship.

"Keep them at bay," Melda commanded over her shoulder.

The dead were banging on the ship with all their might. Some were trying to lift others up onto the deck. They fell right back into the water, only to resurface. More followed, until there were hundreds.

He asked the ship for buckets of water, which he, Vesper, and Captain Forecastle tipped over, onto the dead. They sank again to the sea, hissing, momentarily subdued. But it only bought them minutes.

They tried fire next, which only seemed to annoy the dead. They became more agitated, desperate, sinking their sharp, dirty nails into the wood. Some tried to punch right through the hull.

"Not to worry, ships like this fine beast are practically impenetrable," Captain Forecastle said, just as something smashed below. Wood splintered. "Er, *practically*."

Before Tor could run down and try to keep them from breaking in through the side of the ship, there was a sharp hiss and spin as Engle's line went taut.

It jerked forward, and Engle skidded across the deck. He would have gone flying into the water if it wasn't for Melda's quick arms pulling him back.

Tor rushed to help, Melda holding Engle, and Tor holding her, leaning back as far as they could—

And then they were off. Whatever Engle had caught with

the turnip was big enough to pull the ship free from its frozen place in the water.

The dead yelled and sank below to avoid being run over as the ship sailed away.

Tor looked over Melda's shoulder and could see the shadow of something gigantic beneath the sea, pulling the ship along, hook lodged in its mouth.

"The fishing rod won't last long," Engle said through his teeth, gritting as the beast pulled harder and faster still.

"Neither will we," Tor responded, almost losing his grip on Melda. She groaned as her fingers began to slip, and Engle was pulled forward—

Without any warning, they all flew backward. Tor landed on the deck with a thud, the wind stolen from his lungs. He gasped and gasped until the air returned.

"The line snapped," Engle said, face still red with effort. He stretched out a hand to help him up. Tor took it.

Melda peered over the side of the boat. "I don't see anything," she said. "I think we got away from the dead."

Engle gulped. His eyes were fixed on the horizon. "And how do we get away from that?"

Tor squinted. He couldn't see it, not through the darkness, not miles away. But a second later, he stilled.

A wall of water that bled into the night sky was rushing

toward them, building on its way, already taller than a cliff. A hundred feet high, it swallowed up the sea, swept it all into its wrath.

Captain Forecastle let out a low whistle. "Maybe we should have stayed in our hole, after all," he said to himself.

And maybe they should have listened to the prophecy.

Tor reached blindly for Melda's hand. And she reached for Engle's. "To adventure," he whispered.

"To adventure."

"To adventure."

The wave roared on. Tor had to tilt his head to see its top. There was no way to avoid it, no way out. It was over.

He closed his eyes.

Vesper shook his shoulders and his eyes flew open. "I did steal something," she said quickly, snapping a charm from her bracelet. It looked just like the snowflake they had used on the Calavera.

But this one was in the shape of a cloud.

She handed it to Tor, and he looked one last time at the rushing wall of water, so close he could feel its spray on his cheek, then pressed the charm to the deck.

And, as if carried by a cloud, the ship rose from the water.

Tor dug his fingers into the wood of the deck, steadying himself, melding completely with the ship. They were just inches above the water, and the wave was right there, almost atop them, cresting just above them—

With a groan from the pit of his stomach, he gripped the invisible reins of the vessel and sailed it up into the sky, missing the wave by the length of his hair.

Then higher still, high enough to smirk at the moon.

Only when Tor was sure they were well out of the sea's path did he dare rise from the deck, his legs shaking beneath him. He took a few wobbly steps to the railing and looked down. The sea sat far below, flat as a mirror, and nearly as reflective. The wave had vanished.

"We're...*flying*," Melda said breathlessly, now at his side, shaking her head ever so slightly.

"This. Is. Lightning," Engle said, running his hands through his light brown hair, making it stick up in all directions.

Captain Forecastle planted a heavy hand on Tor's shoulder. "A captain of the clouds." He laughed sheepishly. "Forget what we said earlier." He shrugged. "Impending death...makes ye say things."

Dread coiled in Tor's stomach. It had been too close—too close to dying. He hadn't had a plan, or options, or a way out. He had ignored the book's warning, and it had very nearly gotten them killed.

The thrill of flying wore off quickly, it seemed. Melda frowned and whipped around to face Vesper, who was standing very still, watching the sky around her with quiet awe. "Were you just going to keep that cloud charm you took from the Night Witch's castle to yourself? Didn't think to speak up when those sea zombies almost boarded the ship? Or when we nearly died in the Devil's Mouth?"

Vesper swallowed. "I—I was saving it. For when we really needed it."

"And that was *yours* to decide, why?"

Vesper glared back at her. "I didn't want to waste it."

"No, you just wanted to *steal* it. Probably sell it to the highest bidder! Only gave it up because *you* were about to die, don't pretend you did it for the good of *us*." Melda scoffed. "If it was up to me you wouldn't even be here."

Vesper looked as if she'd just been slapped.

Engle laughed nervously, putting himself between the two. He placed a hand on Melda's shoulder. "Simmer down, *Grim*elda. If it wasn't for Vesper and her sticky fingers, we'd be among those sea zombies."

Melda didn't stand down. She continued to give Vesper a look that could shatter glass before sliding away from Engle and storming downstairs.

Captain Forecastle rubbed his palms together. "Our first

onboard squabble, how delightful!" He frowned. "Say, what's the name of yer ship?"

Tor turned away from him. "It doesn't have a name."

The pirate let out a low whistle. "Every ship has a name, boy. Tis terrible luck if it doesn't."

Tor ground his teeth. He couldn't afford to ignore another pirate's superstition. "Name it what you want," he said.

Captain Forecastle brightened. He ran a hand along the ship's railing, then licked his palm from top to bottom, making Vesper's lip curl in disgust. He nodded, then turned and declared, "This here's *Cloudcaster*."

Engle shrugged. "I like that, actually." He motioned around him. "Not terribly creative, but certainly good enough."

Vesper didn't say a word as she left the upper deck. He hoped she stayed well away from Melda.

Tor leaned against the side of the ship. He never thought he would be looking *down* at the sky. Engle joined him. They both stood staring, clouds like mist around them, the stars bulbous and bright, the moon a disappointed face.

"What are we going to do?" Engle said. He motioned in the vague direction of Melda and Vesper's cabins.

Tor sighed. "Melda really doesn't trust her."

"Well, I don't think her stealing something from the Night Witch helped much."

Tor turned to his friend. He had heard Engle screaming again last night, thrashing in his bed from nightmares. By the time he had gotten up to wake him, his friend had gone silent. Tor had waited up another hour just to make sure. A part of him had hoped that being on another deadly adventure might have been somewhat therapeutic to Engle. Or simply distracting. But his nightmares were relentless.

"Do *you* trust Vesper?"

Engle bit at his cheek, tilted his head at Tor, and turned back to the sky. He reached for a cloud, only for it to go right through his fingers, not anything like the spun-sugar consistency he had likely imagined. He stared at his fingers disappointingly. "Cold. Clouds are *cold*."

"Engle."

He shrugged. "Why would Vesper risk her life by going on this journey if she wasn't really trying to save her people from the Calavera? What could she be hiding?"

Tor closed his eyes against wind that numbed his nose and whipped against his cheeks. His dark hair likely looked a mess. As he and Engle abandoned the deck—where Captain Forecastle laid on his back, hands behind his head, *starbathing*—Tor said, "That's what I'm trying to figure out."

The Golden Comb

The fairest mermaid that ever swam had locks so golden, the sun became jealous. Her hair flowed in a halo, curls draping down her back all the way to her tail, which was made up of scales that glimmered like diamonds.

No one can shine as bright as I, the sun said, so it banished the mermaid below the sea during the day. She could only surface when the moon hung high and darkness turned the ocean black.

The mermaid mourned the brightness and blueness of day—but on one dark night she met a sailor, alone on the deck of a great ship. They spoke for hours, until the sky turned pink with dawn.

Not wishing to be parted from him, the mermaid took a golden comb from her hair and gave it to him. "Comb the water with this, and I will find you," she said.

But before they could meet again the sailor's ship sunk, and the mermaid watched her newfound love die, unable to save him, unable to surface while the sun still shined.

He was lost, as was the gift she'd given him.

It is said that whoever finds the comb, and uses it to brush the sea, will be able to catch a mermaid.

And that mermaid will grant a wish.

8

SIREN'S WHARF

Tor knew the enchantment wouldn't last forever. When he awoke, the ship had already started to sink beneath the clouds. Anyone looking up during the fine, bright morning would see a great ship careening toward the sea, looking like it had sailed straight out of the golden pool of sun.

"Pity," Captain Forecastle said. He was still laid out on the deck, and Tor imagined he must have slept out there, showering in starlight. He claimed it was good for the skin, giving one a glow from within, and Tor thought perhaps he'd been right. The pirate didn't look as weathered as he had before. "Could've spent the rest of our days up here, with want of nothing."

Engle rushed to the side of the ship, grinning as it neared the water. "Make the ride down a bit fun, will you?"

Tor sighed and shifted the boat, commanding it into

a nosedive, wind whipping their hair back. Engle screamed out in delight, and Melda, who had just come up, looked like she might vomit. Tor gripped the mast for dear life as the ship plummeted, plummeted, plummeted—

And landed with a splash large enough to wake a sea monster.

Tor fell back, laughing, and Engle rolled across the deck. Melda tried to scowl, but a grin broke through. "All right, you two have had your fun for the day." She stood, rubbing her back with a wince. "I imagine we made up some time while flying," she said.

At once, the wood was bathed in colors, the map coming to life. Vesper stood a few feet away, shell charm hidden in her palm.

Captain Forecastle's eyes nearly bulged from his face. "What kind of map ye got there?"

They ignored him. And Melda ignored Vesper as she stepped forward.

"You would be correct," Vesper said firmly. "We're just a day away from Perla, with the wind on our side."

In a moment, the map was gone.

Melda nodded sharply, then strode to the lower deck, where Tor had made a breakfast spread appear. Ice bananas, bitterberry porridge, cinnamon spiced yogurt, blueberry juice, and purple avocado awaited. He watched as she fixed herself a bowl, then walked as far away from them as possible, sitting against the last mast. She had brought the *Book of Seas* with her.

Engle made a face. "That breakfast is looking a little light."

Tor rolled his eyes and added a basket of peanut butter muffins and peppermint roll bread.

The pirate hobbled over. "I can't help but notice there's no ale..."

Tor gaped at him. "It's just past dawn!"

Captain Forecastle put his hands up in surrender, then walked away, muttering to himself.

Engle took a break from breakfast only to tilt his head and say, "That looks like a town."

Tor couldn't see anything. Captain Forecastle produced his spyglass, pressed it to his eye, and nodded. "That there's Siren's Wharf," he said. "Nice little town. Devoted to all things mermaid. A few jolly pubs. Good sweets, too." He turned to Engle. "Have ye ever had sea salt caramel bars?"

"Can't say I have." Engle turned to Tor.

"No."

"But you just heard Melda and Vesper. We made up more than enough time."

Tor didn't look up.

"We need to get provisions for the journey!"

"The boat has everything we need."

Engle's eyes narrowed, like he was trying to think of another reason to stop in the seaside village. He brightened. "I read that book! The *Book of Seas*. It says the mermaid's comb was lost to time. Maybe it's *there*. If we can find it, we get a wish, and we can just wish for the pearl! Then we don't even need to go to Perla, or get the compass, or *any* of it."

Tor glanced at Captain Forecastle. "Have you heard any talk of the comb?"

The pirate nodded. "Of course. Every pirate and their captain has searched for the thing."

"And how likely is it that we'll find it in Siren's Wharf?"

Captain Forecastle glanced at Engle, whose eyes were pleading. "Er, there's always a chance, right?"

Engle punched at the air and jumped around.

Tor rolled his eyes. "One hour. In and out."

Maybe a break in a new village was just what they needed.

Melda didn't look pleased as they were docking, very predictably reminding Tor about their deadline. Her protests fell dead in her mouth when she saw a small ribbons shop by the harbor. She gave him a look. "*One* hour."

Once they were off the ship, Engle said, "Not to be a downer, but how do we know no one will steal it?"

Vesper shrugged. "Because we're taking it with us." Moments later, the ship was tiny in her hand, and she stuck it in her pocket.

Captain Forecastle blinked. "Brilliant emblem, lass."

"Yes," Melda said, mouth tight. She turned to Vesper. "*Do* try not to steal it and sail away without us." She walked briskly toward the ribbons shop.

Vesper sighed and ducked into a shop advertising enchanted cream to shield from the sun. Her shoulders had turned a bright, painful-looking red.

Siren's Wharf was a small village with a harbor that could only fit a few nice-sized ships. Many more rowboats crowded the dock, which seemed to be arriving from just down the coast, where a neighborhood of houses had been built along a sandbar.

The town square looked modest, but crowded. The wooden shops had been long stripped of most of their color, courtesy of the salty breeze, and stood no taller than Tor's hut back home. Most only fit a handful of people at a time, but that didn't stop them from crowding inside. Many seemed content simply to point out objects in the window. Tor scrunched his nose. Down the boardwalk, a fish market had been set up, and something smelled sour.

At the center of the marketplace Tor saw something that stood out altogether in the humble village, in its shining richness—a giant statue of a mermaid, perched on a rock, hair reaching her waist.

"They idolize them," Captain Forecastle said. "Which only means they've never seen a real one in the wild." He shook his head. "There're many species of mermaid, ye know. Most don't know that. Sirens are the *worst* kind." His shoulders twitched like a chill had snaked down his spine. Then, he grinned, gaze landing on a pub called the Crusty Barnacle. "Excuse us, boys."

Engle shrugged and headed toward a shop that looked entirely made of gingerbread called Lolly's.

Tor grabbed him by the back of the shirt. "None of that. We're here to find the comb, like *you* suggested. Remember?"

Engle sighed, then followed him through the town square, all the way to the siren statue. A small fountain was positioned at the bottom of her tail. She stood so tall, Tor had to lift his chin to see her face.

"It looks like she's combing her hair, doesn't it?" Tor said, studying the statue closely. Her fingers were positioned right at the top of her tresses and were stuck together, like they had been holding something.

Perhaps the comb had once sat right in the siren's grip.

Tor sighed. If it had, it was gone now.

"Throw a coin in, and your wish will come true." Tor turned to see a hunched over old man standing there, with a wide, toothless grin. "This here's an ancient, enchanted wishing fountain."

Engle immediately went for his pockets, only to find nothing but crumbs. Then, his eyes narrowed. "Hey, there isn't a single coin in this *wishing* fountain." He turned to the old man. "Are you taking them?"

The man quickly hobbled away, just as Melda strolled across the square. Her typically unruly black hair had been fashioned into a single braid at the side of her head; a glimmering golden ribbon weaved through it. She was holding a large text against her chest, and Tor wondered how she had possibly already found time to locate a bookstore.

"Melda?" Engle said. She brightened, a finger going to her braid, as if he might say something about it. "Do you have *dobbles*?"

She glared at him and sighed. "Yes. Ever since last time, I've made a habit of carrying currency with me." Engle opened his mouth, but she stopped him with a hand. "And *no,* I won't be gifting you any."

Melda walked away, and Engle trailed after her. "Not gifting! Just *borrowing*. I'll pay you back!"

Tor walked into the bookstore. It smelled of paper and salt and had a muggy feel to it, like a library at the bottom of a ship. The space was small but efficient. Shelves reached all the way to the ceiling, and across the walls was a wallpaper of book spines. A silver spiral staircase sat at its middle, and Tor watched the woman atop it. She reached for a book at the other end of the shop, and the staircase suddenly moved, spiraling like a top beneath her, gliding across the wooden floor like ice skates before coming to a stop.

She looked down at him, glasses slipping to the bridge of her nose. “Can I help you?”

“What do you know about that statue?” he asked, pointing behind him at the siren.

The woman pursed her lips. “A lot, I suppose. It was the first thing built in Siren’s Wharf. And it’s the most solid, tallest thing in the village. No shop or house is allowed to be built taller than it, out of reverence.”

“Has the statue changed over time?”

She raised her eyebrows at him. The woman was thin, with a head of curly white hair, like a living dandelion. “It’s made of stone, boy.”

“I know. Just—” He stopped himself. Better to be specific. “Did it used to have a *comb*?”

The woman smiled. “You’re observant, I’ll give you that.”

She pursed her lips again, deciding something. Then, she shrugged. "Yes, she did. It's the lore of our village, but some truly believe it. Believe Siren's Wharf was built around it, founded on the power of the comb." Tor must have looked hopeful, because she frowned at him. "Now don't go running off on a treasure hunt. Even if the stories are true, that thing is long gone. Probably in a museum somewhere. Or at the bottom of the sea, for all I know."

"Thank you." Tor rushed out of the shop. He remembered the blood queen's words—the enchanted compass could find anything someone had lost.

If the siren statue had once held the comb, perhaps they could use her and the compass to find it.

And if they found the comb, all they would have to do was wish for the pearl.

Engle was right. Wishing for the Pirate's Pearl seemed a lot easier than having to compete with the Calavera, a Swordscale traitor, and a spectral to find it...

Most importantly, by changing their plan, perhaps they could change fate and avoid the oracle's deadly fortune altogether.

Yes—they needed the comb. Tor swallowed. To use the compass to find it, the siren statue would have to be holding the enchanted device. But they couldn't afford to come back to Siren's Wharf once they located the compass... He could ask Vesper to shrink the statue, but stealing the town's prized possession seemed like it would bring them endless trouble.

Tor brightened. Maybe, they didn't need the entire statue for the compass to work, just a piece of it.

He approached the statue once more, looking for something. A crumbling bit, small enough no one would notice it was gone—

"Looking for a souvenir?" The hunched-over old man was back again, this time holding up a transparent pouch full of powder. "Shavings from the siren statue," he said, lifting a small blade, grinning. Tor saw he did have one tooth, hidden far in the back. "Said to bring luck. All sailors would be wise to keep a piece of the siren statue on their ships."

That might work, Tor thought. If they put the shavings on the compass, it might lead them to the comb that had been stolen from the siren statue. "How do I know it's genuine?"

The man looked offended. "That's my work, right there." He pointed to the siren's tail, to its very tip, where part of it had been clearly shaved down.

The old man bartered until he was blue in the face, before finally accepting Tor's offer of the only thing he had in his pocket—a single dobble.

Tor took the small sack and clutched it in his palm,

hopeful. They might not have found the comb, but if he was right, this was the next best thing.

Now, all they needed was the compass.

The market had flooded with more and more customers, most happily sipping their large mugs of salted ale, window-shopping and chatting in the sun. A few street vendors fried fish right on the street, along with kelp kabobs and grilled shrimp, coated in an apricot chili glaze.

His mouth was watering by the time he reached the harbor, where he found Vesper surrounded by a small crowd. A woman had her by the wrist.

"Your *hair*!" she cried out. "Siren silver, it is." She turned behind her and motioned furiously. "Come, take a look!"

Another woman boldly reached out a hand to touch her head, and Vesper bared her teeth at her. But it only seemed to make the women happier.

"Just as I'd imagined one! Could it be? Have your kind evolved to walk like us?"

A young woman looked around in a panic. "If that's true, maybe they're all around us! And we didn't even know it!"

"How *old* are you?" a young boy said, clutching his mother's skirts.

Vesper pulled away from the crowd. "I'm *not* a siren," she said sharply. But part of her look frazzled. Unbalanced.

She rushed to the harbor, the crowd at her heels, then threw the ship into the water. It grew from charm to full-blown ship in half a blink, and, before the townspeople could gasp at the sight, she was climbing up its ladder and hiding herself below.

Melda strolled down the dock, Engle at her side. He was holding a caramel bar. Tor wondered how much whining he'd had to do before Melda had caved.

"Where's Forecastle?" Tor asked.

She shrugged, tying one of her old ribbons around her mermaid book, then to her wrist, perhaps to make it easier to carry while she climbed up the side of the boat. "You *did* say an hour. I wouldn't be too gutted if you decided to leave him behind."

Engle carried the rest of his caramel bar between his teeth as he followed her up the ladder.

Tor didn't know why he expected timeliness from a pirate. He rolled his eyes and headed straight for the Crusty Barnacle.

The door wasn't cut correctly for its frame, allowing the sounds of shouting and bad fiddling to seep out into the street. Glass shattered, and laughter followed, along with calls for another serving of ale. Tor took a breath and stepped inside.

A thick, wooden bar dominated the pub, and behind that was an intricate wooden carving that ran the length of the wall.

Five mermaids were perfectly crafted, laid on their sides so that their tails served as shelves, filled with all sorts of elixirs.

Captain Forecastle was seated at a round table, surrounded by a horde of sailors. Glittering pieces of some game Tor wasn't familiar with were laid before him. But not nearly as many as there were in front of everyone else.

"We're good for it!" he was saying, as he demanded more pieces. "Trust us, we're more than good for it, look—"

He caught Tor's eye and raised an eyebrow. "Thought ye'd be sailing off by now."

Maybe they *should* have left without him.

Tor crossed his arms. "We have a bargain. Remember?"

Captain Forecastle shrugged. "If ye want to be rid of us, we'll take no offense. This here's a good village. And we've got new friends." He grinned at a table that most certainly didn't grin back. He tilted his head at Tor and said through the corner of his mouth, "Got any dobbles, boy?"

One of the sailors stood. "I *knew* it." The men at his right and left stood, too. "You're not leaving this pub until you've paid what you owe, pirate."

Captain Forecastle laughed nervously and stood, hands coming up in defense. One of the men flinched. "That's a *nasty* lifeline you have there."

The other men looked, too, and gasped.

Tor hadn't seen it yet. But now was no time to investigate. "Run!" he said, and they bolted for the door.

The pub owner made a move to block them, then shrugged, as if it wasn't worth the effort.

They barreled through the door, and down the block, the sailors at their heels.

As they ran, Tor swore he saw something from the corner of his vision: a floating hat, just like the one the Calavera captain wore. He turned abruptly, careful not to slow down, but whatever he thought he saw was gone.

Melda was on top of the ship, mouth ajar.

"Ye better get that thing moving quickly!" Captain Forecastle yelled, gasping like he hadn't run in a great while.

"*You* just focus on hanging on," Tor yelled back.

The moment they reached the boat, Tor leapt onto its ladder, climbing just high enough for the pirate to fit beneath him. Then, with a quick close of his fist, the ship's sails puffed up, and they bolted away.

"Farewell! So long! Good, bloody day!" Captain Forecastle said to the sailors shouting at him from the dock, turning to wave his hat in the air, just one hand and foot on the ladder.

Tor climbed the rest of the way with anger hot in his stomach. If they didn't need the pirate to help them find the compass in Perla, he'd have gladly left him to the wrath of the sailors.

Melda stood waiting, eyebrow up.

"Don't ask," he said, walking past her downstairs. He suddenly had a raging headache, and all he wanted was a nap. Just as he passed Vesper's room, though, he heard a hushed voice.

It sounded like she was *speaking* to someone.

He pressed an ear to her door.

"*Please*," she said. "I'm begging you—"

The plank beneath his weight groaned and she cut off. Tor knocked on her door a few moments later, and Vesper answered, face flushed.

"Yes?" she said moodily.

Tor peered inside. The room was tiny, no place to hide. She was alone. The large conch shell she had found on Indigo Isle sat on her desk.

"Lunch," he said simply, before snapping his fingers and making a tray of food appear in her room.

Then, he turned on his heel to talk to the only people on the ship he could trust.

Melda listened to Tor recount what he'd heard with flared nostrils. She undid and redid the ribbon in her braid, which gleamed brightly in the waning sunlight.

Less than a day away from Perla. From the compass.

And, possibly, with the statue shavings' help, just hours away from the pearl.

For a moment, Tor allowed himself to imagine what it would be like to return home to his mother in one piece. To sleep for a week straight, to possibly pretend like he was normal.

Then, Melda snapped her fingers beneath his nose. He blinked and she rolled her eyes at him. "Daydreaming, at a time like this?"

"Sorry—that's it. That's all I heard."

She shook her head and turned on her heel, making small circles on the upper deck. She turned suddenly. "I *knew*, I just *knew*, something was off about her." She threw her hands in the air. "And we can't just send her packing. We need someone from Swordscale."

"Maybe we don't." He turned to make sure the rest of the deck was clear, then unearthed the tiny sack from his pocket. The shaved rock sat inside.

Engle peered at it. "Is that..."

"Shavings from the statue at Siren's Wharf. The owner of the bookshop said it used to have a comb and that it was *stolen*."

Melda straightened. "All we need is the compass then. We can use the siren's shavings to find her lost comb. And if we find the comb, we get a wish. And if we get a wish—"

"We get the pearl." Engle finished.

They all grinned at each other like thieves.

"Good," Melda said. "I didn't like relying on Vesper to find the pearl. We can't trust her. *Or* Captain Forecastle, for that matter."

Heads lowered, they huddled together. "When we find the compass, we can say goodbye to them both," Tor said. "Until then, it's best if we act as if we know nothing."

Engle shrugged. "I can do that."

Melda smiled sweetly at him. "Without much effort at all."

Tor rolled his eyes. "We already have enough enemies on this ship," he said quietly. "Let's not fight among friends."

● ☽ ◗ ☾

Before dinner, Tor found Engle at the back of the ship, squinting down into the water.

"See anything good?" he said.

Engle kept staring. "I think something is..." He shook his head. "Never mind."

"What is it?"

Engle turned away from the water and blinked long and hard. “Nothing. Just those stupid nightmares. I think they're seeping into true life and making me paranoid. Making me see things...”

Melda took a break from reading her new mermaid book and made her way over to them.

“Do you want to talk about it?” Tor asked. “I've been meaning to ask you—”

Engle shook his head again, then waved away Tor's concern with a lazy hand. “It's nothing,” he said. “Just need to sleep better at night.” Melda neared and he said loudly, “Melda's snoring certainly hasn't helped.”

She gave him a look. “If anyone snores, it's *you*, and you also talk in your sleep,” she said.

Engle paled. “I do?”

She smiled deviously. “Yes, and I can hear it all right through the walls.” Melda regarded her nails. “What interesting things I hear...”

Engle stormed off, and Melda laughed. She turned to Tor. “He doesn't talk in his sleep,” she said.

“I know. I'm in the cabin next to his, remember?”

She sighed, grin disappearing. “I've tried to talk to him about it, you know. He refuses. He doesn't think the nightmares are a big deal.”

Tor watched his friend walk to the opposite side of the ship and peer into the water again. "I'll talk to him," he said.

She nodded. Then, she motioned toward her new mermaid book. "Apparently, there are several species of mermaid."

"Captain Forecastle said so, too."

"Each is as deadly as the next. Only very few are the friendly, helpful type. Some are green with nails as long as spikes, some are half human, half octopus, some are such beautiful singers they make sailors jump off their own ships—the Melodines we've already encountered, in the middle of a desert of all places."

Tor laughed without humor. He remembered their purple gem eyes and voices like maple honey. They would have drowned him in the oasis if it hadn't been for Melda and Engle.

Melda continued. "Some, like the story in your mother's book, sing nightmares to life."

Tor stilled. Was that what was tormenting Engle? Was a siren whispering nightmares into his ear from the sea, making him see terrible things in the daylight?

"It says that they can affect one during sleep, too," Melda said, nodding like she was thinking the same thing. "Maybe that's why his dreams have been so bad on the ship."

"Okay—how do we stop them?"

She opened the book to a dog-eared page. "An elixir for bad dreams. It's in this book and works to banish them, no matter the cause."

They spent the next hour putting together the mixture. It required a handful of sea foam, a silver hair (which Vesper begrudgingly provided), a slice of moraberry, wood from a ship, and spit from a pirate, all mixed in an oyster shell.

Though elixirs could typically only be made by those with elixir emblems, the sea seemed to have its own rules. Tor stirred the mixture once, and it bubbled blue, then green. Then boiled away, leaving only a thin, transparent paste.

"We rub it on his pillow...and no more nightmares," she said. "From a mermaid or otherwise."

They decided not to tell him. Engle had been rather defensive about his nightmares recently, no need to embarrass him further, Tor reasoned. During dinner, when Engle was ravenously finishing off an ear of charred, buttered, and nut-crusted corn on the cob, Melda excused herself. She returned without the elixir and nodded silently at Tor.

And that night, for the first time, Engle slept in silence.

Maladies at Sea

Sicknesses at sea can be far crueler than those on land. Disease spreads with ease in close quarters, and soon the entire crew is covered in scales. Stormscale is known to kill in less than a day. Grimgrey takes its time, crumbling bone until the skin just sags. Palestye starts with a pain in the side, then ends in coughing blood.

Many a pirate have gone to distant lands in search for cures—and some have found them. But many more have succumbed to their malady, and now rest in their watery graves beneath the sea.

9

BLUEBRAID

The next morning, Engle was grinning. He stretched his arms high above his head as he strode across the deck, then came to a jumping stop in front of them. He disheveled Tor's hair with one hand and pulled Melda's new braid with the other.

She looked like she was trying very hard not to smile. "You look well."

Engle bounced around on his toes like someone about to go into a battling ring, full to the brim with energy. "I feel amazing. Refreshed. Had my first good sleep in a while."

Tor and Melda shared a quick look. "Good," Tor said. "Today's important."

Perla was just a few miles away. While Engle had snored loudly next door, Tor hadn't gotten a wink of sleep. His insides had been twisted up—hope, fear, and worry all intertwined.

Today, they could have the pearl. If everything went right.

Tor swallowed. By now, he knew things rarely went as planned.

"So, sightseer, anything on the horizon?" Melda asked. She was fully smiling now, watching Engle run across the ship, staring out at every direction.

Tor was smiling, too, watching Engle trip on an uneven board, then burst into laughter. He hadn't seen his friend look so high-spirited in a while. Maybe he was okay now. Maybe, just maybe, they could put the past behind them.

Captain Forecastle surfaced from below, a finger in his ear. "What's all the commotion?" he said. He opened his mouth to say something else, then gasped. His head twisted unnaturally upward, chin to the sky, as if his hair had been pulled back. Melda screamed, her head whipping back the same way.

And Tor felt the unmistakable smoothness of a blade across his throat.

● ☽ ◗ ☾

Captain Forecastle grinned. "Hello, Bluebraid," he said. And like a curtain falling, a dozen pirates suddenly appeared beside them, swords drawn. A vessel was anchored nearby, with thick ropes strung between it and *Cloudcaster*.

The pirates had swung aboard without a sound—even Engle hadn't spotted them.

Somehow, they had been invisible.

"That emblem never gets old," Forecastle said. The woman holding a blade to his neck spit at his boots. She had a captain's hat just like Forecastle's, and skin as tanned as Tor's, covered in various tattoos that looked faded and colorless next to her gleaming silver invisibility emblem. It would have taken an extraordinary amount of power to also make her crew and ship invisible. Tor wondered where she had learned to wield her ability so expertly.

Her voice was raspy when she spoke. "You have the gall to speak to me so casually, after what you did? I should take your tongue, fool." She drove the blade even closer to his neck, and Captain Forecastle's throat bobbed nervously.

"No need, no need. The watery hole gave us time to think...to...*repent.*"

Bluebraid laughed thunderously, without humor. "Save those lies for the fish." She nodded roughly toward one of her crew—a boy who looked not much older than them. He wore a ragged leather vest, shorts, and worn brown boots; his hair was so long it reached past his shoulders. "Search them."

The boy went to Tor first, and he tensed, waiting for him to draw a weapon—but the young pirate made no move to put a finger on him. Instead, he put his hand out, then dropped it. "Nothing of value," he said in a voice far too deep to belong to a child.

There was still a blade to Tor's throat, so close he didn't dare breathe deeper than necessary. The arm that held the sword was crusted over and scaled like a fish. Tiny shells dotted the pirate's knuckles.

Tor swallowed and felt the cool metal against his larynx.

The boy moved onto Melda.

"Just a few dobbles," he sneered.

When the boy approached Engle, he twisted his face in disgust. "Just crumbled, stale pastries."

Vesper was still in her room below. It seemed like they hadn't discovered her yet. Maybe she had made herself incredibly tiny. Or maybe she had escaped, somehow, deep below the sea when she'd heard the commotion. Either way, Tor wasn't surprised.

At last, the boy reached Captain Forecastle, who laughed nervously. "He's gotten very good..."

The boy glared at him. "Yes," he said, voice full of poison. "I've had twenty years of practice."

"Twenty?" Engle seemed to not have been able to help himself.

Bluebraid turned her sharp gaze to him. "Twenty years,

our lifelines have been frozen." She dug her blade hard enough against Captain Forecastle's throat that it produced a tumbling droplet of blood. "Twenty years of agony. Not being able to sleep or leave the sea." Her nostrils flared. "Usually, lifelines mean nothing out here. But the curse that binds us is relentless."

"But shouldn't your curse have ended, like the others?" Engle wondered. Tor wished he would stop talking.

"The Night Witch didn't do this to us... No, we had to make a deal with a deeper darkness for a chance to set us free." She grinned down at Forecastle. "And *that's* where you four come in." She nodded at the young pirate boy, and he lifted his hand.

And smiled.

"You've got something *quite* valuable, don't you, Forecastle?"

"*Captain*—" he began to correct.

But before he could finish his sentence, the boy stuck a hand into the inside of Captain Forecastle's jacket and pulled something from one of its hidden pockets.

A compass.

The compass.

Tor forgot all about the sword then. He thrashed against the man's grip, catching him by surprise. For a moment, he wriggled free. Then, the pirate's scaled arm sliced against Tor's as he fought to get ahold of him. “You lied to us!” he screamed out, as the blade found his neck once more. “You were using us to gain passage to Perla, then you were going to lose us and find the pearl yourself!”

Captain Forecastle shrugged. “Never make a bargain with a pirate that isn’t inked in blood.”

Bluebraid grinned. She released Forecastle, pushing him to the floor, then stepped over him. She walked slowly to Tor, her boots echoing loudly against the deck. Closer, Tor could see that her thick, blue braid was dotted with a dozen diamonds. She smiled. “What do you know of the Pirate’s Pearl?”

Tor stiffened. He said nothing.

She kept smiling as she snapped her fingers, and the young pirate boy took Engle by the front of his shirt. He hauled him to the edge of the ship. “We’ll throw him overboard. And I’ll make him more than just invisible. He’ll cry for help, but you won’t hear him. You’ll search for hours, but you won’t see him. Not until it’s too late...”

Engle’s eyes widened. Tor had never seen him look so afraid. He imagined his friend was replaying that day in the Lake of the Lost—when he had almost been lost forever. When he had been dragged deep beneath the gray water, with no hope of ever surfacing.

No.

Never again.

They needed to get away, but Tor's plan would mean losing the compass. He looked at his friend—

And made a decision.

Tor met Bluebraid's gaze. He lifted his arms, and the ropes flew to him, startling the pirate holding the sword to his neck so badly that Tor was able to step away. Even Bluebraid seemed shocked, her eyes wide as he pushed his hands down as hard as he could, like he was trying to break through concrete with just his fingers, groaning at the effort. And the ship followed.

"Hold your breath!" he screamed.

The mermaid at the bow plunged headfirst underneath the water.

There was a roar as the ship dove deep through the sea, fast as lightning. Tor closed his fists, and the other ropes found Melda, Engle, and, begrudgingly, Captain Forecastle, holding them secure. Connected to the ship, he could sense Vesper below in her room. The force of the ocean swept Bluebraid and her crew away, left in *Cloudcaster*'s wake. The ship continued to sail down through the deep seas, bubbles erupting in streams behind them.

Then, seconds later, Tor pulled on the ropes, and they rushed toward the surface.

Sunlight neared, then exploded in his vision, and Tor collapsed onto the planks, fully drained. The ship groaned beneath him as it righted itself. The ropes dropped Melda, then Engle, to the deck, and they coughed and coughed, only stopping to take deep breaths in between.

Melda slumped against one of the masts and lifted a weak finger at Tor. "Don't you ever do that again," she said.

Engle scoffed. "Why'd you save him?" He motioned to Captain Forecastle, who was looking around desperately for his hat. He found it, dripping and mangled between some of the lines.

"I don't know."

The latch to the bottom level opened, and water spilled out, followed by Vesper, who simply wrung her hair dry.

"Thanks for the help," Melda said sarcastically, hands in fists, voice still hoarse. "Were you just going to wait until they killed us all? Escape back to your watery world?"

"I—"

Melda cut her off with a glare that could pierce a diamond, and Vesper retreated below once more. Melda turned her wrath to Captain Forecastle. "And *you*—you lying, filthy, unforgivable *pirate*."

Engle was by her side; he placed a gentle hand on her arm. "Land ahead," he said softly.

They stopped in the first port they encountered, a good-sized one with a sign that welcomed them to Tortuga Bay. The name was familiar—Tor thought Melda might have mentioned it a while ago.

Captain Forecastle began to spin lies and make excuses, but when his words were met only with glares, he climbed down the side of the ship, and they left him on the dock.

Tor watched the pirate until he was just a dot, then turned to his friends. "What now?" he said. Every step they'd made had been wrong. Every person they'd trusted had been wrong.

But Tor did not regret his decision to choose saving Engle over the compass.

Melda look at her tiny hourglass, which now held much less purple sand than before. "It's over, isn't it?" They had gone to great lengths to find the enchanted device, it was the key to finding the pearl. Without it, they had nothing.

And it had been lost to Bluebraid and her crew.

Engle grinned. "Who's giving up now?" he said. Then, he pulled something from his pocket.

The compass.

Man without a Mouth

The sea is an endless soup, though the cauldron it sits in is a mystery. Many a pirate and sailor have attempted to chart every mile of bright blue water, every island, every faraway land. But some seas are deadlier than others—and some lands, too. It is said that far across the ocean, there is a place completely devoid of color. A pirate made the mistake of piercing the wall that had kept that land separate from the rest—and it shattered his ship to pieces. A single sailor survived on driftwood to tell the tale.

And it is a tale many have chosen not to believe.

The man claims to have seen a land of fire and smoke, of nightmares and dreams. He says the hole the ship made in the wall allowed many things to escape. Including a man without a mouth. A spectral. He burned a path through the sea, water turning to steam, and walked across its bottom easily.

Many dark creatures from that land have been spotted throughout the sea in recent years. And it

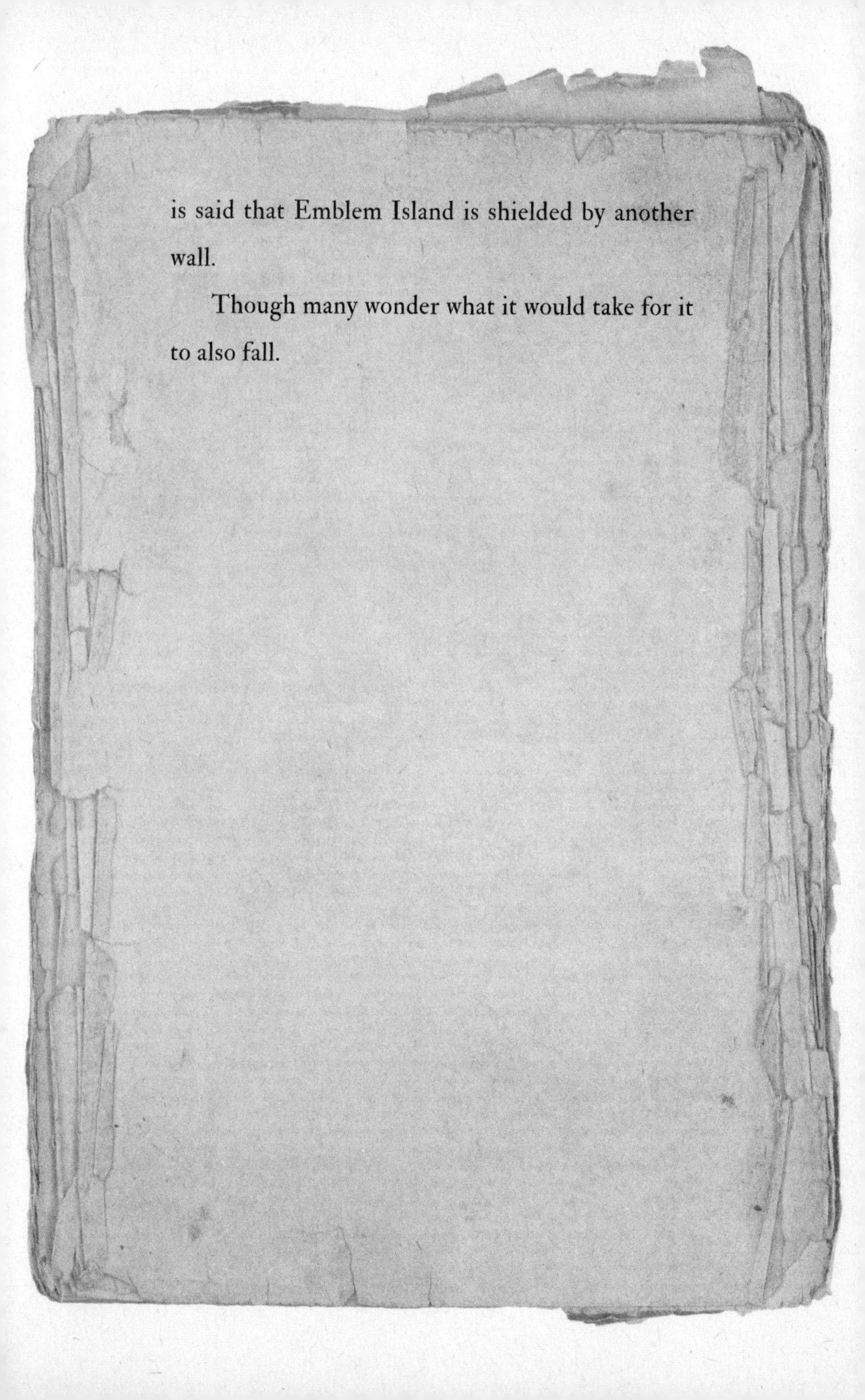

is said that Emblem Island is shielded by another wall.

Though many wonder what it would take for it to also fall.

10

THE TOYMAKER

The compass glimmered like a jewel. Its dial was crafted from mother-of-pearl, its needles from solid gold. A pattern of fish, shells, and moons decorated its interior, between four symbols—N, E, S, and W.

"Nicked it from the strange pirate kid," Engle said, shrugging. "Right as you sent the ship down." He smiled wider. "That was lightning, by the way."

"*And* terrifying," Melda added. Her tone was smooth, but her eyes had gone wide, staring at Engle. Impressed. A little surprised.

Tor grinned. "Maybe you *are* becoming a pirate." He felt around in his own pocket and was relieved the boy hadn't been able to sense the sack of powder's value. He supposed it *was* just a bit of dust from a statue, not too important unless one knew its purpose.

Unless he was wrong... He banished the thought. This had to work. The future of Estrelle relied on it.

Engle was famished, and he begged for food before they enacted the next part of their plan. Tor allowed it, still shaken from their encounter with the pirates. He was just finishing his glass of stormberry juice when something below shuddered, and Tor lurched forward. The ship silently pulled on their thread, and Tor grabbed on. He felt around, as the ship, and something pooled around him. He winced.

Vesper burst from below. "We have a leak," she said. "A big one."

Tor felt as much. The side of the vessel had been scratched badly in the Devil's Mouth, a thick tear across its hull, and it had gotten worse when the ship had soared to the skies, then landed. It seemed as though their trip underwater to escape Bluebraid and her crew had finally made the rip tear open.

"Can you make the hole smaller?" Tor asked. The ship groaned beneath him, and he could feel the water burst through its side.

She nodded. "For a little. But my fix won't hold long. We have to get it repaired."

That would take ages. Time they didn't have. As if on cue, Melda silently reached for her arenahora, grimacing at the sand left. It was nearly halfway gone.

"We don't have the time," he said.

Vesper looked down below, where Tor could hear water bursting in, filling the hallway. "We don't have a choice," she said, before running down to do what she could.

Melda sighed. "She's right. If we don't get the ship repaired, then there's no way we'll be able to follow the compass." She turned to Engle. "See anything close by?"

The sightseer studied ahead. They weren't far from the coast, after leaving Captain Forecastle behind in Tortuga Bay. He nodded. "There's a town, with ships, not far. Should have someone to be able to patch up old *Cloudcaster*."

Vesper returned, her pants wet to her knees. "Closed. But not for long." She opened her shell map, and they saw all up and down Emblem Island's west side, villages and cities dotting the coast.

The village Engle had spotted up ahead was labeled Gargyle. Tor had never heard of it. He glanced at Melda, and she shook her head—she didn't recognize it, either.

"Never seen a town like that before." Engle said.

Gargyle was built completely on docks that jutted far out into the water. There were dozens of them, crisscrossed, and built not on a grid, but wayward, as if a giant in the sky had dropped a handful of bridges from the clouds, and people had decided to make a town of it.

Tor moored the ship awkwardly in the mess of a harbor, squeezing dangerously close to a shop that was located on the end of a neighboring dock. The building drooped low, heavy with what looked like clocks, just a few pounds away from falling into the sea.

A woman peeked her head through the shop's window, smiling widely. She had her hair still in curlers and wore an apron, like she had just been in the middle of baking. "Nice to see you, might a timepiece be of interest? We have clocks that cluck, clocks that talk, clocks that walk—useful if you have a hard time getting out of bed—clocks that tell you the wrong time, if you're in the habit of being late. Clocks that sing, clocks that ding, clocks that ring, clocks that bring you coffee, clocks that—"

"No, thank you, we're quite all right," Melda said, holding up her arenahora.

The woman frowned. "Now *sand* isn't *my* first choice, but, to each their own..." She was about to leave when Tor spoke.

"Is there a ship repairer here?"

She pointed a finger across the way, then firmly closed her window.

Tor went to the place the woman had indicated while the rest stayed on board—everyone except for Engle, that is, who wandered into the town despite Melda's insistence he stay put. Even reminders that he didn't have a single dobble in his pocket didn't stop him.

The man in the ship repair shop had a reed sticking out from his mouth and tipped precariously backward in his chair when Tor walked into his shop.

"You need my help, I presume," he said arrogantly, straightening.

Tor nodded. "My ship is badly damaged on one side, sliced open."

The man grinned. He had yellow teeth, some much sharper than others. Tor looked quickly for an emblem, but didn't see one. "Now how did that come to be?"

"Just some rocks."

The man still smiled as he nodded. "Just some rocks... Let's see..."

He followed Tor down the docks, to the ship. Melda and Vesper now leaned against it. The waterbreather's enchantment was just about to run out, the crack widening before their eyes.

The man let out a low whistle. "That's a bad break you have there. Might not be worth fixing at all." He turned to Tor. "Why don't you let me take it off your hands? I'm afraid this looks beyond repair. I'm in a giving mood. I'll pay fifty dobbles, just because I feel bad."

Melda scoffed. "You're joking, right?" She looked around. "Empty harbor, lack of customers? Not our fault. Don't think you can con us."

The man turned to face her. He looked around, then bent so he was her height. He grinned, rotten teeth on full display. "Right as you may be about a lack of customers..." He turned to his left, and right, dramatically. "I don't see another shipfixer in this town, either." The man laughed as he regarded the gash in the hull. "And you won't be sailing anywhere else to get another quote, with a tear like that. Best take my offer. And now, I'm thinking I'll pay forty."

Melda seethed.

And, just as the man opened his mouth again, he fell into the water, the planks below his feet suddenly shrinking to an inch across. Vesper took a step forward and smiled at him through the new hole in the dock. The man cursed loudly, drenched and covered in the trash that had accumulated underneath the pier. "How's the water?" she said. "I've been dying for a swim."

Just then, Engle walked up, laughing hysterically. He peeked into the hole, at the shipfixer still cursing as he tried to climb out, and laughed some more. "You made her angry, didn't you?"

Melda had a very small smile on her face as she glared

into the hole. A moment later, she sighed. "What are we going to do now?"

As terrible as he was, the man was right. He was the only one in town who could help them, and their ship wouldn't make the journey to another.

Engle shrugged. "Lucky for you, I've already scouted the place." He cupped a hand to the side of his mouth. "*Mean* people here, wouldn't even give me a taste-try of fudge!" He shook his head, disgusted.

"And..." Melda said pointedly.

"And I think I have an idea! Vesper, shrink the ship, will you?"

Melda looked unconvinced, but Vesper did as Engle said.

He led the way down the dock, which dipped too far into the water for Tor's liking in some places. The dock split into two. One side led across the stretch of sea to another mess of overlapping docks, and that was the way they took, right onto a floating dock that had to be pulled by a man on the other side using a rope. He tipped his hat at them as they passed.

Finally, they reached a small cluster of shops, all crowded together on the same pier.

"How on Emblem did you find this place?" Melda asked.

"I just...explored," Engle said, lifting a shoulder.

In front of them sat three buildings. A small gallery, with

paintings that were multilayered, enchanted so that they held multiple works of art that played on a loop. Most of them, unsurprisingly, depicted the sea and a maze of docks that was unmistakably Gargyle. Next to the gallery stood a restaurant. The smell of spices spilled out of an open window, scents Tor didn't recognize, so spicy even a whiff burned the inside of his nose.

Engle walked into the third shop—a toy store.

Melda sighed and rolled her eyes.

The toy shop had striped spinning tops that were enchanted to never stop, streamers that changed color and whipped wildly around—nearly hitting Tor in the face as he entered—galloping wooden horses, and kites that seemed to be flying themselves. A group of dolls were arguing on a table, then turned suddenly when they saw they had visitors. Their frowns quickly disappeared, and they smiled brightly, curtsying as one unit.

"What beautiful hair!" one doll said in a tiny, high-pitched voice, blinking its eyes very quickly at Vesper with eyelashes made of curling black feathers.

Another subtly pushed past her and said, "Silver is the best color, I think! Look, just like my dress!" She twirled for good measure.

A third doll laughed, and Tor saw her pinch the other as she skipped past. "You're about the prettiest person I've ever seen! We'd be great friends, I think."

"I don't need friends," Vesper said curtly, before walking away.

The dolls turned to each other, and Tor had to listen closely to hear them arguing again.

"Your fault, always yours!"

"Her hair wasn't even that pretty, plain if you ask me, just like your dress!"

Tor continued through the shop. He picked up a ball that immediately bounced against the wall, then back into his hands. He moved swiftly out of the way of a tiny train that produced real smoke and didn't seem to require a track. Engle was at the very back of the store, where an old man had appeared from behind a curtain.

"Didn't I tell you not to come back?" the old man said, sounding exhausted. Tor wondered how many things Engle had broken.

"I didn't touch anything this time! I swear it!" Engle said. Then, he motioned for Vesper. "We need help. Do you think you can fix this?"

Vesper held up the tiny ship, slice down its side, which did, in fact, look very much like a toy.

The old man squinted at it through his spectacles. "I suppose. I have a woodshop..." He looked uneasy.

"We'll pay you," Engle said, though Tor didn't know how.

Melda was the only one who had currency, and it wasn't more than a few dobbles.

The old man sighed. "No payment. Just promise never to come back to my store."

They followed the man into another room filled with wood, machinery, and buckets of paint. He sat at an old desk and placed the ship carefully in front of him.

With a sharp creak, he turned a giant magnifying glass attached to the table so it was in front of his eye. His eyebrows came together, and he squinted, as if not believing what he saw.

He turned to look them all up and down, his gaze landing at Vesper. "You're a magnificate, aren't you?"

She swallowed, then nodded.

The man turned back to his desk without saying a word.

Using tiny tweezers, he lifted the hatch of the ship, then turned it over, releasing a stream of seawater. He mopped it up with a rag, clicking his tongue. The boat now dry inside, he grabbed blindly for a long, silver tool that resembled a quill. It hissed when he pressed its end, and a tiny spark of power came out its other side.

The toymaker grunted as he ran the strange instrument along the hole in the ship's hull, sealing it. Still not looking satisfied, he stuck a finger into a gray plaster from an open container, then smeared it on top, his eye never leaving the giant magnifying glass.

He muttered to himself as he got up to walk to the other side of the room. When he returned, he had a tiny bucket of dark paint, and a brush so small it seemed to contain just a handful of hairs.

He painted over the mark, then nodded, pleased. "Can still tell it's been broken, but this is the best I can do in such a short amount of time."

"It's perfect," Tor said. "Thank you."

Following the terms of their agreement, they turned to leave. Everyone except for Melda, who was staring at the old man.

"Yes?" he said, tired.

"That's an animator emblem," Melda said, motioning toward the man's finger. There was a tiny golden spark there. "Can you really make any inanimate object real?"

"No."

Melda reddened, clearly disappointed. "Oh."

She turned to go, and the old man said, "There are levels to animation." He sighed. "The item itself decides whether or not it wants to be real."

"And if it doesn't?"

The man shrugged. "Then it never wakes up." He peered

at the ship in Tor's hand, then at them, before sighing once again. "Sometimes, when I animate something, it has a lot to say. I took a trade for an old nutcracker this morning, and it gave many warnings. In its place in a store window in Siren's Wharf, it had seen someone appear and disappear. The Calavera captain, it claimed."

Tor stilled. When they'd been in Siren's Wharf he could have sworn he'd seen the captain's hat, in the corner of his vision, just before they left.

Were they being followed?

The toymaker shook his head. "I would go inland, if I was you," he said. "If the Calavera's curse has been broken, the sea and its cities are not safe places to be."

They were silent on the haphazard walk back to the marina. The toymaker's warning rang through Tor's head.

He wished they could heed his advice and go inland. Instead, they had to sail toward danger, into the eye of the storm.

And hope the Calavera captain, the traitor, and the spectral didn't beat them to the pearl—or didn't attack them before they had a chance to find it.

The toymaker's fix had worked brilliantly. When Vesper grew the ship in the harbor—making sure to avoid the shipfixer, who had drifted and was still trying to climb back up onto the docks—the hole was completely sealed.

"Just looks like it has a scar, doesn't it?" Engle said. He patted the ship on the side as he climbed up the ladder. "You look absolutely menacing, *Cloudcaster*."

Once aboard, Tor, Melda, and Engle gathered at its helm.

"We have the compass," Tor said. "And part of the siren statue. I think we should look for the comb first. If we use it to find the pearl, we might avoid the prophecy, since we changed our plan. If it doesn't work, we can always use the compass to go straight to the pearl." He looked down at the enchanted object in his palm. "If I'm right, and the siren statue originally had the comb, then this should lead us right to it." And if the legends in the *Book of Seas* were true, using the comb to brush the sea would attract a mermaid who would grant them their wish for the pearl.

Engle grinned. "Let's go, then."

Tor carefully dipped his finger into the sack from Siren's Wharf. A bit of dust stuck to his thumb. He pressed it to the instrument's glass and held his breath, waiting.

If it didn't work, they would have to rely on Vesper. She would need to hold the compass, which, according to the prophecy, would take them on a journey not all of them would survive. And, there was the Calavera captain, the Swordscale traitor, and the mysterious spectral. For all they knew, they could be hours away from finding the pearl, or even on their tail...

No, it had to work.

Tor watched the compass intently—hoping he had been right.

And its needle began to whir.

When it finally stopped spinning, it pointed directly west.

Relief almost brought him to his knees.

"We don't need her help anymore, do we?" Melda whispered, motioning vaguely below deck toward Vesper's room. She had gone there as soon as they had boarded. He wondered what she was doing down there. Likely speaking into that mysterious conch shell.

Tor nodded. "No, we don't. But let's not do anything until we've found the comb. And then the mermaid." He knew the warnings. Though there were dozens of species of mermaids, according to Melda's book, they all had one thing in common: a reputation for being wicked, deceiving creatures. The wording of their wish had to be precise, leaving no room for loopholes.

They remained on the deck for hours, watching the compass move ever so slightly. Vesper came up for food, and

Tor did not take his eyes off the pirate's instrument, even as he ate, its thin golden needle guided by an invisible force.

Every once in a while, he sprinkled bits of the statue's powder on its glass, when the wind had all but blown it away. He led the ship the same way he had once watched giantesses lead their horses. It groaned slightly beneath him, its blue and silver sails always filled with wind, even when there was barely a breeze on his cheek.

Tor wondered why the Night Witch had ever had use of a vessel like this. Had she sailed on it hundreds of years before, when she had been just a girl and not a legend?

Had she understood the draw to the sea that Tor had always harbored in the pit of his stomach?

Soon, staring at the compass became tiring. They decided to take shifts, to ensure there was always powder on the compass. Melda and Engle were below, taking their break.

Tor had just leaned his head back against the mast when he heard a splash.

He was on his feet in an instant.

Vesper was in the water, staring up at him, as the ship passed by. "Don't worry, I'll catch up to you," she said, diving deep into the water.

Tor felt a pang of jealousy. He had daydreamed about his time in the forgotten underwater city, down in depths he would never have been able to explore without his new emblem. Breathing in the sea was completely different than simply swimming in it. He wanted a thousand years just to see every inch of seafloor, to encounter every sea creature at least once.

As promised, Vesper climbed up the ship's ladder just a few moments later, dripping a trail of water across the deck as she walked toward him. "Pity you have to be the captain," she said. "The water's warm."

She sat cross-legged on the deck and wrung her hair out. "You have no idea how strange it is to do this," she said, making a puddle beside her knee. "I've never had to dry myself in my life."

"Tell me about Swordscale," Tor said.

She dropped his gaze like a weight. "It used to be magnificent. I remember it all, as a child. It was so nice, so beautiful. Back then, we lived in harmony with mermaids."

Tor raised his eyebrows, and Vesper gave him a sidelong glance.

"Not the type you've heard about. These were torrytails, not much different from you or me. They breathed underwater and had a fin, but their tails... You could see legs within them. Stuck together, but there, so similar to us. They have their own origin story, a frightening tale." She bit her lip.

"One of them was my best friend. Salma. Our fathers, they ruled Swordscale together."

Vesper closed her eyes, and Tor was surprised to see a tear slip down her face, getting instantly lost in her silver hair.

"One day, we were attacked. My father locked me in my room to make sure I didn't try to fight; I was too young. By the time I broke out, my parents were dead."

Tor bowed his head, not knowing what to say. He settled with, "I'm sorry." He remembered Vesper yelling after her grandmother, but not her parents. He should have suspected.

She shrugged. "And all of the torrytails had fled. They left and never returned. Swordscale was badly damaged, and without solid leadership, it crumbled further. Things... changed. Our rules had relaxed over the years, but leaving Swordscale again became forbidden, for fear of spurring another attack. Still, I would sneak out, and I never saw anything to be afraid of."

"Who attacked Swordscale?" Tor dared ask.

Vesper shook her head. "I have no idea. No one speaks of it. And most of those who might have known are dead." She shrugged. "As I told you before, Swordscales are superstitious. They believe writing about bad things will make them happen. Speaking them is worse."

"I'm really sorry, Vesper," Tor said again, knowing it wasn't enough.

She took a deep breath. "My people are already weak, already broken. If the Calavera succeed, waterbreathers will be all but extinct. We're the last settlement I know of." Her bottom lip quivered, and she bit it, holding it still. "My parents *died* protecting their people." She lowered her head, her green eyes blazing. "I won't let their sacrifice be for nothing."

● ☽ ◗ ☾

Later, the sea was still. It felt heavier around the ship as Tor navigated it, requiring more effort than usual. He was alone on the deck, compass in his palm, when Melda appeared. She offered to take over while Tor rested, but he declined. He wasn't tired, and he liked watching the water, especially when afternoon turned to evening.

"It always looks a little lazy this time of day," he said, staring out at the ocean. The few waves that did form around them had rounded crests, as if the sea was ready to get off work.

Tor couldn't fathom ever getting tired of watching it. Each mile they sailed, the water looked a little different.

He turned to her. "You know, maybe Vesper isn't so bad. Maybe we can trust her."

Melda gave him a look. "Are you going off facts? Or are you biased, because she's a waterbreather, like you?"

"What's that supposed to mean?"

Melda shrugged. "You've wanted this marking your entire life, and she's the first person you've met who has it. I get why you'd want to trust her."

"*No*, I just—" He wanted to tell Melda about Vesper's past, but stopped himself. Doing so felt wrong. It wasn't his story to tell.

Melda walked over to him. "Are you enjoying it, at least?" She nodded at his emblem.

Just a month ago, Melda had scoffed at Tor's wish for a waterbreathing marking. Now, he saw no judgment in her gray eyes. He frowned at the sky. "It feels wrong, knowing the cost. And circumstances." He looked up at her. "But—yes. It's just like I thought it would be." He straightened. "Sandstone—you should have seen it, Melda. It was bigger than Estrelle, like Zeal, even. But...down there." He was grinning. "Breathing underwater, it's incredible. It's just like breathing air, but it's thicker, you know? Sweeter, almost. And things are different underwater. You can walk, just like on land, or swim, and—" He stopped himself, took a breath, then slowly slumped over. "I know I sound strange. But I can't explain it. I've just always been drawn to the ocean, like something's waiting for me out here." Tor shrugged. "Do you know what that's like?"

Melda was looking past him, focusing very intently on a spot far away. Her fingers found the base of her throat, where her necklace once sat. Before she had sacrificed the rare drop of color it held to save Engle. "I do, actually," she said.

Then, they were flying through the air.

Tor hit the side of the ship and bone snapped—his arm erupted in pain, like fireworks going off beneath his skin. He screamed out, and Melda crawled over to him. Engle jumped up from where he had landed, on the opposite side.

Something had struck the boat.

"What *was*—" Before Engle could finish his sentence, a long tentacle whipped out of the sea fast as the casting line of a fishing rod and across the deck. It landed with so much force, Tor, Melda, and Engle went flying backward once more.

The bone in his arm stuck out in a strange direction, almost through his skin. He cradled it as he rose, barely resisting the urge to cry out in pain.

Engle swallowed. "That's a capsizal," he said. "Five tentacles. Fifty feet long. Carnivorous." He shook his head. "I *knew* something was following us. I wasn't just imagining it."

Melda screamed as another tentacle spiraled from the water and smacked against the ship, this time slithering down its side, underneath the vessel, all the way back around. "It's going to smash us to pieces!" She turned to Engle. "Does it have a weakness?"

He nodded. "Terrible eyesight. Can only sense movement."

Another tentacle had joined the others. Then another. And another. Its suction cups made sticking sounds as they fastened firmly against the wood—its tentacles went taut, and the boat cracked, a fracture running straight down the deck like a bolt of lightning. It was going to split the ship in half.

Tor recognized the creature—it looked just like the giant squid from Sandstone. He wondered how Vesper was doing below deck and hoped she would be able to escape through a window, if the vessel was crushed further. "How many of these exist?" he yelled over the growl that shook the ship, pain a pulse in his arm.

Engle was shaking. "Only one at a given time."

Just then, Vesper surfaced from below deck, pushing heavily against the latch, which one of the tentacles had partially covered.

Tor took a step toward her and couldn't believe he had just tried to convince Melda that Vesper could be trusted. "You took it, didn't you?" He remembered Captain Forecastle's words about the ship's golden-edged sails; he had said it meant something aboard had been stolen. Tor had assumed the sails had sensed the Night Witch's stolen cloud charm, but now—

"Took what?" Melda yelled. The sea at their sides bubbled like the ocean was simmering, a big soup they were about to be boiled in.

"The fortuneteller's skull." *That* was why the monster had attacked in the library. And also why it had followed them all this way. "Give it back!" Tor yelled.

Vesper hesitated.

"You'll kill us all!" Melda said.

Vesper reached into her pocket and made the skull grow into its full size. Then, she threw it into the water.

One of the tentacles retracted to fetch it. The sea stopped boiling.

For a moment, Tor thought the capsizal might just leave.

But then, the rest of the capsizal's tentacles tightened. It seemed the creature wasn't done with them yet.

The ship cracked again under its grip, and Tor winced, feeling the ship at the brink of breaking.

Vesper ran to the edge of the deck, and Tor imagined she was about to abandon them, before she yelled, "Jump!"

Melda looked like the last thing she wanted to do was follow Vesper, but they had no choice. They leapt into the sea.

By the time Tor landed in the water, the ship was no bigger than his thumb.

Its tentacles now gripping air, the capsizal fell behind them, roughly into the ocean. For a moment, there was just a faint buzzing in Tor's ear, a bee that had made its way into the sea. He tasted salt in his mouth, having swallowed water that once would have burned his lungs.

The capsizal was right in front of him, and every one of Tor's bones itched to swim far away... But he remembered Engle's warning, and forced himself still. Even as his arm throbbed in blinding pain, made worse by the impact from jumping. The creature's tentacles blindly reached through the water, desperate to grip one of them. *Engle. Melda.* Tor searched for his friends, wincing in pain, hoping they were able to not only stay still, but also survive the near thirty seconds underwater.

Time continued to click by, and Tor nearly shuddered in pain, a motion that might give him away, when the capsizal finally gave up.

With a final push of its massive tentacles, it disappeared into the deep, taking the fortuneteller's skull with it.

The Cursed Sea and Its Forgotten Cities

The sea has its secrets. Tucked deep below, creatures roam; beasts that have never before surfaced. Entire cities go unnoticed.

Unless one is invited.

It is said that those worthy of a visit might come across towering gates in the middle of the ocean. An invitation.

And that those with the power to venture underwater might discover great riches and even greater secrets. But each has a price. For the sea takes twice as much as it gives.

Sailors are willing to bargain with the ocean, just for a taste of it.

The only way to overcome fear is to face it.

And the only way to live is to sail to different places.

A pirate's heart is restless.

They would rather die than look in death's eye and think their life was wasted.

11

STORMSCALE

Tor was back in his room on the ship without any recollection of how he had gotten there. It was warm as summer inside, though their journey had gotten colder as they had traveled up the coast. Had they changed direction for some reason? Melda hovered above him, about to place a thin piece of linen against his forehead. He was burning from the inside out, like the damage to his arm was an ember that had spread into a fire. Sweat trickled down his forehead.

The linen was cold as ice against his face and brought a whisper of relief.

"He's awake," Engle said, walking into the room and rushing to his side.

Tor looked down at his arm, which was pulsing with pain. None of them were curadors; they would need to find someone with a healing emblem to right the bone. It would be difficult, but every major city had one, and there were plenty of thriving coastal towns nearby. But, as his blurred vision cleared, he saw that his arm didn't look like an arm at all.

"We saw it when we ripped your sleeve off, to survey the damage," Melda said quickly. "You passed out."

His skin was covered in dark scales, from his shoulder down to his fingers, where tiny shells had replaced his knuckles.

"It's spread like wildfire. We've *watched* it grow. A few hours ago, it was just your elbow—"

"The pirate who held the blade to my throat, he had this," Tor said quickly. "Do you know what it is? Is there anything about it in the book?" He vaguely remembered a chapter about sicknesses at sea.

Melda nodded. "We think it's... We think..." She broke off in a sob and quickly turned away.

Engle looked equally gutted. He sat on the edge of Tor's bed and said, "We think it's stormscale, mate."

Tor squinted. Stormscale. He remembered the passage now. No known cure, or at least one almost impossible to find...proven deadly in less than a day. "But that doesn't make sense, that pirate had definitely had it longer than a *day*."

Melda had wiped away her tears. Her eyes were

bloodshot. "They were cursed, Tor, their lifelines frozen. His must have been frozen right in the middle of his illness, keeping him alive."

Less than a day. He dared a glance at the window, its panes dark with night. He had encountered the pirate that morning, which meant he only had a few more hours.

Tor remembered the prophecy. One of them would die. It had been fated.

Somewhere deep inside, he was happy it was him and not one of his friends.

He tried to smile. "It's all right," he said. "Don't stop sailing, okay? Try to find the pearl. Save Estrelle. And tell my mother—" His voice cut off, a lump in his throat. He swallowed. "Tell her I—"

But his vision blurred again. He tried to speak, but—

Tor tumbled into darkness.

● ☽ ◗ ☾

Something waited in the abyss. The darkness moved and scattered, revealing a woman in a dress that was now tattered at its ends.

The Night Witch.

"Just a whisper from death," she said slowly, taking him

in. "Only my power keeps you alive. But it, too, will soon extinguish." She shook her head.

Tor looked down and found himself whole. His arm did not pulse with pain; he did not feel hot all over.

In fact, he felt cold. Dangerously so.

"I want to show you something."

She walked toward the darkness, the train of her ruined dress trailing behind her.

Tor followed.

He stumbled—and fell into a different world, like plunging through a portal. Before him, he saw a girl far in the distance. She climbed out of a boat that had washed upon an island devoid of color, as if a storm had swept through and taken all of its best parts for itself.

This was Emblem Island, thousands of years before.

And the girl was Estrelle, founder of his village.

"The charms she used to bring the island back to its former glory, the ones she used to create the first emblems..." The Night Witch was floating next to him, right on the sea, watching the young girl stumble across gray sand. "Did you ever wonder where they came from?"

Tor remembered the story. "Her grandmother," he said.

"Yes, but who was her grandmother? *What* was the place Estrelle came from?"

Tor had never questioned it. Before a month ago, he had never even believed the stories, let alone examined them.

The Night Witch turned to face him. "After destroying this island, darkness found Estrelle's home. She was the only one to escape, and she took her people's most powerful talisman with her."

The necklace. The one that held the charms that would become emblems.

She nodded, hearing his thoughts, and continued.

"Estrelle's grandmother and the rest of her descendants sacrificed themselves, used all of their abilities to trap the darkness in their lands in their attempt to vanquish it. And for more than a thousand years, it was dormant. As Emblem Island's power grew under Estrelle's influence, the darkness back at her home faded, until it was almost gone."

The Night Witch nodded toward the island, which had transformed. A new girl stood at the coast, watching them. She had white, peculiar hair.

"Then, I was born with the first deadly emblem. The power to kill with a single touch, balanced by the power to bring anyone back to life. I could have been the key to killing the darkness across the seas for good—but instead, after the murder of my father, the darkness in *me* bloomed. Darkness feeds on darkness, Tor. Unknowingly, the more sinister and powerful I became, the stronger I made him, until he was resurrected."

Him. Tor had so many questions. Was the darkness a person? A thing? Where had it come from? What had Emblem Island been before it had been destroyed, before Estrelle had landed on its shores?

She turned to him. "It's up to you now Tor, to stop the same stories from being told once more."

"But I'm dying," Tor said. "I can't help anymore. I can't save the island." He took a shaking breath. "You picked the wrong person," he said. "I'm not enough. I wasn't even able to face being the leader of my village, let alone protect all of Emblem Island. I'm not *enough*."

She frowned at him and pointed at something in the distance. "You have something I never did," she whispered. "You have help."

With a whoosh, she was gone. Tor continued to stare at what she had pointed out, something in the night, sitting on the distant seas. Tor walked toward it, water slippery as ice beneath his feet. As he came closer, he realized the object in the distance was a ship.

Cloudcaster. Anchored in the middle of nowhere. He heard voices, rushed and loud—muted and echoing. Chaos.

Soon, he saw Melda, Engle, and Vesper on the deck. All running as if the ship was sinking.

"Hurry, he's almost gone!" Melda screamed. She was facing Vesper. Were they working together?

Had Melda forgiven Vesper for taking the skull and endangering their lives?

Before Tor could put together what she was doing, Vesper jumped into the water right in front of him. Not seeing him at all.

Tor thought heavy thoughts and plunged beneath the sea, following her down, feet pointed toward the abyss.

A mangled shipwreck rested on the seafloor far below. Vesper darted inside with impressive speed, eyebrows furrowed. "Come on, come on, come on," he heard her say to herself, over the clatter of things she moved and pushed away deep in the belly of the ship. It was grand, bigger than *Cloudcaster*, with a large bird on its helm, wings spread wide.

Tor wanted to get closer, to see what she was doing. What she was looking for. But before he could, Vesper bolted out of the skeleton of the vessel. He followed her, back up to the surface.

"I have it," Vesper shouted to the deck, her head bobbing out of the water. Tor stood on the ocean once more, watching

Vesper climb up to the second step of the ladder, then crouch, one hand still gripping the railing.

The other held a golden comb. She reached down and lightly brushed it against the surface of the sea.

Silence.

Nothing stirred. The waves continued to lap against the anchored ship, lazy and undisturbed.

"Try again," Engle said desperately. "You have to, this *has* to work. *Please*."

Vesper reached down once more, expression wary. But before she could comb the sea another time, a pale hand broke through the pitch-black water and gripped her wrist.

Vesper gasped in shock, and the comb fell, disappearing beneath the water.

A head broke through the waves. She had hair golden as sunlight spun into silk, the comb now dug into the crown of her head. The siren's eyes were the pink of dusk, and much larger than even Melda's, framed by lashes so long they touched her cheeks.

Vesper blinked, as if struck by her beauty. "We—we—"

"You've found it," the siren said, her voice buttered velvet. The mermaid's tail briefly stuck out of the water behind her in a happy swoop. It was covered in bright, glittering scales, her fins a gauzy, feathery salmon pink. "Make a wish—and make it count."

Melda spoke from the deck, her words guttural and desperate. "Save our friend, Tor. Cure him of any sickness or injury," she said. "Please."

No. He wouldn't let them waste their wish on him. Not when they could find the pearl. He wasn't worth it. He rushed forward, running atop the sea, wanting to object, to give the mermaid another wish.

The siren turned to watch him as he approached, like she could see him. Her head tilted to the side in curiosity, before she nodded at Melda.

And he was yanked by his feet to the bottom of the sea.

A Warning to Untested Pirates and Sailors

Sirens are not the only temptresses of the sea. In the vast blueness, one must rein in greed—and desperation. For both lead to mistakes. And mistakes, at sea, are nearly always deadly.

Orangebalms are a trail of tiny islands meant to tempt pirates and sailors into lowering their anchors. Dwarf fruit trees line their shores, sprouting golden apples, honey mangoes, and purple peaches. More than enough to tempt a dry, hungry mouth. But these fruits are plump with poison—even the thick, sweet-smelling liquid inside the tree's branches is deadly to the touch. The sand beneath them is volcanic, hot enough to burn through flesh. And beyond those plants, vicious creatures await. Vampire leeches, flies that feast on eyeballs, and snakes with venom that dissolves skin and bone.

These islands can be easily recognized by the orange ring of rocks around their coast, a pretty feature that often makes them more attractive to the unknowing. They are the exact inverse of an oasis and should be unquestionably avoided.

Treasures also pose risks. Many a golden coin has been misenchanted, injected with dark power. Pirates who have come across these cursed riches have found themselves stunned permanently, shrunken to the size of a grain of sand, or transported alone into the middle of the ocean. Those with cursesensory emblems are prized crew members, for only they can smell the bitter scent of misechantment. That is why treasure is often carried in wooden chests—for a smart pirate does not touch their loot until a cursesensor can be consulted.

It is also why thieves rarely survive long on pirate ships.

Perhaps the greatest warning of all: For those willing to steal from the sea, the consequences can prove deadly. Guardians lurk below, giant creatures that can swallow ships whole.

The ocean is full of ancient beasts who awaken when someone has taken a treasure they cannot keep.

12

PERLA

Tor hurtled off the bed, landing on the floor. He heard steps on the stairs, then Melda burst in, quickly followed by Engle and Vesper.

Melda threw her arms around him and sobbed into his shoulder. "You—you were *gone*, Tor! You were dead, you were so *cold* and blue..."

Engle embraced him next, and Tor was shocked to see his friend's eyes rimmed in red. Engle nodded gravely. "She's right, Tor. You died. We all thought..." He straightened and nodded. Tried and failed to smile. "But you're here. You're okay."

Tor didn't have the heart or energy to tell them that they should have wished for the pearl. That maybe, that way, their mission wouldn't be doomed.

Because the prophecy had been right.

One of them had died—only to be brought back.

Which meant that the other half of the prediction would also come true. They would fail on their quest to find the pearl.

Part of Tor had wanted to give up the entire journey, even as he sailed forward. But now, having seen the sacrifice his friends had made, he realized it wasn't about him or his Night Witch abilities.

It was about them. And he would die a dozen deaths to make sure they never did.

All of Emblem Island was counting on them.

He turned to Vesper, who watched him, wide-eyed, from the other side of the room, arms across her chest. Her hair was still wet, forming a small puddle at her bare feet. "Thank you," he said. "I know you didn't have to help me, so thank you."

None of them asked how Tor could have known how Vesper helped. She simply said, "I'm glad you're all right," before leaving the room.

Tor turned to his friends.

Melda sighed. "I don't trust her for a second. But she's not so bad, I suppose."

Engle nodded. "And we need her, now."

His friend was right. With the wish used up, they now had to use the compass the way the blood queen had intended—with someone from Swordscale holding it. Only then could the compass lead them to the pearl.

They just had to hope that the spectral, the Calavera captain, and the Swordscale traitor hadn't found it yet.

Though grateful for Vesper's part in his rescue, Tor couldn't help but play back the night's events, starting with the capsizal.

Why had Vesper taken the fortuneteller's skull?

He rested through the night, sleep sweet like sapphire and thick as syrup. He slept all morning, too, almost through the afternoon. By the time he surfaced, Tor was starving, and they were nearing land. Ships passed by, leaving and entering the harbor in front of them. He thought it must have been a busy port.

"Tor!" Engle said, smiling wide. He ran down from the upper deck. "How did you sleep?"

"Well, thanks," he said, his voice coming out raspy and cracked. He was thirsty—and had just realized it. "Are we stopping?"

Vesper appeared, holding the compass. "We've been going where it leads us." She opened her map, and Tor frowned down at the markings running along the planks at his feet.

"The pearl is in *Perla*?"

Engle shrugged. "According to the compass, at least."

"How did the ship sail without me?"

Melda strode toward him. "We didn't think it would—but we explained the circumstances to the mermaid, and the ship listened. It was still tethered to you, of course, can't sail without you." She swallowed. "When you were *gone*,"—Melda shuddered—"the ship stopped moving completely. The sails went out. That's how we knew."

Tor felt very much alive, but could not fathom the moments Melda and Engle had thought him dead. If anything happened to either of them...

No. He banished the thoughts. He was saved, for them—to help the two people who had continuously risked their lives to be there for him, without question. Using the comb to save him was a debt he could never repay—but he *could* make sure they succeeded in finding the pearl, saved their village, and got home safely.

And that was exactly what they were going to do.

Perla's harbor stretched across an entire mile of coast, capable of hosting over a hundred vessels. Ships three times the size of theirs perched merrily in their own dedicated slots, each carved from luxurious wood that looked smooth and new. He noticed they were grouped by figurehead. Some ships had a roaring lion, plated in what looked like gold. Nearby, there was a small fleet of vessels helmed by horses. Then, warriors. Great serpents. And, finally, birds.

Perla's port was bustling with trade, the market starting far out into the docks. They disembarked and took their ship with them, only to meet a variety of merchants, each one yelling louder than the last.

"Fresh cod, the flakiest on Perla!"

"Oysters, the best you'll find on Emblem Island!"

"Rare tiger-striped mackerel, with lemon slices included!"

"Genuine enchanted fishing rods, guaranteed to catch you dinner tonight!"

"Fried fish with fried potatoes and purple pickles!"

"Does Perla have a queen, like Zura?" Engle asked Melda, eyes wide with hunger as he surveyed the stands of food.

"No. Perla is run by the five top merchants, who are said to hoard the best enchantments in Emblem Island, imported from every coast." She shrugged. "Honestly, I'm not surprised the pearl's here. It's probably in one of their palaces." She pointed up at a cliff that framed the city. Five palatial houses were built in its side, each connected by a bridge.

"How on Emblem are we supposed to get up there?" Engle asked.

Tor didn't know. It looked like the houses were well guarded. "Let's just keep following the compass."

Vesper held it firmly in her hand, glancing down at her palm every few seconds. The needle led them down the docks and past luxurious seaside apartments and town houses, made of striking white marble. It was a city of wealth. The streets were perfectly crafted in stone, not a crack in sight. Shops lined the streets at the bottom floors of town houses, their products neat and simple inside. Through windows, Tor saw spider silk clothing, jewelry made from gems the size of small potatoes, a hat shop with hats enchanted to do all sorts of marvelous things, like whisper into the user's ear the name of approaching strangers or warn the wearer of impending danger. Or so the man standing outside advertising them claimed.

Everyone in Perla wore a hat, some in strange shapes, like bows and birds. Each in a range of colors: lavender, butterscotch, indigo, violet, blush, and juniper.

Someone with an illusion emblem stood in the center of the road and painted the sky with an invisible brush, creating floating ribbons and balloons that burst, only to appear once more. By the looks of it, Perla was preparing for a celebration.

"They certainly like chocolate here," Melda said. Every block had a chocolate shop, with prices in the windows that made Engle's eyes bulge.

"Ten dobbles for a chocolate bar?" he yelled. "It better be made of gold!"

"It is," Melda said, reading the sign.

"The City of Seekers," Tor said softly, remembering what Captain Forecastle had called it.

Melda smirked. "Indeed."

"This way." Vesper turned onto a narrow side street, and they followed, squeezing past women wearing dresses that took up practically the entire block.

Melda studied them, fascinated. "I've never seen fabrics like these," she said quietly. "They're enchanted." One of the dresses turned from ice blue to pink, then shortened to its wearer's ankles when she encountered a small puddle on the road. Another grew sleeves and a cape when the woman complained of the slight breeze.

Vesper turned again, this time onto a street lined with pubs that looked nothing like the Crusty Barnacle. She stopped, and Tor ran into her back. "It's...moving a lot," she said.

The needle whizzed this way and that, as if confused, before finally settling on a direction.

"That means the *pearl* is moving," Melda said.

Tor nodded. "Which means someone has it on them."

Vesper walked faster now, almost running down an alleyway. Perla's chatter and fine music fell away as they traveled to its seediest part, which, even then, was nicer than most villages.

The streets were nearly empty. The shops all looked closed. Even the sun seemed to shine less here, blocked by the taller buildings closer to the harbor. Tor spotted a sign on the corner of a street, marking the place as Galaway Lane.

"Seeking something?" A man wearing a fine long coat stood behind them. He wore a hat that had real flames burning on its rim, yet somehow the fabric remained unscorched.

"No," Melda said firmly. And they continued past him without another word.

Engle swallowed. "I don't like this place." He looked around, squinting into the distance. "I feel like someone's following us."

Tor wished they could turn back around. He felt uneasy, too, like they were all being watched. Yet, the compass' needle continued to lead them farther down the street, deeper into the darkest part of the city.

A scream echoed down another alley, not far away. Followed by another.

Melda winced, her hands in fists. "There are rumors," she said quietly, "that the city is so rich because it runs on the profits of dark enchantments."

Tor's mouth went dry. He had heard about dark enchantments once, from a classmate who had gotten sent home after the teacher had heard him talk about them. They were born from pain—usually from forcing someone to enchant an object. And they always required blood.

The compass swung toward an alley.

Everything in Tor screamed to run. But they had made it this far. They were so close. So they walked down the alley, only to find a solid wall at the end. Nowhere else to go. And no sign of the pearl.

The compass needle stopped moving.

"What happened?" Engle asked. Something dripped nearby. A rusty door creaked. Smoke billowed from the building next door.

Vesper shook the compass, trying to get it to work again. But the needle went limp. "I don't know. I didn't do anything differently."

Melda looked around. "It must be this place. The number of enchantments might be affecting it somehow."

Tor turned to walk back down the alley and froze.

The Swordscale traitor stood there, next to the Calavera captain. His floating hat was now coated in flames, just like the man from the street. Tor's stomach dropped. He watched as the Calavera captain pulled a matchstick from his pocket, lit it with the blaze on his head, then whispered a word into the flame. It glowed purple for the briefest moment.

Then, it extinguished, along with every streetlight.

In the near darkness, Tor could barely make out a figure who appeared in a flash of mauve.

"Spectral," Vesper hissed.

The Calavera captain and the Swordscale traitor were gone. Vanished.

Another flash, and a different spectral appeared. And another. They blocked the alley completely.

None had a mouth, the skin pulled taut where one should have been. Still, Tor felt them as they stepped closer, reaching into his mind, prying it open like a stubborn oyster.

We're here to collect you, a slithering voice said right into his brain.

Melda tensed next to him. Engle gasped.

Vesper let out a sob. He wondered what they had said to her.

They backed into the wall, nowhere to go. And the spectrals inched closer, their dark robes dragging behind them.

Vesper raised her hand as if to make them small, but her fingers shook. She groaned with effort, but seemed frozen in place.

Are you ready to watch your friends die, Tor Luna?

The spectral was standing in front of him now, the skin of his face stretching up like he was smiling.

Tor cried out, cradling his hand. His lifeline—it was shrinking right before his eyes. Vesper had said that lifelines weren't reliable at sea anymore, which was why theirs hadn't changed at all during their journey, even moments from death...

But they were on land now. The rainbow line shrunk smaller and smaller still, until it was barely there. Engle and Melda's were practically gone. The spectral took a step forward.

And crumbled to ash as an arrow hit it.

Another arrow whizzed right past Tor's nose, finding its next target. The third remaining spectral sent a cloud of smoke up as a shield, then threw a mighty beam of purple fire through the air, aiming for where the arrow had come from.

But another pierced it, from the opposite direction.

And the spectral fell to pieces.

Tor's lifeline grew again, back to what it had been before, an agonizing process, the rainbow lines stitching themselves back into his skin. There was a clatter at the mouth of the alley.

The man from Galaway Lane who had spoken to them appeared. He lit a match on his hat and neared the three piles of ash as if to reignite them. But a voice from above said, "I wouldn't," and the man ran away.

Tor recognized that voice.

A moment later, a figure dropped down from the roof, holding a rope.

Captain Forecastle. He wore a shirt without sleeves,

revealing a long arrow emblem that ran the length of the inside of his forearm.

There was commotion on the roof of the opposite building, and Forecastle quickly lifted his arm wrist-side up, pulled back with the other, and released—the arrow emblem shot out down his palm, then became real as soon as it left his skin, only to be replaced by another.

Engle's mouth hung open.

Melda didn't look as impressed. "How did you find us here?"

The pirate scratched at the back of his head. "No thank ye for saving yer lives? Suppose we deserve that." He sighed. "Had terrible luck in Tortuga Bay... Lost every gamble we made, every fight we started, every dobble we stole..." He looked pensive. "Began to realize double-crossing ye after ye freed us did something terrible to our karma." The pirate shrugged. "So we're here to make amends."

Melda raised an eyebrow at him. "That doesn't answer my question."

"Started asking around for the pearl, heard some chatter about dealings in Perla. We figured it was here, and that the compass would lead ye to the City of Seekers. So we waited. And followed ye from the harbor. In case ye needed us."

Engle *had* mentioned feeling like someone was following

them. The pirate must have been well hidden for Engle not to have spotted him.

Captain Forecastle nodded toward the three piles of ash. "Dangerous enemies ye've made."

Vesper shook her head. "So they have it, don't they? The compass led us here. Right where they were."

Tor blinked against a sudden flash of nausea. If the traitor, the captain, and the spectrals had the pearl, then Estrelle's fate was already sealed. They could destroy the town in minutes with its power.

His family—

"Not necessarily," Captain Forecastle said. "According to chatter, the Calavera captain, that silver-faired fellow, and spectrals have been all over the city, searching. They've been gathering information from merchants, pirates...even assassins. Don't think they've found it yet."

Vesper shook her head. "But the compass—"

"The compass is a fickle thing that will double-cross ye in an attempt to get wherever it wants to go..." he said. "Trust us, we know. If ye lose yer focus on what ye've lost for even a *moment*, it will pull ye in its own direction..."

Melda shot a scathing look at Vesper, but didn't say anything, and Tor was grateful for that.

Still, Vesper's mistake had almost cost them everything.

The spectrals had appeared in moments, though none of them had been the one he had seen on the Calavera ship. No, that one was larger than the others, more powerful...

Why wasn't the larger spectral with them? What deal had the Calavera captain and traitor made with it?

If the Swordscale traitor and Calavera captain were in Perla, it could be close by. Tor remembered mention of the spectrals in the *Book of Seas*. If the more powerful of them could do half of the things the story described—

"We need to leave. Now," Tor said.

Captain Forecastle nodded, eyes darting to the surrounding rooftops. "Good idea."

They hurried out of the alley, Captain Forecastle at the front, his arm long in front of him, ready to shoot an enemy with an endless supply of arrows. It was dark now, and Galaway Lane seemed to be waking up. Shop doors were propped open, and seedy characters stood outside. Men and women wore hats covered in cobwebs, black diamonds, ice, smoke, bones, and even snakes. Women who wore dark gloves to their elbows laughed wickedly as they approached, their voices high-pitched like the creak of a closing door.

Tor sighed in relief when they stumbled onto the main road. Wealthy Perlas regarded them haughtily, dressed in their evening best. Some wore gowns with gems woven right into the fabric. They were walking toward the docks in droves.

At the front, Melda tried to squeeze through, but the crowd was too thick, and they got pushed to its edge, against a row of town houses. Tor turned in all directions, searching for a flash of purple. More spectrals could appear anywhere. Or the Calavera captain, with his long sword at his side. A captain famed for bloodshed... Nowhere was safe.

Captain Forecastle cursed as a spectral appeared at the outskirts of the crowd, searching it intently.

Tor opened his mouth, just as a hand covered it.

"Don't move if you want to live," a voice said into his ear, before he was dragged through a door.

He had been pulled into a townhouse foyer. Melda, Engle, Captain Forecastle, and Vesper stumbled in behind him. The door slammed shut. Through a gap in the window shutter, Tor saw a spectral pass by, hood covering most of its head, looking for them.

"I take thank-you payments in dobbles, gold, and chocolate," a voice said. The same one that had just spoken into his ear.

A young woman stood before them. She wore an impressive three-tiered pink hat—three bows stacked atop one another—and a white dress with a ribbon at the waist that was puffed out at the bottom like one of Tor's father's soufflés.

She quirked an eyebrow at him. "Not what you expected? I know the dress is a bit over the top... It's a pain trying to fit in, in a place like Perla."

In a quick movement, she untied the ribbon at her waist, and the bottom half of the dress snapped off, revealing a much more practical pair of pants and boots. She kicked the skirt away with disdain.

"Now, then." She smiled widely. "Nice to meet you. I'm Violet, and I'm an assassin."

The Sundrop Salmon

The sun cried, just once. And its first and only tear formed a fish that fell from the sky. It landed in the sea and had golden scales, each more glittering than the last. It blinded the other fish as it passed, its radiance never before seen.

The other fish, consumed with jealousy, formed a plan to take all of the sundrop salmon's scales that night, so that it would be dull, like them. While the golden salmon slept, the first fish went to pry off one of its scales—

And fell dead. The would-be stolen scale turned silver. And none of the other fish approached the salmon again.

It is said that this scale is enchanted. Gifted by the moon, who protected the sun's fish. For the attack happened at night, while the sun slept. The moon's scale amplified the fish's innate ability to stun other fish, protecting it from danger.

And some say that if wielded by an Emblemite, it would magnify their abilities, too.

To this day, the golden fish swims, known to trail pirate ships, chasing treasure that shines as brightly as its creator.

13

VIOLET, THE ASSASSIN

Tor heard Engle gulp behind him. Melda said, "Excuse me, what?"

Captain Forecastle laughed. "Should've known by the hair clip," he said. "Which house?"

Violet beamed. "Crimson."

He nodded, then bowed. "An honor, then."

She bowed her head back at him.

"Do you have the slightest idea what's happening?" Tor heard Vesper ask Engle.

He shook his head. "Not a crumb of a clue."

The pirate turned. "There are five houses of assassins, ye see, each with their own code. Rules, if ye would. We pirates intersect with them quite a bit."

"And what code does the Crimson house follow?" Melda asked.

Violet motioned for them to follow her farther inside, and, as she casually strode down the hallway, she pulled an impressive amount of weapons from her person. A dagger from her chest, three knives disguised as pins from her hair, a full sword from between her shoulder blades. Along with many other trinkets Tor didn't recognize, undoubtedly enchanted to be lethal.

She led them to a large sitting room with a cozy couch, fluffy pillows, and thick blankets strewn about.

Violet slumped into a chair with a groan, kicking up her feet onto the marble coffee table. "What a day," she said, shaking her head. She ran a hand through her long brown hair, then said, "Oh, missed one!" before pulling a three-inch-long knife, disguised as a hair clip, from behind her ear. She dropped it onto the table with a clatter. "Now, then, what's your name?"

She was looking at Melda, who blinked. "Grimelda Alexander. Melda, for short."

Violet smiled. "Well, Melda, House Crimson has very simple rules. Never kill for pleasure, never kill the innocent, and never miss a target." She shrugged. "That's it."

Vesper tilted her head at her, an eyebrow raised. "And who determines who is innocent?"

"Good question. *I* do, of course. I only kill the despicably dreadful." She picked at a piece of lint on her top. "In a city as corrupt as this one, it's one of the only ways to get them to stop hurting innocents."

"Corrupt?" Melda's forehead was a folded up fan of lines. "Who is corrupt?"

"All of them, I'm afraid." Violet leaned in. "I've gotten assignments from housewives, lawmakers, aristocrats...even *children*, if you can believe it." She saw Engle's expression and shook her head. "I don't take them, of course." She squinted. "Well, not *all* of them."

"How does one become an assassin?" Tor asked, curious. He had never really heard it thrown around as a job prospect.

She smiled, revealing a row of dazzling white teeth. "You get *exceptionally* good at killing."

Tor leaned back on the couch, and the assassin laughed. She smacked her lips together, resting her chin on her hand. "It's lonely though," she said wistfully. "Hard having friends, in my line of work, can make things...complicated. Especially when you have an enemy, and they try to use your loved ones as bait." She shook her head. "Can get *quite* messy." She rubbed her palms together, and Tor saw that she had an extremely long lifeline, a fact that must have put her at ease in her profession. "Anyway. Should we discuss the bounty on your heads?"

Tor froze. Had they walked directly into a lion's den? Was she just as bad as the man with the fire-brimmed hat?

Violet raised her eyebrows. "Oh, I'm not trying to collect it," she said, lowering her head. "I suppose I never made that clear." She tapped at her bottom lip. "All of Galaway has been looking for you. Which means you and I might just be on the same side."

Tor swallowed. The Calavera captain, the spectral, and the traitor must really have wanted them dead if they had gone so far as to put a bounty on their heads.

"And what side is that?" Tor asked.

Violet frowned. "Spectrals have been in and out of this city more times in the last month than the last ten years. They're planning something, and I want to stop it."

Engle looked suspicious. "Why?"

"I have my reasons, sightseer," she said, spotting his emblem. "On one assignment, I lived on a ship among pirates. And heard plenty about the Calavera. That captain must be stopped. With the pearl, he would ruin all that is good on Emblem Island. Including all of the places I've made my home." She swallowed. "But, more importantly, an enemy of the spectrals is a friend of mine."

Captain Forecastle said, "Thank ye for opening yer door to us."

Violet whipped to look at Melda and said, "Don't you know it's impolite to stare?"

She reddened. "It's just...that marking, on your wrist."

Tor saw it. A band of silver, like a smear of melted moonlight. He had seen some just like it before.

She grinned. "I trained with the giantesses, until adulthood," she said. "This is just one of the bands I earned there."

Melda brightened.

Engle rolled his eyes. "Here we go..."

"We visited them, quite recently! Do you know Valentina?"

Violet nodded. "Of course! She's a good friend."

"She taught me to use a sword! Just for a few minutes, but I was very surprised by its weight..."

Melda continued to speak to Violet about the giantesses, and Tor found another marking on the assassin. This one, an emblem. He could have thought of a dozen different abilities that would best serve a killer, but this was certainly not one of them.

"You're an aniboca," he said, interrupting one of Melda's many stories. Melda glared at him. "You can talk to animals."

Vesper raised an eyebrow. "Is that useful in your... profession?"

Violet swept her long hair back in a single motion. "Well, it helped me find you lot, didn't it?"

Tor frowned. "It did?"

Violet whistled, and a small bird came flying through the house. A blue and gray lark. It landed on her shoulder. "She told me Crowmus was on the prowl. He's the one with the fire on his hat." She rolled her brown eyes. "It looks ridiculous, doesn't it?"

"So they're your spies?" Vesper asked.

"Much more than that. But, sure—they're my eyes and ears in this city and beyond," she winked at them. "Now, enough shoptalk. Is anyone hungry?"

Tor hadn't eaten since before he had died, he realized, with a hollow pang in his stomach. Engle—who had surely eaten some of Vesper's sea snacks just hours before—answered with an enthusiastic yes.

"Perfect! I don't cook—I deal with enough knives on the job, if you know what I mean—but I'll grab something from across the street. There's this lovely little restaurant; the chefs are from Zura and brought all sorts of spices over. I'll get a variety." With a final smile, Violet walked to the foyer, tied back on the bottom of her dress, and strode out the door into the town square, which was crowded, but not nearly as much so as before.

Melda shrugged. "She seems nice."

Engle gaped at her. "She's an *assassin*!"

The lark had been left behind and squawked angrily at Engle.

"What?" he said to it. "It's true!"

"Stop it," Melda said.

Engle scoffed. "You only like her because she trained with your beloved giantesses!"

In fact, Melda had never taken off the ring the giantesses had given to her, as a token to remember to be strong. She twirled it around her finger as she huffed, then leaned back on Violet's exceptionally comfortable couch.

Vesper shrugged. "I think she's the fish's scales."

Engle turned to her and blinked. Tor figured it was some sort of Swordscale compliment.

Captain Forecastle made himself comfortable on the couch and wriggled his toes in his boots. "Wouldn't believe the places we stayed, when ye left us at Tortuga Bay." He looked around. "Now *this* is luxurious."

Engle scoffed. "I suppose *killing* is a profitable business."

Melda glared at the pirate. "Don't you dare try to steal anything."

Captain Forecastle laughed. "Steal from an assassin? Have ye lost yer head? Wouldn't dream of it." The lark squawked at him loudly, and he sighed, then pulled a ruby-hilted dagger from his pocket—a dagger that surely hadn't been there before they had entered the house. He placed it on the table, and lifted his hands in silent surrender. "All right, all right."

Soon, Violet arrived, juggling three baskets of food in her hands, along with a large box of Perla chocolates.

They ate dinner in her dining room—garlic roasted potatoes, buttered fried dough, mushroom soup, fresh salmon covered in an array of colorful spices, steamed vegetables Tor had never tasted before—until the chatter of the streets died down.

After much prodding from Melda and Vesper, Violet explained how her job as an assassin worked. Through the sliver in her door she would receive a white letter with a red seal. If she refused the job, no further action was necessary. If she accepted, she wore long red gloves to the market the next day, where someone would be watching.

Acceptance by mail was risky, she said. Clothing choices could hardly be used as evidence in court.

Upon acceptance, detailed instructions would be placed within the wrapping of a fish she purchased.

Then, it was up to her to deliver.

"And what are the other assassin groups?" Melda asked. "What are their principles?"

Violet pursed her lips. "We're each named after a shade of

red. There's Crimson, of course. Then Garnet, Ruby, Scarlet, and Vermillion." Violet frowned. "Let's just say, the only thing we have in common with the others is the killing. Our methods, reasons, and morals...differ greatly."

Captain Forecastle nearly choked on the ale Violet had found him. "*That's* one way to say it," he said, sputtering drink as he laughed.

Violet suddenly turned to Vesper and tilted her head. "What is it?" she asked.

Vesper only blinked.

"I've been trained to study body language very carefully. You have a question. Ask it."

Vesper pressed her lips together. She looked unwilling to speak, and moments ticked by. But Violet was patient, waiting until she said, "Your emblem. It has nothing to do with killing. How did you end up an assassin? How was it even an option for you?"

Violet sat back. "Ah." She pursed her lips. "I hate fate and destiny and everything predetermined. My emblem isn't the best for an assassin, but I made it work for me. I *evolved.*" She shrugged. "Any emblem's use can be reimagined for nearly any role. What's yours?"

"I'm a magnificate," she said. And Tor was surprised she didn't say waterbreather.

Violet snapped. "Fantastic! Much of my job is about disguising myself and certain objects I don't want discovered." She thrummed her fingers on the table, her nails painted deep red. "If I had your ability, I would not just do the *obvious*, which would be disguising things by making them very small. No, I would hide them in plain sight. Make them so unusually large, make them look like something else entirely, that no one would think to look twice." She blew air roughly through her mouth, thinking. "And if I was in a fight, I wouldn't do what they might anticipate, which would be to make myself small or large. I would change my *enemies'* size. Because they wouldn't be expecting it." Violet shrugged. "You see, in my line of work, there are some that can shield against an emblem's power and others who can sense things that one is trying to hide, so the element of surprise is invaluable."

"How about my emblem?" Engle asked enthusiastically. "What would *I* do if I was an assassin?"

Violet glanced at the spyglass on his skin and shrugged. "You'd be the lookout. Nothing surprising about *that*, I'm afraid."

After their plates were empty, Violet offered them a place to stay for the night. "I have plenty of rooms," she said. "And a penchant for guests."

Though Tor wanted to, they couldn't. Melda produced the small arenahora from her pocket. "We have a long way to go and not much time," she said.

"I see. Another time, perhaps." Violet peeked through a sliver of exposed window. "I don't see them anymore, but who knows what's lurking out there. I'll take you through the back way."

Violet led them down to the bottom level of the town house. It looked like an ordinary bedroom until she slid over the bed, revealing a hatch.

"These tunnels run all through the city," she said, opening it. "And are only accessible by a select few." She whistled, and her lark flew into the room. "She'll show you the way," she said. "If I can ever be of help to you, just say my name to the nearest bird. Word will get to me."

Tor thanked her, and climbed in first. The tunnel was made of stone and was small enough that Captain Forecastle would surely have to hunch over. Melda, last to say goodbye, jumped as the bird sped past her, down the corridor. It led them like a guiding star, beneath the many dangers—and wonders—of Perla. Already close to the docks, it took just a few minutes before the lark showed them to a door that emptied out in a quiet corner at the base of the harbor. Engle went first, to make sure the coast was clear. The bird chirped a last goodbye, and Tor watched it fly back down the tunnel.

Then, on swift wind, they finally left the City of Seekers.

The Young Princess

There once was a princess who lived in a castle on the coast. The young royal spent hours in one of the castle's towers, eyes fixed on the water. She stared so long at the sea that the sea began to stare back.

Come closer, child, it said.

So one night, she snuck out of bed. She creeped past guards and down to the sand, which had always been forbidden.

Three heads bobbed within the waves, and the princess knew them to be mermaids.

It was rumored that long ago, one of her ancestors, a king, had lured a siren from the sea and made her his queen.

The call of the ocean had been passed on to the princess, and she took a step into the water, unable to resist.

Come closer, the sea said, and the mermaids smiled.

With each step into the water, the princess found herself changing. She yelled out as her legs

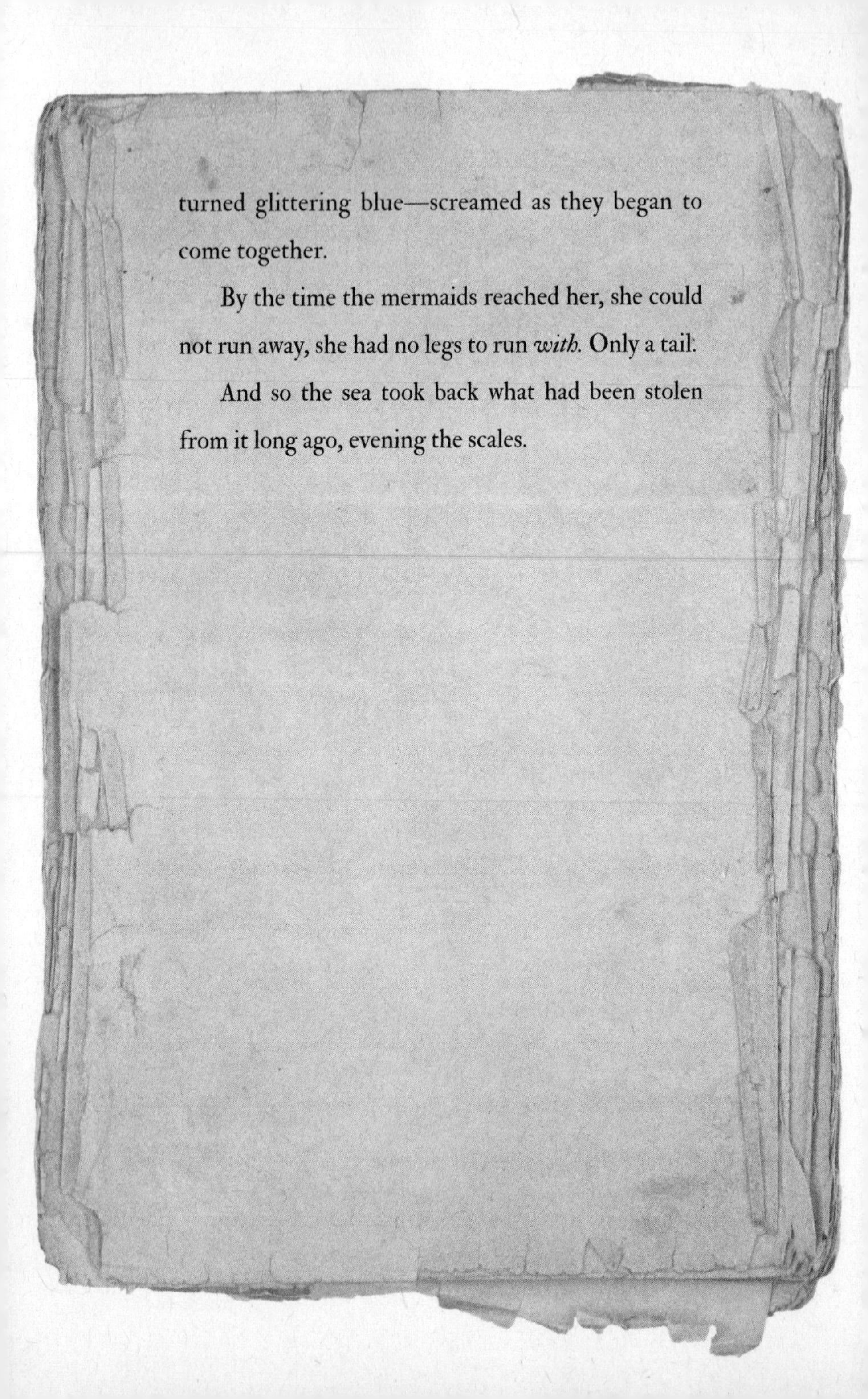

turned glittering blue—screamed as they began to come together.

By the time the mermaids reached her, she could not run away, she had no legs to run *with.* Only a tail.

And so the sea took back what had been stolen from it long ago, evening the scales.

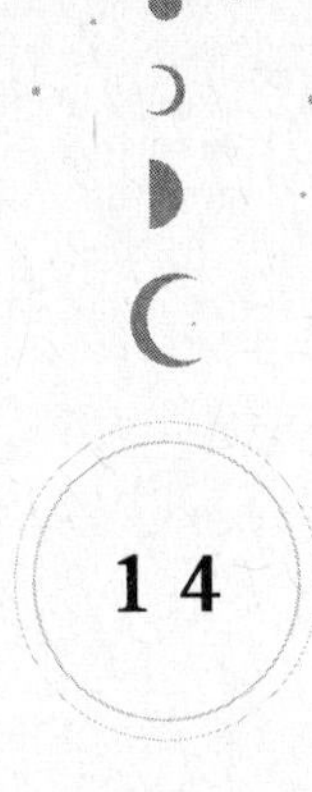

14

THE SILVER SCALE

Captain Forecastle kicked his feet up onto a barrel on the deck as if he had never left.

"I suppose he *did* save our lives," Engle said, shrugging. "If he wants to help, we should let him."

The pirate was the least of his worries. Melda's hourglass had emptied considerably since they had been attacked by the capsizal. If they were to have any chance at finding the pearl in time to save Estrelle, they needed to find it soon.

If the ice keeping the Calavera at bay unfroze before they returned, it was all for nothing.

Tor thought about the Night Witch's visions and what the assassin had said. The spectrals were planning something... Is that what the Night Witch was so afraid of? What she had warned him about?

He remembered that Vesper had said something about them on the first day of their journey. He took her aside.

"What do you know about spectrals?"

She raised her eyebrows at him. "Why?"

Tor ground his back teeth together, wishing she could just give him a simple response. "Swordscale bans writing about violent topics, yet you know about them. How?"

Vesper stilled. She was silent for a moment, before saying, "Why do you ask so many questions, Tor?"

He saw Melda out of the corner of his eye walking toward them. Tor didn't want to worry Melda or Engle about the Night Witch's visions, not yet. Not when they had so much else to consider.

"Never mind," he said and joined his friends.

Melda seemed in a better mood than usual, which Tor imagined had everything to do with the assassin's mention of the giantesses. "Are you ready?" she asked Tor.

He raised an eyebrow at her.

"To chart a final course." She called everyone to the helm.

Engle pulled the compass from his pocket and handed it to Vesper. She closed her eyes, and, as per Captain Forecastle's instructions, thought very hard about the pearl.

"A drop of blood would help," Captain Forecastle said quietly.

Without hesitating, Vesper made her dagger charm large enough that Tor could see its blade and pierced her hand with it.

Blood dripped onto the compass' glass.

They held their breath.

The needle whirled around and around, fast as lightning, as if invigorated by the blood. It swung this way and that, in endless sweeps, before finally settling on a direction. North.

Tor commanded the ship to follow.

Finally, *finally*, they were headed for the pearl.

Captain Forecastle yawned and murmured about needing a good night of sleep. Before he could leave, Melda stopped him. "What else did you hear about the pearl in Perla?"

He shrugged. "Just that those three characters were looking for it there. The captain, the spectral, the silver-haired one, like her," he motioned toward Vesper.

"That's all?" Tor asked.

"There was something else about the Calavera captain... He was sniffing around for an enchantment..." Captain Forecastle gave him a pointed look. "Something to melt ice."

Tor stiffened. "Did he find it?"

"Couldn't tell ye."

Melda began walking in small circles, head down. "This is good. If they had already found the pearl, they wouldn't be looking for a melting enchantment. They could simply unfreeze the sea themselves." She brightened. "We still have time then, we could still find the pearl before them."

Tor hoped she was right.

They didn't know where they were going—so they didn't know when they would get there. All they could do was go forward, blindly following the compass.

And hope time wouldn't run out.

Tor ran into Vesper in the hallway before bed. "Has it healed?" he asked. The cut she'd made in her palm had looked deep, and Melda had concocted a simple elixir to soothe it. Vesper had shrunk the compass and now wore it on her charm bracelet.

She looked at him, dazed, like she might not have heard him.

He lowered his head. "Are you all right, Vesper?"

She blinked. "Um—yes. Of course. Just...tired." She gave him a curt nod, then retreated to her room.

Tor noticed her green eyes had been slightly swollen and pink at the creases.

Like she had been crying.

The next day, Tor woke up shivering beneath his sheets. They had kept traveling north throughout the night, and the weather had turned, quite suddenly. He asked the boat for thicker clothing and piled the layers on before leaving his cabin.

Melda was on the deck, wrapped in her blanket, sitting beside Engle. Tor snapped his fingers and a mountain of jackets appeared, along with a pile of wool blankets, socks, and a table lined with warm drinks—hot chocolate, canela tea, and hot rum for Forecastle.

The pirate merrily tilted his hat at Tor, then went straight for the drink.

"You know, lots of really interesting fish live in temperatures like this," Engle said after taking a jacket and hot chocolate, which he finished in an impressive gulp. He peeked over the side of the ship, and Tor wondered how far into the sea he could see. "Ombré haddocks, longtail connies, lemon sea snails, giant salmon, ribbon-tailed flounders."

Melda quickly turned to face him, intrigued. "And how would you go about catching a giant salmon?"

Engle frowned. "Those types are very sensitive to movement, so if I wanted to catch one, I would make lots of motion in the water to try to attract it."

Melda beamed at him. "Great. Catch one." She undid the bright golden ribbon from her hair and handed it to him. "And use this as bait."

Engle frowned, then shrugged.

Tor looked at Melda as she walked over to him. "You really think it's out here?" He knew exactly what she was hoping Engle might catch, only because he had finished the *Book of Seas* in the last few days. Engle clearly hadn't.

She shrugged. "It's worth a try, isn't it?" She took a hot chocolate, topped it with a fat dollop of cream Tor had thought up, and sat down to watch Engle make a plan. "If anyone can catch a mythical sea creature, it's him."

Vesper joined them on the deck twenty minutes later, sitting next to Captain Forecastle, who was brushing through his beard with his miniature sword. The waters had gotten so cold she couldn't swim in them, and she stared down at the sea longingly.

"We're waiting, boy," Captain Forecastle said to Engle from across the deck, rum sloshing around in his mug.

Tor grinned. "I hope you don't plan on using yourself as bait instead of the ribbon."

Engle stuck his tongue out at them. He had been trying to come up with a plan for almost half an hour. At first, he had wanted to jump into the water himself and splash around. Melda had quickly shot that idea down, citing not only the sharks that had trailed the ship for the last few miles, but also the freezing water. Engle had asked Tor to ask the ship for a number of things, none of which he had touched.

Tor watched Engle lean over the ship, his belly on the side, and cup his hands around his mouth. He started yelling, then singing, butchering some of the pirate songs Forecastle had a habit of singing in the morning.

"There once was a fiddle
That smelled like a...riddle?
And played music sweet as a gem...
Enchanted it was,
to make songs that we love
Until something...something happened..."

Captain Forecastle winced at Engle's pitchy voice and took another swig of drink.

"Wait, I actually know this one!" the sightseer said.

"There once was a captain
Who'd been everywhere I'd been
From Tortuga to Perla to Estrelle...
Though one day he made port
Ran into the wrong sort
And fell victim to a blood queen's spell
From that day and on
His luck was all gone

And his ship was swept into a tempest

In the hurricane he resides

Each year taking more lives

For the crew of his stormy ghost ship!"

Vesper rolled her green eyes. "If you want to catch a salmon through movement, your voice won't do much, *lovely* as it is. It doesn't travel well—from the surface down into the sea, it barely makes a vibration."

Engle stopped his singing and turned to her. "What would you suggest, then?"

She sighed. "We're going to need some planks."

"Ready?" They were all stationed at different points throughout the ship, two planks in each of their hands. Engle looked behind him, making sure they were in position, then said, "Now!"

In one solid rhythm they beat their planks against the ship's sides like it was a giant drum. Vesper had explained that the vibrations made would attract fish much better than singing. Tor was surprised Captain Forecastle agreed to help, and he smirked as he watched the pirate half-heartedly thump his instruments against the wood. They continued beating, Tor's arms quickly getting sore, before he saw Vesper was right.

Dozens of curious sea creatures approached the boat, surfacing from the great below. A few sharks, with heads he'd never seen before. Some long, exactly like a saw. Some squished, their eyes on opposite sides. Some with two eyes on one side, like a flounder. Some with two giant, sharp front teeth like a vampire.

Tor had now slowed the ship to a crawl, almost completely still.

"How much longer of this, boy?" Captain Forecastle asked, barely hitting the side of the ship yet looking just a few breaths away from passing out.

"Just a little longer!" Engle said. He drummed more enthusiastically than anyone else, seeming to have an endless stream of energy. "I've never seen a giant salmon," he said dreamily. "Wait, is that an optagorp?"

"What's an optagorp?" Captain Forecastle asked at the other end of the ship, still thrumming, sounding out of breath.

Engle squinted intently, then brightened. "Vesper, get ready!" he yelled, grinning at the sea, fishing rod with the ribbon in his grip, seeing something no one else could. Vesper rushed to his side, dropping her planks to the deck.

She waited, hand outstretched. They all stilled, stopping their drumming until Engle yelled at them and they kept playing. Hands moving at a rapid pace, Tor stood on his toes and watched as something bigger than even the sharks surfaced, golden and sparkling, like the sun reflected onto the sea. Before it could swim away with the ribbon, Vesper shrunk it down, then floated it to the deck.

As soon as it touched the wood, it expanded, and Tor jumped back.

In its full size, the fish was bigger than Tor. It thrashed and splashed around wildly, and he thought it might simply jump back into the water.

The sundrop salmon's golden scales were mesmerizingly bright. They were reflective, fracturing sunlight into miniature, blinding rainbows. For a moment, Tor was frozen, spellbound, the same way he had been dazzled by the Melodine's song over a month before.

Only one scale was a different shade—the silver of swords.

His first reaction was to take it. But Tor froze. He had read the story and knew what had happened to the fish that had tried to steal the salmon's scale.

His breath caught in his chest as he realized they probably should have made a plan. The salmon thrashed violently along the deck, whipping this way and that. They would likely have to simply let it go, the scale wasn't worth one of them dying trying to get it...

"Stop," Melda commanded, her loud voice shocking the fish still.

Part of Tor wanted to tell Melda that her leadership emblem didn't work on animals...but the salmon had listened. Her marking couldn't control the fish, however. It only had the ability to convince.

Melda inched closer, reaching a hand toward it, careful not to touch. "Your scale. Would you be willing to part with it?"

The salmon jolted.

Melda stumbled back. Tor thought it might attempt a jump off the ship or bite her, but there was a glimmer, and the silver scale slipped off, a golden one waiting just beneath it.

"Quick, we don't want to kill it!" Engle said.

Vesper shrunk the salmon again, then deposited it back into the water in its full size. It promptly swam away, joining the rest of the fish, which had left after the drumming had ended.

"Everyone else must have tried to simply steal it," Melda said quietly. She bent down and carefully took the scale between two fingers. It looked slightly translucent, and smooth, similar to the mother-of-pearl inside the compass.

"What does it do again?" Vesper asked. She eyed the golden ribbon, still in the water, as if finally realizing why

Melda had insisted it be used as bait. The salmon they had caught was no ordinary fish, clearly. Tor thanked the universe again that Melda had read the stories so carefully.

Melda pressed a finger against the scale, and it shimmered. "According to the *Book of Seas*, it magnifies an emblem's power." She admired it from all angles. "It's a rare, coveted treasure." Jaw very tight, Melda handed it Vesper. "Here."

Engle blinked in shock. Tor didn't dare say a word.

Melda shrugged, her nose very high in the air. "You should hold it...for now. None of our emblems can truly be amplified to make much of a difference, but yours..." She sighed. "Even Violet said it, there are other ways, beyond the obvious, that your power is useful."

Vesper raised an eyebrow, surprised. A moment passed before she carefully took the scale. It glowed in her palm. She nodded, then shrunk it down, adding it to her bracelet for safekeeping.

Engle grinned. "I did it," he said triumphantly. "*I* caught a mythical sea creature. And practically all by myself."

Melda gave him a look.

Engle ignored her and skipped to the table of warm drinks, grabbing himself a handful of congratulatory marshmallows meant for hot chocolate. With three in his mouth he said, "Hey, Forecastle, how'd you end up in that hole, anyway?"

Captain Forecastle sat on a barrel, and it groaned beneath his weight. "That there's a long story."

Engle turned toward the helm, squinting. He faced the pirate again. "Nothing for miles. We have time."

Captain Forecastle shrugged. "All right then."

Tor, Melda, Vesper and Engle sat on blankets before him, the pirate looking quite pleased to have an audience.

"The *truth* please," Melda said. "No exaggerated hogwash."

Captain Forecastle grinned. "Not to worry, young leader. This story hardly needs embellishing."

He cleared his throat.

"Thousands of years ago, something on Emblem Island erupted, charring the whole island. Chunks of its original enchanted core went flying like mad, and were lost in the sea—unmatched treasures...jewels coated in power. The first pirates hunted these to their watery death. Why? Because just *one* had enough ability to topple cities, to end the greatest of enemies." He took a long swig of his drink. "Over time, these ores of energy were split into many more pieces, then forged to make The Twelve. Objects, they were. A necklace, a ring, a pocket watch, a sword, a fork, even! Wouldn't know it was so powerful unless ye made the mistake of touching one. Each pirate king received one, to be passed along his line. To split power equally.

"What they didn't know, the fools, is that some of those jewels coated in magic were also coated in curses. A third of the families were struck by these curses, strong enough to be passed along through their family line for generations. One had all of their descendants born half fish. One was cursed with insatiable greed. One was cursed with having anyone they fell in love with perish.

"*We* are descended from one of those original twelve pirate families. One of the four that received a cursed jewel."

Engle swallowed. "What was your family's curse?"

Captain Forecastle shrugged. "A frozen lifeline when we reached adulthood. Back when those things mattered out on the sea."

Engle frowned. "That doesn't sound so bad."

He nodded. "Certainly not the worst. We never thought of it as a curse. Got to be young almost forever." He pressed his chapped lips together. "But then, we fell in love with a woman destined to die. Her lifeline was nearly gone when we met. The blood queen agreed to transfer our curse to her, thinking it would save her life."

Captain Forecastle looked past them, at something far away. "Didn't know that when the blood queen transferred the curse, she made it worse. It froze our love's lifeline, but it cursed her entire crew and trapped her in the sea. Forced her to watch her family age and die from afar and did not let her sleep. Without any rest for years, she went mad." He lifted his palm, and Tor saw what had terrified the gamblers back in the Crusty Barnacle. Captain Forecastle's lifeline began as a tiny line, then stopped, leaving a large gap across his palm. On the other side, it continued in a mess of mountains.

"It was Bluebraid," Melda said quietly. "That's why she hates you."

Captain Forecastle nodded solemnly. "It's forbidden for curses to be transferred, so that's how we ended up where ye found us."

Melda tilted her head to the side. "What did Bluebraid mean that she had to make a deal with darkness to have her curse removed?"

Captain Forecastle looked down at the deck. "When something erupted in Emblem Island and charred it, sending power flying into the sea, something was unleashed. Something *broke* through, that day. She made a deal with whatever that is."

Tor swallowed. "What else do you know of this darkness?" he asked carefully.

Captain Forecastle shook his head. "Not much. And we'd like to keep it that way."

He stood, bones cracking loudly as he did. He wiped his

hands on his pants. "Well, that's our tale," he said. Captain Forecastle smiled, but Tor saw it didn't reach his eyes. Not at all. He nodded at Engle. "Want to learn how to catch firefly shrimp, boy?"

Engle nodded enthusiastically. He followed Forecastle to the helm of the ship.

Melda murmured about taking a warm bath and disappeared below.

Vesper was biting her bottom lip, lost in thought. Staring at her palms, covered in pale lifelines.

"Do you...want to talk?" Tor asked. It seemed as if she had what his mother called a worm in her thoughts; a crawling anxiety that invaded one's mind.

Vesper looked at him, eyes wide, as if desperate to say something. But then, the light in them dimmed once more, and she looked at the deck. "No," she said sharply, getting up. "I appreciate your concern. But I don't need a friend."

The Girl with the Frozen Heart

There once was the daughter of a sailor who could never tell a lie. She was born and raised on the sea and saw truths tucked between the waves.

The girl could tell a woman she was with child, a thief how he would die, and a newlywed that his happiness was a lie.

The little sailor's truthtelling emblem became so famous, Emblemites would crowd ports when her family's ship docked, begging for a bit of truth for themselves.

But, as she learned, the truth can cause more chaos than good.

She witnessed families torn apart, people gone mad, leaders fall, all because of her gift. The girl caused so much devastation that sadness consumed her, an inferno of guilt and worry constantly blazing in her chest.

To stop the pain, she asked a boy with a snowflake emblem to turn her heart to ice.

From then on, she spoke truths without feeling any sorrow at the ruin she left in her wake. She felt nothing at all. Then she left, in search of a place as cold as her heart.

She traveled north until the ice was as blue as a cloudless sky. And there she lives, still offering truths to those that dare the journey to find her—and who have had enough of lies.

15

THE TRUTHTELLER

The compass never pointed anywhere but north, and they traveled farther than Tor could even picture on a map. Three days passed without encountering land, and the breeze became a chill.

Melda had finished her book on mermaids, but kept going back to different chapters, a pen in hand, writing in the margins. Tor got the sense that she was distracting herself from her arenahora, which had been reduced to just a few pinches of sand. Vesper looked more tired by the hour, as if the days out of the water weighed heavily on her. Engle slept soundly.

Tor had a habit of standing at the helm of the ship most of the afternoon, as if doing so would make them sail faster. He tugged on his connection to the boat, willing it to speed through the narrow channel they had just entered, between two expanses of snow that went on for miles.

"Would you look at that," Captain Forecastle said, making everyone else stand.

Up ahead, glaciers floated in the water on both sides, surrounded by long shards of ice. Atop each sat a mermaid. They had ice blue tails and white hair that floated around them, the same way it would if they were underwater. Their fins were silver and solid, like freshly cut diamond. They whispered to each other in a language Tor didn't understand.

"Melda?" Tor asked. "Are they in your book?"

She looked fascinated. "They're wintresses. Mermaids who thrive in the cold and draw power from its frigidity."

"Are they dangerous?"

She pursed her lips. "Only if you try to take their ice. They have quite sharp teeth and nails."

"What do they eat?"

"Frozen fish." She gave him a look. "Why, what are you thinking?"

He shrugged. "I don't know, Melda. Would you say the ice here is as blue as the sky on a cloudless day?"

Melda let her eyelids droop, instantly recognizing the description. "You can't be serious. We don't exactly have time to spare." She held up her arenahora for good measure.

"I know. But the truthteller might say something that makes a difference. That changes fate." Tor swallowed. Most of the time he spent at the helm, he worried about the prophecy. It had predicted his death, which he had somehow survived.

And it had also predicted that their quest would be fruitless.

There had to be a loophole for that, too. Some way to get to the pearl before the captain, the spectral, and the traitor.

Melda didn't look happy. But she let out a long breath and nodded. "Want me to come with you?"

"No. I think I have to do this alone."

Tor stopped the ship and let Melda explain to the others where he'd gone. He stepped off the stairs and carefully onto a giant sheet of ice that had floated near their ship, mostly intact. It led all the way to the mermaids, sitting casually on their glaciers. He whistled, and Melda dropped the basket of frozen fish he had made appear just seconds earlier. The ice was slippery beneath his boots—one foot slid forward and his other leg buckled, but he steadied himself, worried about cracking his head open on the unforgiving ice.

The mermaids watched him curiously, hands busy braiding their floating white hair. Their bell-voices hitched as he neared, some barring teeth sharp as daggers.

Tor approached and placed the basket at his feet. He

knelt, not taking his eyes off the mermaids in case they leapt to attack, and blindly reached for a fish. He picked one up by its tail.

The wintresses' voices changed then, their chimes now rushed with excitement.

"I'm looking for the truthteller," Tor said slowly, wondering if there was any way they could understand him.

One of the wintresses looked up at him, as if trying to understand. With surprising elegance, the others began taking fish from the basket.

Tor stared at the curious wintress.

She clearly did not speak his language. He gritted his teeth and began trying to pantomime what a truthteller was, but stopped when he remembered his emblem. He pointed at it, showing her the marking. Surely it would mean something to her.

Immediately, the wintress nodded with understanding.

She ducked under the water, and Tor had to run to follow, his feet slipping and sliding as he rushed to catch up. The sheet of ice came to an end, so he jumped on another, nearly falling into the water when it tipped to the side with his weight. Before he could plunge into the glacial waters, he leapt onto another shard of floating ice. The wintress did not look up or over her shoulder; she simply kept swimming, light blue tail moving swiftly behind her, at times splashing out of the water.

He knelt and used his hands to paddle the piece of ice closer to what looked almost steady as land, wide and solid in front of him. Just as he jumped and made it onto the field of ice, the wintress swam beneath it. Tor saw her through the frozen water. This new sheet of ice was half transparent and half frosted over, surprisingly sturdy, even with cracks running down it like marble. He followed as the wintress swam underfoot until the ship was barely visible behind him, and it began to snow.

He stopped when she did. The wintress turned to face him, smiling through the ice, then darted away.

He had arrived at a cave made entirely of ice.

Icicles sharp as swords guarded its entrance, looking ready to fall and skewer an intruder. He walked to its mouth, then lingered, not daring to step through. From what he could see, the entire inside was a geode of ice crystals, glowing in a supernatural bright blue.

For a moment, he considered turning around. He remembered the legend from the *Book of Seas* and its warning. The truth often led to chaos.

What if the truthteller told him something unforgivable? Something that changed everything?

Or, worst of all, a truth that Tor wished he wouldn't have known?

He took a step back, his boots imprinted on the snow in front of him. He had doubted himself the entire journey. His worthiness of being the Night Witch's successor. His wariness of everything that came with that.

But he had made a decision to sail forward, no matter the cost. Which meant he had to make peace with the consequences that could follow.

"Hello?" he called inside and heard his voice echo once, then twice.

The voice that answered was cold as frost. "Enter."

So he did.

Beyond the entrance of the cave sat a stately home, crafted completely of sparkling ice. A woman stepped down a flight of frozen stairs. She had long, white hair, and Tor couldn't decide her age. She wore a crown of icicles and a gauzy, blue-white dress.

The truthteller did not look surprised to see him. She didn't look...*anything*.

"I suppose you are here because of my abilities?"

When Tor nodded she unsheathed a long sword from her back, and sliced a piece of her stair's railing with vicious speed. It fell and slid to Tor, coming to a rest against his boots.

"Let that melt in your hands, and I'll study the puddle."

Tor knelt down to grab the chunk before the truthteller could send him away. He immediately felt the bite of the ice in the center of his palms. It melted slowly—agonizingly so. He gritted his teeth, trying to get his mind off the shocking pain. "Aren't you wondering who I am?"

She glanced at him. "No."

Eventually, the ice pooled in his palms, leaving only a small solid piece in its center, like the yolk of a cracked egg. He waited, hands frozen and throbbing, until it was completely thawed. Only then did he drop the water at his feet.

She walked over, and Tor saw her emblem, a white circle, bright on the top of her hand. She knelt and her dress pooled around her. She dragged a finger through the puddle for just a moment, then stood.

"No questions. I will tell you three truths. And then you must leave."

Tor nodded.

"First. The prophecy will ring true."

Tor knew as much, though its confirmation made his stomach sink. Did that mean they would not find the pearl before the spectral, the Calavera captain, and the Swordscale traitor? That there was no chance at a loophole?

The truthteller continued, bored. "Second. The prophecy

has not been fulfilled. Your fleeting death was not what it referred to."

Tor's breath stuck in his throat, his vision blurred. If the prophecy was true, and it hadn't been fulfilled...

He or one of his friends would die soon.

Tor almost forgot there was one truth left, until her voice echoed through the cave one final time.

"And third—the Swordscale traitor..." Tor could picture him in his mind's eye, disappearing with the Calavera captain and the spectral. "He is your waterbreather's brother."

The First Mermaid

Once upon a different time, a curious girl had a cruel father. He was rich beyond measure and overly protective of his daughter. To keep her safe, he built a palace atop a cliff on an island accessible only by a land bridge that disappeared in high tide.

When the tide was low, the father locked his daughter in her room, for fear she would use the bridge to leave. She watched the sea from her balcony and marveled at its beauty.

She whispered so many nice things that the sea fell in love with her. It danced beneath her room, sending swells so high she could almost touch them.

One day, she managed to break the lock to her room and fled the palace, intending never to come back. She ran down the land bridge barefoot.

Just as the tide was rushing in.

It swallowed her up, pulling her to the bottom of the ocean.

But she did not drown. The sea asked if she

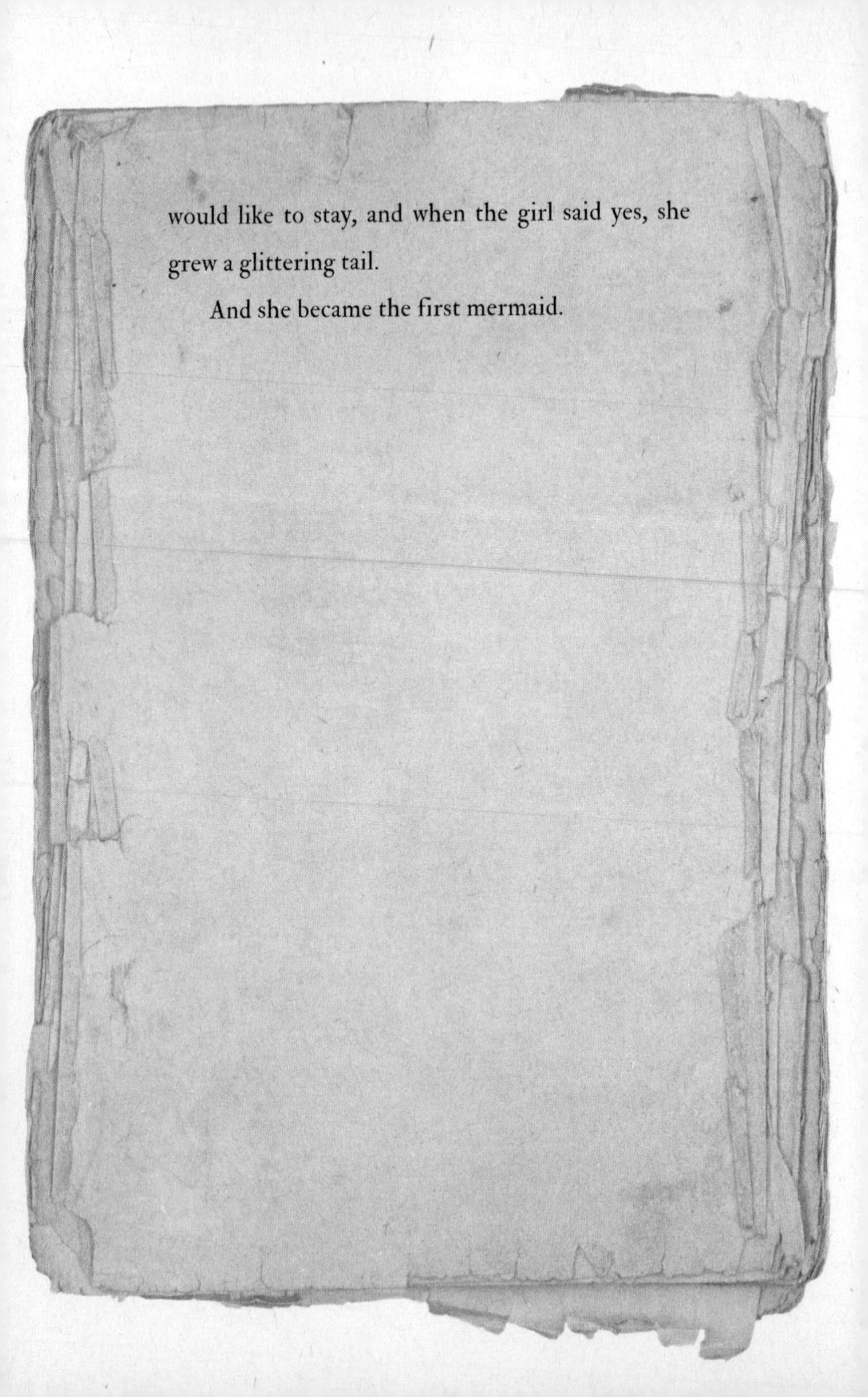

would like to stay, and when the girl said yes, she grew a glittering tail.

And she became the first mermaid.

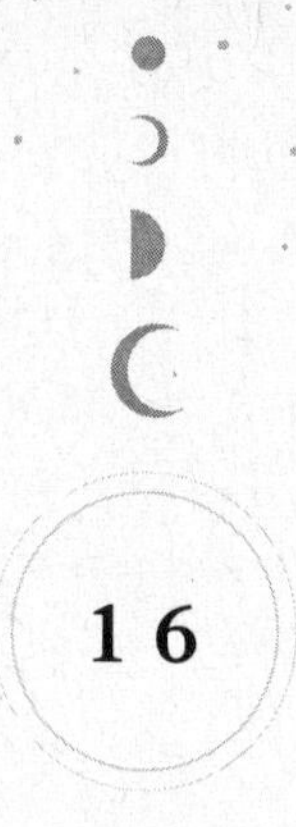

16

FROZEN

Tor walked over ice, feeling a connection to the harsh landscape. He, too, felt frozen solid and fractured through. Weightless, yet dense. And very close to shattering.

He had *trusted* her. Even after everything she had done, after all of the signs he had chosen to ignore, he had believed her story.

Tor climbed up the ship with shaking hands and stormed over to Vesper, who was glancing down at her map, likely searching for any upcoming land.

"Are you working with them?" he demanded, his own voice surprising him.

Vesper straightened. "Working with who?"

Melda and Engle were behind him a moment later. "The

people who captured *your* kind, the ones that put a bounty on *our* heads."

"Of course not," she scoffed.

Tor seethed. He couldn't remember being so angry. "Is he your brother?"

Melda stilled. She said very quietly, "Is who her brother?"

"The Swordscale traitor."

Vesper had her held head high. Her arms were shaking slightly by her sides.

She nodded.

"What?" Melda yelled. "How long have you been playing us? Was this the plan all along? To spy and let us figure out the way to the pearl, so you could report back to your brother?"

Vesper shook her head. "No. I—"

"Do you deny trying to contact him, using the conch shell in your room?"

"I did, but—"

"You have been lying to us from the moment you washed onto Estrelle's shores. You called him the Swordscale traitor, even though he's your brother, and you have been working with him—"

Vesper yelled, "I'm not working with him. I'm trying to save him."

There was a moment of silence. Melda glared at her. "I don't believe a word you say."

Engle stepped forward, putting a careful hand on Melda's shoulder. "One chance to explain yourself." He turned to Tor and Melda. "Right?"

Melda fell back next to Tor. They both said nothing.

Vesper nodded. Her fingers shook—was she nervous because she was about to tell another lie? Or upset she'd been found out? "Ever since my parents died, my brother has been...troubled. He knows who killed them and what happened that day. He's been searching the seas, against all of our city's rules, for a chance at revenge. The blood queen turned him down, I'm not sure why. When the Calavera curse was broken, he sought them out, and offered the pearl in exchange for their help at vengeance. When they found that the pearl wasn't where it was supposed to be in Swordscale, that it had been stolen, I suppose he offered to help them find it...

"I only learned this when it was too late, when they had already invaded. He seemed to believe they wouldn't harm us, but I told him we couldn't trust them, so he locked me in my room, the same way my parents had, years before. My grandmother let me out and told me to flee. I tried to warn others, but a Calavera intercepted me on my way out of our palace—and put his sword through my side. I was able to get to the portal to the ship just off Estrelle, and you know the rest."

Melda shook her head. "I don't believe you," she said. "Why wouldn't you tell us?"

"You already didn't trust me. I thought if I told you the truth, you would find another way to the pearl, one without me. You were my best chance at finding my brother—and stopping him."

"So, you used us," Tor said.

Vesper laughed without humor. "Only as much as you used me. You don't think I knew you were going to leave me somewhere once you found a way to the pearl that didn't require a Swordscale? You used *me* for the compass, to even get this far." Her eyes narrowed. "And don't pretend you all have been perfectly honest. You're not even honest with each other."

Engle took a step forward. "Now that's where you're wrong."

Vesper stood her ground. "Ask your friends about your nightmares, then."

Tor froze. Next to him, Melda quietly gasped.

Engle turned to face them. "What does she mean?"

"It's nothing," Melda said. "We made an elixir for you. To *help* you."

"What?" The sightseer's face twisted. "You gave me an elixir without telling me?"

"You wouldn't talk about it," Tor said. "You were suffering. We just wanted to help. And it worked."

Engle backed away from them. "By going behind my back? Both of you?"

Melda's eyes were wide. "Don't you see what she's trying to do? She's trying to distract us, divide us—"

"I'm not doing *anything*," Vesper said. "You three are so quick to judge me, to mistrust me, but if you all looked deep within yourselves, I'm sure there is something you'll each find there that you have been keeping from your *best friends*. For good reasons, I'm sure. Just like I had mine. This is my *brother*." She kept her head high. "I would do anything to protect him, *far* worse things than I've already done. And I'm sure you three can understand that, too."

She walked across the deck, then stopped just short of the stairs.

"I lied, I stole, and I know how it must look—but I'm not working with them. I want to find the pearl and keep it out of the hands of the Calavera just as much as you do."

Engle wouldn't speak to them. Even after Tor had made a feast appear that ran the entire length of the deck, he stayed below.

After dinner, Tor made an entire platter of desserts appear in Engle's room, with his favorites: sapphire pie, emerald-cream meringue, diamond-dusted doughnuts. But a few moments later, Tor heard Engle's door slam shut and found the plate of sweets outside.

Melda and Tor sat on the deck, wrapped in layers of fabric, both unable to sleep.

"For a long time, I disliked him," she said staring at the moon, just a crescent in the sky. "Even before I knew him. Engle."

"Why?"

She sighed. "I was so excited to start school, so proud to be a leader. I knew how rare it was, and, when I learned there would only be one other person in my class, it made me even more excited."

Tor gave her a look. "Melda, you *hated* having me in leadership."

She scowled at him. "Would you let me finish?" She took a breath. "School was always a welcome relief. I love my brothers, and I'm glad they're better now, but I didn't always want to be home. I never really got to play or make friends, because my mom always needed help with them. School was different. I *had* to go. So, when I saw only one other person in leadership, I thought—" She cut off and rolled her eyes, like she was embarrassed. "But then, I saw you with him. You already had a best friend. You two ate lunch together every day, even when everyone else sat with their emblems. So...I disliked him."

"Melda, I had no idea."

"I know, I know. I'm not saying this to guilt you. I'm saying it because I get it. I get why you've been friends with Engle for so long. I know he's family to you."

Engle *was* family. Since his parents worked far from Estrelle, at the Alabaster Caves, he stayed most nights at the Lunas' house. Engle came to every dinner, was there for every breakfast.

"I've underestimated him plenty of times." She looked tentatively at Tor. "I think we *both* have."

He realized she was right. Tor still saw Engle as the joking, class clown kid he had been in the first few years of their friendship. But Engle was so much more than that. He was fiercely loyal...and cunning, when he wanted to be.

For the last year, Tor had been obsessed with swimming and waiting for Eve to make his wish. He wondered if that had put a wedge between him and his best friend. Tor knew Engle better than anyone else, yet still was surprised when he had admitted to being affected by the Lake of the Lost.

The last month, Tor had been focused on his own pain. His own regret. His own anger at what the Night Witch had done to him. He should have asked if Engle was all right. Tor should have realized that his friend had been hiding his hurt behind jokes and laughs. He had done it before, whenever he was upset that his parents were always away.

"Melda," he said suddenly. "Are *you* okay?"

She blinked at him. "No. Not really..." She swallowed. "But if we all get home in one piece, I'll find a way to be."

They stayed on the deck all through the night, trading stories about Engle, until the sightseer surfaced. It was barely dawn.

Melda and Tor stood immediately. He stepped forward. "We're sorry. We never should have never done it behind your back. We should have talked to you about it."

Engle nodded. "Yeah, you should have."

There were a few moments of silence.

"Do you want to talk about it?" Melda asked, voice quiet. "The Lake of the Lost?"

The sightseer stared down at the deck for a little while, biting the inside of his mouth. Then, he nodded.

Engle sat down next to them and frowned. "I don't think I've ever been afraid of anything, not really." He shrugged. "I never thought about dying."

Tor knew as much. During their last journey, Engle had been the bravest of them all.

"But then the Lake of the Lost happened, and I thought I was going to *die*. I thought that was it, I was a goner. It hurt, and I was afraid. Really afraid." Engle lolled his head back and stared up at the sky. The sun was just starting to peek over the horizon. "When we got back, things weren't the same. Mom was home for a little while, and I pretended to be okay because I wanted her to go back to the Alabaster Caves. But I'm not. Every night, I dream of it. Every single night, I get dragged down into the lake by the bonesulkers."

Melda took his hand. "How can we help you?"

He shrugged. "Just...this," he said. "Talking about it. We..." He swallowed. "We didn't really talk about it afterward."

Tor realized he was right. They would meet up at the beach most mornings, but mostly sit in silence. Lost in their own thoughts.

They had each dealt with the aftermath of their journey alone.

Tor nodded. "I promise to talk about it all from now on. Even the bad stuff."

"Me too," Melda said.

Engle smiled. "Me three."

"Which reminds me," Tor said. "There's some more...bad

stuff." He told them everything the truthteller said. By the end, Engle and Melda were both pale and silent.

"So that's it, one of us is going to die?" Melda said, looking somewhere past Tor.

It felt like a knife was being twisted in his stomach. The lump in his throat made it impossible to talk. He nodded.

Engle bowed his head. "I don't want to die," he said softly. "But if it's this way, saving one of you or Estrelle, that would be all right."

A tear slid down Melda's cheek. She shook her head. "No. I don't want to keep going. I—I don't want one of us to die. Not if we're going to fail anyway."

Tor imagined Engle was going to call Melda a hypocrite. But Engle surprised him by sighing. "Mel, we have to at least try. Estrelle is counting on us."

Melda's bottom lip quivered. "But she's the truthteller. And she said one of us would die and we won't get the pearl. What the point?"

"You know what? What if the pearl is destroyed? What if it doesn't even exist? What if we find something else that can save Estrelle or defeat the Calavera?" Engle sighed. "There are a thousand possibilities that fit the prophecy. And if, in the end, we still stop them from invading Emblem Island, then it's worth it. We can't give up now."

Melda blinked. "Since when are you the voice of reason?"

Engle grinned. "When our voice of reason isn't being reasonable."

Tor laughed, just a little. But inside, his chest felt like it was concaving. Because even though he had made the decision to charge forward whatever the cost, he couldn't imagine living without one of his best friends.

Isla Pomme

When pirates die, they hope to go to Isla Pomme, a place made completely of treasure. The sand is gold dust. The water is miles of strung-together sapphires. Goblets never run dry. The sun never burns. The creatures never bite.

And some are lucky enough to visit Isla Pomme while still living. It is said that when a want is bright enough, the island will appear, to offer a bargain to those desperate enough to take it.

Once, a pirate's wife drowned, and he missed her so much, Isla Pomme revealed itself, with a way to bring her back. Without hesitation, he inked his name in blood, linking his life to the contract. He was reunited with his love, but at a cost.

He had to replace the life the sea had lost.

When the man and wife had a child, the ocean called in its debt.

Pirates still hunt the island, searching for a heaven that does not always require death. Though, more times than not, death is the cost. Isla Pomme

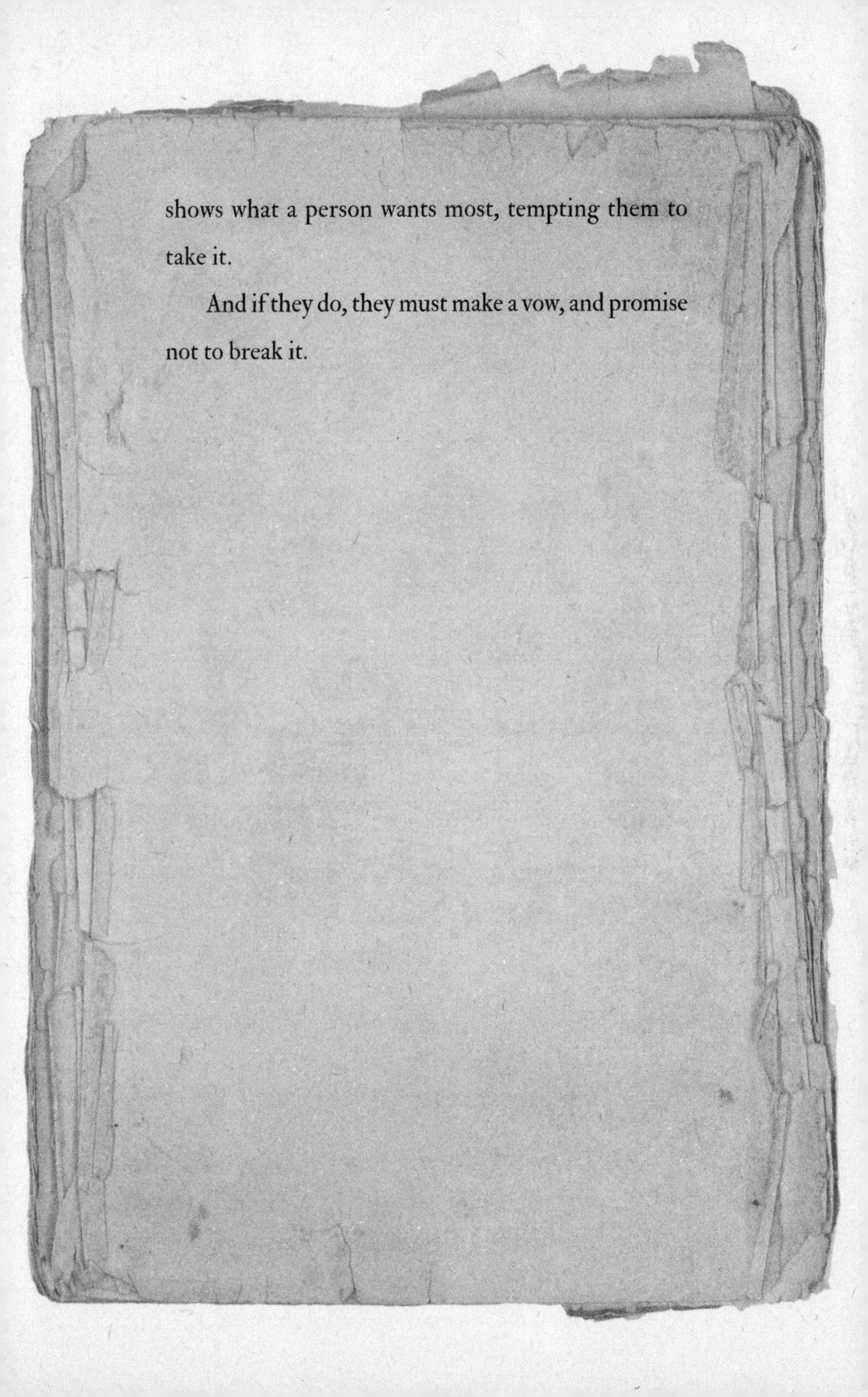

shows what a person wants most, tempting them to take it.

And if they do, they must make a vow, and promise not to break it.

17

DREAMWALKER

Tor, Melda, and Engle had talked until the sun came out and Captain Forecastle surfaced, frowning. "You three cost us beauty sleep," he said. He pointed beneath his eyes, where two impressive purple rings had formed. "Just look at 'em! Look at 'em!" He hobbled over to their group, then bent down, a hand cupped to the side of his mouth. "So, we getting rid of the waterbreather?"

Melda glared at him. "I suppose second chances only apply to you then?"

Captain Forecastle straightened. "Second chances? *Ye* who dislike her so dearly are so quick to forgive?"

She laughed without humor. "Forgive? No. But I will admit, if she isn't completely lying to us, I understand her." She sighed. "I would do absolutely anything for my brothers."

"I think she is telling the truth," Tor said. Melda shot him a look. "The compass, when she held it, led us to Perla. I don't think it was because she lost focus. I think it was leading us to her brother."

Engle nodded. "Something she lost. Makes sense, I guess."

Captain Forecastle let out a low whistle. "Another strike against her! She almost hand-delivered ye to yer enemies! Now, if it hadn't been for our arrows..."

They had discussed it at length, finally coming to the conclusion that, good intentions or not, they could not trust Vesper. She would surely choose her brother over them, if it came to that.

Still, leaving her behind now, so far north, would be a death sentence. So they decided to proceed with caution and watch her very carefully.

"She's staying," Tor said.

Captain Forecastle shook his head. "Yer kindness will cost ye out here, it always does. Everyone, absolutely everyone, only cares about 'emselves." He snorted "Might as well have a fortunetelling emblem, us! Can tell ye for certain, if ye want to predict a person's next actions, just think of what they want most. They'll do whatever gets 'em closer to it." He walked away murmuring, "What if we'd been kind to the thief who nearly lopped our head off! Or the sea beast that wanted our arm?"

Tor made breakfast appear so Forecastle would stop talking. He also put a platter in Vesper's room, expecting she wouldn't surface.

But, surprisingly, she did, just as they finished eating.

Her face solemn, she flung open the shell charm. The map spilled to her ankles, and spread, coating the deck in color. It was only snow and ice as far as the eye could see.

"The compass changed directions," she said, showing it to them. For days, its needle had pointed north. Now, it pointed east.

Tor looked at the map, searching for any landmarks in that direction. And he found that if they kept going, they would reach only one place.

The very northern tip of Emblem Island.

Finally—a destination.

A chill danced down Tor's spine. "How far?"

"We'll be there tomorrow afternoon."

Tor nearly collapsed in relief. Melda's arenahora was nearly out of sand. Their time was almost up. If they were going to find the pearl and save Estrelle before the ice melted, it needed to be tomorrow.

Vesper lingered. She looked like she was trying to make

a decision. Tor could practically see her mind spinning behind her eyes.

Finally, she turned to Engle with a sigh. "I know you don't trust me. But I think I can help you. As a peace offering."

"Help him with that?" Melda said, her voice poisonous.

"His nightmares. The elixir you made will only last so long. Dreams like these don't just go away by themselves overnight."

Engle looked down at his empty plate. "How?"

Vesper snapped a charm off her bracelet, then made it grow in her palm. It was a star with silk string across its inside, like an instrument "This is a captura," she said. "My mother made it for me when I was a child and enchanted it with her emblem."

"What was her marking?" Tor asked gently.

"She was a dreamwalker. She could go into anyone's mind as they slept, to see what they saw, and to interfere, if she wanted."

Engle eyed the mysterious star. "This will keep me from having nightmares?"

She shook her head. "No. It simply traps your worst dreams in its strings. So a dreamwalker might visit them with you, to change them...and hopefully stop the nightmares at their source."

"But none of us are dreamwalkers," Melda said. There was an edge to her voice. "Unless you have a third emblem you haven't told us about."

Vesper sighed. It looked as if she was working very hard to keep from having another fight with Melda. "My mother enchanted it, so we might be able to use her power to go into one of his dreams. Once." She turned to Engle. "That is, if that's what you would like."

Engle bit his lip, thinking. He eyed the web, then Tor. Then Melda. "Okay," he finally said. "Will it hurt?"

Vesper shrugged. "Not physically." She stroked the captura like playing the strings of a harp, and it created a melody, dark and melancholy. "It's been trapping dreams this whole time, since you've been in proximity to it," she said, not stopping her song. "Just close your eyes, as I find Engle's worst. Just close your eyes, and focus on the music..."

Vesper's voice fell away, and Tor was sucked forward, toward the captura, with a flash of wind. Part of himself had been peeled off, and he felt his body fall onto the deck behind him with a loud thump.

Then, he was spinning, skin cold as ice, his head filled with clouds and cobwebs. There was another wind, one that pulled him down, and then he landed somewhere solid, legs buckling beneath him.

When he opened his eyes, he saw himself across a body of water.

They were at the Lake of the Lost. Melda had just traded the blue color of her eyes to a goblin in exchange for use of his boat. They had just started paddling, unaware of the creatures that lurked below, circling them, readying their attack.

He heard Melda gasp. She wasn't just in the boat, she was also standing next to Tor above the Lake of the Lost. They watched themselves make their way across the water.

"Welcome to my nightmare," Engle whispered from Tor's other side, eyes fixed in front of him.

They were still rowing, but Tor saw something move below. Something he and his friends in the boat were blissfully unaware of.

Engle shook—his teeth clattered together, his words stumbled. "It's—it's coming," he said beneath his breath. "It—"

Tor stepped in front of him. "It doesn't kill you," he said. "Melda saved you, remember?" He pointed at her face. "She gave up her drop of color, for you."

Melda took Engle's hand, then Tor's. "I would do it a million times over because you *lived*, Engle. And the bonesulkers will never hurt you again. I swear it."

Engle swallowed. "I know. I just can't stop seeing them,

feeling their nails cut across..." He shivered, and his hands gripped his chest.

There was a scream. Tor turned in time to see one of the bonesulkers reach into the boat and pull Engle out by his neck. He was gone in an instant.

Engle fell to his knees, mouth open, hands shaking at his sides.

From their view, Tor could see underwater. Could see the bonesulkers dragging Engle down, down, down. Could see his friend, reaching up for help.

Tor knelt, trying to sink into the water, but it was hard as glass beneath him. He watched Engle get pulled deeper below, watched his friend struggle. And he couldn't help him. He banged on the water, knowing it wasn't real, but still unable to just sit and do nothing.

Engle, beside him, was silent, eyes wide as he watched himself nearly die.

No, this was bad, this was making things worse—

There was a crack close by, like a mountain splitting in half.

Vesper appeared, coated in gold, a falling star wrapped in flames. She walked past them, then flung her hands down against the water.

Gold flashed through her fingers, in wide sweeps of color.

A hundred screams ripped through the dream, and, in a flash, the bonesulkers disappeared, fracturing into a million balls of light. Even the lake seemed to shatter.

And Vesper sank down into the Lake of the Lost, still glowing. She swam quickly, right to Engle. The bonesulkers hadn't yet sliced across his chest in bloody streaks. She pulled him up out of the water, into the boat.

"You're okay," she said. "You're fine." Then, she pressed a hand against his chest.

Light billowed out of him in streams like woven gold, and Tor saw that they contained memories. Little pieces from Engle's mind, from the time he rode the zippy to the moment he broke his arm on the Twinetrees. Most were bathed in light, but a few, small enough that he couldn't see what memories they held, were tinged in darkness. Vesper handled the moments with care and stretched them out like wet fabric. She worked quickly, making the good ones bigger and the bad ones smaller. Then, finally, she came upon the dripping memory of the Lake of the Lost. It was folded a dozen times, and when Vesper expanded it fully, Tor saw it was huge, taking up most of the space in Engle's mind. Once unfolded, she shrunk it down, so small that all of the others smothered it.

Then, she walked out of Engle's nightmare, leaving only a trail of sunlight behind.

The Pirate and the Turnip

Once, there was a cruel pirate, obsessed with the sea. He refused to port, even when his crew was sick, opting instead to throw them off the ship. When his men threatened to rise up against him, he procured a talisman that forced them to be loyal and unable to ever try to leave him again.

The pirate, though enamored with the sea, loved a land food more than any other—a root vegetable. Turnips. He ate them by the barrel and always wanted more. He forced the cook to put them in his every meal and made his men buy barrels of them at the shore.

He would trade any treasure for the vegetable, so sailors made a habit of stopping by his ship when they went past, to make advantageous deals. This made the crew hate their captain even more. They watched him exchange gold coins they had gone to great lengths to find for the turnips he adored.

The crew wanted the pirate dead, so they devised a plan. They set a net with bait and waited for months.

Until one day, they managed to catch a mermaid.

They presented the siren to the captain, and the pirate knew it meant he might be granted a wish. "I wish to live beneath the sea, like you," he said.

The ship buckled beneath him, and he fell right through its hull. For instead of turning into a merman, the pirate had become a giant, hideous fish.

The crew had counted on the captain's foolishness. But when they refused to release the mermaid, wanting wishes of their own, she turned them *all* into sea creatures.

And so the crew was doomed to follow the pirate captain wherever he roams.

18

LAST CHANCE

That night, Engle slept peacefully, without the elixir on his pillow. Tor was not so lucky.

The Night Witch visited him once more.

He was back on the cliff, in front of her castle. She stood outside it, staring at Tor with a strange expression on her face.

She looked pained. Afraid.

"Tor." Someone touched his chest, and he gasped, almost falling out of bed.

Melda was standing there, hand still outstretched. "It's me," she said. "Are you okay?"

He nodded. Sweat dotted his forehead. "Yeah, you just surprised me." She was still wearing her nightclothes, and her ribbons were knotted in her hair. "Is something wrong?"

"We stopped," she said.

Tor stilled for a moment. She was right. He got out of bed immediately. "Have we already reached the northern tip?"

Vesper was waiting in the hallway. Her silver hair was in a braid, tied up with a piece of ribbon Melda had lent her. "No," Vesper said. She followed him up to the deck, where Engle and Captain Forecastle were waiting. It seemed he had been the last one to notice the ship had halted its course.

It was still dark outside, the stars thick like a blanket the sky put on at night to keep warm.

He rubbed the sleep from his eyes, then squinted ahead. There was an island that ran across the entire horizon.

"It doesn't stop for miles," Engle said, shaking his head. "It's like...a wall. Blocking us from sailing any farther."

Vesper opened her shell, the colors pooling around their feet lazily, as if they, too, had been asleep. "It's not on the map. Not anywhere."

Tor scratched the side of his head. The island was long, but not far across. It looked plain, just a stretch of golden sand. Not much more than a sandbar. "I suppose we're going to have to walk over it, then," he said.

Engle turned to look at him with a strange expression on his face. "Tor, what do you see?"

"What?"

"What do you see on the island?"

He frowned. "Nothing, it's just sand."

Captain Forecastle laughed beside him. He shook his head. "We see gold, boy. Mountains of it. And jewels the size of potatoes, growing from the ground."

Melda sighed. "It's clearly Isla Pomme. It'll show you whatever it thinks will tempt you to make a deal with it."

Vesper was very still. "I see my brother," she said.

They went below to change out of their nightclothes. Tor thought about Melda's words—the island would show him what he wanted most.

Then why did he see nothing?

Melda and Engle were waiting for him in the hall. "We need to talk," she said, craning her head to make sure they were the only ones still below. "Going across Isla Pomme isn't a good idea."

Engle gave her a look. "Of course it isn't! It wasn't our first option, was it?"

She glared at him. "You heard Vesper. She saw her brother, which means the island will try to make a deal with her to save him."

Engle shrugged. "That would be good, right?"

Melda gaped at him. "The island is bloodthirsty, and she said, *very clearly*, that she would do anything to save her brother."

"So what do we do?" Engle asked.

"We make sure she doesn't sign a contract," Melda said steadily.

Dressed for the day ahead, they gathered on the deck, and Vesper made the boat smaller around them, until it was just larger than a dinghy, tiny enough to calmly wash ashore. When they disembarked, Vesper clipped the ship onto her bracelet.

"Whatever it offers, don't take it," Melda said sternly.

Captain Forecastle surprised Tor by nodding, seconding Melda's warning. "Anything the sea gives, it takes back twofold."

Tor still saw nothing. The island was smooth and flat. Not even a tree in sight. He began the short walk across it, wondering what everyone else saw. What could possibly tempt Melda? Tor watched her as she walked, her gaze catching on things he couldn't see. She shook her head, then held it high, walking past whatever had appeared.

Captain Forecastle rolled around the sand, laughing and filling his hands with invisible treasures. He howled like a wolf at the moon, and continued to splash around, sliding on his stomach along what Tor imagined might be an avalanche of diamonds.

Engle looked miserable, arms across his chest as he was forced to walk through what was no doubt the most delectable spread of food imaginable. Melda had made him read the Isla Pomme story before they left, and he knew that taking just a bite of the food offered would mean entering into a deadly bargain.

Still, he looked like he was considering it.

Vesper had tears rolling down her face, falling straight into the sand. She walked silently as she cried, not turning to look at Tor when he asked if she was all right.

He was going to ask again when he saw that his island was not empty after all. Something sat at its very edge, so close to the other side a large wave could have swept it away.

An oyster. It flipped open to reveal something that made Tor sink to his knees.

A pearl.

The Pirate's Pearl.

"It's yours," the breeze said into his ear. "If you want it."

A piece of parchment appeared from nowhere, unraveling beneath his nose.

Tor read the contract.

The Pirate's Pearl is a treasure of the highest value. In exchange for it, we ask the following:

Tor Luna, heir to the Night Witch's power, will forfeit all of his inherited gifts, properties, and power.

Tor Luna will never return to Estrelle.

These terms are nonnegotiable. The term date is ten thousand years.

At the end, there was a place for his signature.

He looked over his shoulder. Melda was now staring intently at her feet, scowling. Vesper was still crying.

Tor asked for a quill. One immediately appeared in the air, and he dug its sharp metal tip into his palm without hesitation. Crimson broke through skin.

Before his blood could pierce the page, the parchment went flying, landing in the shallow water.

He turned to see Captain Forecastle there, arm raised. "Have ye lost yer head?"

Melda rushed over. Tor realized they might not have been able to see the illusion of the pearl, but they could see the very real contract, wet in the water, an arrow sticking it into the sand. She gaped at him, furious. "Were you going to sign that?"

Her eyes found the blood dribbling from his palm, and a hand found her mouth.

He ground his back teeth together. "It's worth it. It's a deal I'll make."

Tor had never wanted the Night Witch's powers to begin with. He would gladly give them all up, especially if it meant saving his people by getting the pearl. Being banned from Estrelle would hurt, but he would live anywhere if it meant stopping the Calavera from destroying his home and harming his family.

Melda stormed over to the contract and tried to read what

was left of the parchment. She scoffed. "Did you ever think to wonder *why* this terrible island *wants* your abilities?"

Tor was silent.

"Because it wants to offer it as a temptation, in order to get *them* to also sign a contract. The Calavera captain. Or even the spectral. Or someone worse!" She ran her hands through her hair, face red with anger. "The Night Witch told you how dangerous her power in the wrong hands would be. And you're so quick to go off and trade it? Just because you don't want its responsibility anymore?"

Tor's hands were fists by his sides. "To save Estrelle."

Melda laughed in his face. "You would do it to save *yourself*."

Tor fumed. His face felt hot, though the sun hadn't yet peeked over the horizon. "I didn't ask for any of this! It was forced on me, and I'm supposed to accept it, just because it was given?"

There was a moment of silence, and Melda looked at him as if she didn't believe what she was seeing.

Tor swallowed. He had never seen her look so disappointed.

She breathed out roughly. "Fine. Sign whatever you want, Tor. It's your lifeline. Forgive me for caring about it."

Once across the island, Vesper enlarged the ship. Tor boarded and made no move to return to his cabin. He sat on the deck, listening to the waves.

He had been so close to signing it—he *would* have signed it, if it wasn't for the pirate.

Tor heard a creak behind him and whipped around.

Vesper stood there, eyes bloodshot, as if she couldn't sleep and was looking for the same peace the ocean brought him. She turned to leave when she saw him.

He shook his head. "Don't leave. Not on my account."

She looked like she might leave anyway. Then, she carefully walked toward him and rested her elbows against the rail.

"Nightmares?" Tor asked her.

She shook her head. "I don't get those. Not anymore."

"Because of your mother?"

Vesper nodded. "She made all of my nightmares into dreams, until there was nothing left to be afraid of."

Tor looked at her sidelong. "You aren't afraid of *anything*?"

She gave him a look. "Of course I am. I just don't lie to myself about it." She shrugged. "I find you only get nightmares about things you haven't admitted to yourself you fear." Vesper stared at him, moments ticking by. "I understand, you know. Not wanting something that's been thrust upon you."

Tor said nothing.

"When my parents died, my brother renounced the Swordscale throne. He didn't want it—all he wanted was revenge. He would leave for weeks on end in search of who knows what. Planning to fight, when we're supposed to represent peace." She swallowed. "The crown went to me."

Tor looked at her then. "But you're..."

"A kid?" She laughed without humor. "The throne doesn't mean much anymore. We have a council made up of elders that makes most decisions. But the throne represents the enchantments that have kept Swordscale safe all of these years. My ancestors made the original pact with the blood queen," she said. "If my bloodline dies, Swordscale ceases to exist."

Ceases to exist. That was worse than being born a leader. To have the fate of a people on her shoulders since she was a child... Perhaps she did understand his attitude toward the Night Witch's inheritance. More than he would have ever thought.

"In my village, in Estrelle, my bloodline has ruled for as long as we can remember. We have the leadership emblem," he explained. "I didn't realize how important that was and wished it away. That's what started all of this. That's why the Night Witch chose me."

She looked at him. "I didn't ask to be born into the family

I was in Swordscale. To have its future reliant on my family line. No one *asked* me." She shrugged. "You might not have asked to be the Night Witch's heir, but it happened. It's real. You can either accept it and use what she gave you to change the world for the better, or you can continue to feel sorry for yourself and try to forget what you are."

"I'm *not*—"

Vesper held up a hand. "That first day on the ship, those ropes held you like a puppet. Only when you decided to master the ship, and the powers that came with it, did it release you." She squinted at him. "Are you going to keep being the prisoner of your own destiny, or are you going to stop complaining and become the person the Night Witch knew you could be?"

Tor blinked. He felt like he had been slapped across the face and embraced, all in the same moment.

Vesper shrugged. "Just think about it, Tor," she said. They stood in silence for a long while.

And Tor made a decision. Vesper, harsh as she was, was right.

Whether he liked it or not, he had a dark power. He would continue to sprout new emblems. And he could hide them, the same way he had been hiding his waterbreathing marking, ashamed of what he had become, or he could accept that no matter what power he had been given, he was still Tor.

Nothing could change that.

The sky had turned blue with morning light, and it was cloudless. Tor motioned toward it, grimacing. "You know what that means, don't you?"

Vesper nodded. "It means it's going to storm."

The Forever Storm

There once was a man half crazed from his time in the sun, who claimed to have seen a storm swallow a ship.

Not destroy, not demolish, not splinter, but *swallow whole*—in one quick swoop.

Ten years later, another man claimed to have seen the same ship again, in the center of a tempest, its sails tattered, but still holding together, riding a wave as tall as a tower. The men aboard shouted for help, but before anything could be done, the storm passed, and the ship was gone.

Once every ten years, the ship is seen, cloaked in clouds, winds, and rain, the men still looking the same as they did when their boat disappeared.

There was a riddler who claimed that those who free the ship from its storm would be given a gift.

But anyone who tries and fails becomes part of the crew of the cursed storm ship.

19

THE OYSTER

The ship lurched and spun, stumbling through the storm. Tor knelt on the deck, trying to keep *Cloudcaster* from capsizing. A wave knocked the hull so hard he went flying to the side, landing on his back. His hair was matted to his face, and he could barely see, wind pummeling water straight into his eyes.

The wood groaned, and ropes flew through the air, wrapping around his wrists to keep him steady.

Vesper opened the hatch from below and poked her head out. "We've gone off course!" she yelled. "We need to go east!"

He nodded, turning the ship slightly, and closed his eyes a moment before a wave came crashing over the siren and onto the deck. It might have swept Tor away, but the ropes held firm.

He was trapped between two equally raging storms—the rain that poured violently from dark clouds circling above him like an endless pack of wolves and the sea that seemed determined to reach the heavens.

Melda and Engle had protested when Tor asked them to stay below, but finally did as he asked. Tor didn't mind being alone. He preferred the rain pounding against his head to the thoughts that raged inside it.

Another wave hit the helm, and it showered him in a glacial spray. He couldn't see anything now, the rain blinding him completely, so he sank to the deck and rode the ship like a horse as it galloped across the seas, trying his best to keep it steady with the ropes around his wrists.

"Nearly there!" a voice said through the downpour, and Tor slumped over in relief. He felt the waves get smaller and smaller beneath him, as they navigated out of the open water and closer to the coast.

The rain thinned, and he stood once more.

Just ahead sat a town with a harbor that only fit one ship.

He made port, then went below.

"Tor, you're pale as bone!" Melda said, her rage from yesterday all but forgotten. He stumbled past her to his room, where he changed into fresh clothing and tried his best to get warm. Still, even though he wore many layers, and Melda shoved tea at him the moment he left his cabin, his chest felt hollow as honeycomb.

"Are you sure you want to go now?" she asked him, a worried expression on her face. He must have looked terrible.

"We're so close." Tor said, his own weak voice surprising him. "The Calavera captain and his allies could get here at any moment. We can't wait."

Melda nodded, not looking convinced, but not saying anything more. Engle joined them, and he smiled, though it did not reach his eyes.

"Whatever happens, it was an adventure," he said, outstretching his hand, lifeline up.

"To adventure," Melda said, her voice thick. Tears gathered in her eyes like storm clouds. She pressed her lifeline to his.

"To adventure," Tor finished, holding his palm to both of theirs.

And then they climbed up the stairs toward whatever awaited them above.

The town looked abandoned. It was just a cluster of stone houses and empty streets—yet Tor swore he saw someone rush to close their shutters.

He stepped onto a creaking dock that threatened to

collapse at any moment. Vesper was behind him, holding the compass, which had gone deathly still.

She took a step off the ship, and Tor watched the needle whip to the side. He followed where it pointed, and froze. Something at his core yawned and stretched, slowly awakening.

There was an isle a mile away from the docks, connected to the town by a narrow land bridge, ocean raging on either side. He felt connected to it, tethered by an invisible piece of thread. And something on the other side tugged him forward.

"It's a tidal island," Melda said. "Just like in the book. The land bridge is only visible during low tide." It was made up of a single, looming mountain, with a tower at its very top.

"We better start walking then," Engle said.

The land bridge, crafted from sand and crushed-up shell that crunched beneath their boots, was so narrow only two of them fit across. The sea lapped at its either side, splashing them with spray. Rain pummeled them in painful streaks, the wind roaring in Tor's ears, angry like the ocean, which was a terrifying, deep blue—impossible to see through. When they were halfway across, Tor looked around. He was far out into the sea. Tor felt like he was walking on water—just like he had once done with the Night Witch—rather than on a narrow sand bridge through it.

"Do you see a way up?" Melda asked Engle, nodding toward the mountain ahead. It was larger than Tor thought, the tower atop dwarfed by its size.

Engle nodded. "There's a path, an ancient staircase that doesn't look very sturdy."

Gray-tinged, angry clouds had trailed them, taking turns cracking open. A flash of lightning illuminated the tower, and Tor saw a long window at its very top.

He wondered if the pearl was in that room.

"Can you see into the tower?" Tor asked. Sightseers' eyes were much more sensitive than others', since they worked so much harder. It would require Engle to use his see-through vision, something he could only do occasionally, when the weather was right.

A roar of thunder shook the ground underfoot. Tor swallowed. The weather definitely did not seem right.

"No. I can't."

The sea sloshed even more furiously now, the ocean beginning to encroach on the land bridge, though it was still low tide. Tor walked faster, body already aching from steering the ship through the storm. He looked at his friends, heads down against the wind, shoulders hunched, pushing forward nonetheless, and he became resolute as marble.

Whatever happened didn't matter. If his friends survived,

that would be enough. That would *always* be enough. He chanted the words on a loop in his head until they reached the base of the mountain.

A tiny ring of sand circled the towering peak, and, as they stepped upon it, even more clouds broke open and soaked the ground beneath their feet, as if already grieving something terrible.

"This way," Engle said, wiping long strands of light brown hair out of his eyes. The stairs began at the left end of the mountain and wrapped around its back, all the way up to the tower. Engle was right, they looked ancient—each step a misshapen rock, barely holding on.

"Careful on your way up," Melda said, tying her hair back with one of her ribbons. "The rocks are slippery, and falling would be deadly."

The higher they climbed, the truer her statement became. One wrong step, one fallen stair, and they could all go tumbling to their deaths. The sea crested wildly, all whitecaps now.

"Watch out!" Engle said, as a wave fifty feet high rushed right toward them. Tor pressed himself against the mountain, trapped, nowhere to go but up. But Melda was at the front, and she stood frozen in fear, staring at the rushing water.

Just short of them, the wave finally crested and crashed against the cliff, right below their feet. The ice-cold spray showered Tor, and Melda gasped. Salt in her eyes, she took a wrong next step and fell—

Only for Engle to grab her by the back of her shirt. "The water's rising," Engle said, voice trembling. "Go, go!"

Melda turned and began running up the steps, her boots squeaking against the wet stone. Engle was behind her, then Vesper, then Tor. Captain Forecastle was at the very end, coughing as he rushed to keep up. Tor's chest felt frozen solid, his lungs hurting with every breath. He was soaking wet and freezing.

He slowed down to wait for the pirate, but Forecastle waved him away. "If we're meant to go, we'd be happy to be buried in the sea."

Another wave crashed, higher, inching closer with every moment. Rock crumbled from the mountain, down into the abyss. Tor knew he couldn't drown, but wondered if he would survive falling into the frigid water.

He watched the tide pull out the water below them to form another massive wave, leaving hundreds of rocks, sharp as knives, in its wake. He swallowed. He might not drown, but if the freezing water didn't kill him, those would.

The rain blurred his vision almost completely now, coming at him sideways. He didn't dare stop and kept his eyes on his feet, his hair wet and dripping across his face. Thunder rumbled above his head, followed by a long strike of lightning that seemed dangerously close.

"Just a few more steps!" Melda yelled from the front. Then, sooner than Tor had expected, he heard the loud creak of a rusty door opening.

He tumbled into the tower, slipping and falling onto his knees. He coughed, his chest incredibly tight.

The thread pulling him to the isle tugged yet again. Tor looked up and saw that the tower was a lighthouse with spiral stairs to its top.

"There," he said, voice barely making a sound. "It's there." He started up the stairs, and the rest followed. "No." He turned around. "Stay. Please. We don't know what's upstairs or what will happen. We don't all have to go."

Melda stepped forward. "No. You did this last time. Engle and I stayed behind and you had to face the Night Witch alone." She shook her head, resolute, and Tor knew there was no changing her mind. "Never again. We go together."

With Tor at the front, they ascended. At the top, there was a hatch.

He opened it.

The peak of the tower was large and domed. The window Tor had seen from below was carved into its side, huge and completely open, the storm raging on just beyond it, some rain making its way inside, pounding hard against the smooth stone like knocks on a door. The room was empty, save for one thing.

An oyster shell, sitting in the middle of the floor.

Tor could feel its power buzzing around him, the frenzied ocean waves drawn to it, rushing toward it.

The Pirate's Pearl. It was inside the oyster shell.

He moved to take it.

A fiery burst of purple lightning lit up the room, striking Tor right in the chest.

"Tor!" Melda screamed, rushing to him. Engle fell to his knees.

But Tor did not move again.

The spectral appeared out of thin air, the Calavera captain at his side, and the Swordscale traitor at his other.

Vesper turned to the spectral and bared her teeth. She made a move to strike him—and, in an instant, the spectral summoned purple flame in his palm, then aimed it at her head.

It flew, but missed, tearing a gaping hole right through the tower instead.

The Swordscale traitor had pushed the spectral aside.

Seeing his chance, Captain Forecastle shot five arrows, one after the other. But this spectral was stronger than the others—it had a smoke wall up in less than a second, blocking every single one. The pirate continued to fire, getting closer.

The lighthouse wall on the opposite side was crumbling, disappearing before their very eyes as it tumbled into the sea. The storm found them inside, lightning illuminating the room in terrifying flashes and rolls of thunder masking Melda's sobs.

Captain Forecastle aimed more arrows, one after the other, pushing the spectral back, getting close enough to make a deadly blow. The spectral narrowed its eyes, and, with a whip of his wrist, brought up a new barrier, purple as his fire. The two arrows hit it, then ricocheted and pierced the pirate right through the stomach. He slumped to the floor.

On the opposite side of the room, Vesper was approaching her brother, who had just saved her from the spectral's fire. "Calder," she said. She reached out a hand to her brother. "Please, don't do this. Not to Swordscale. Not to *me*."

For a moment, he hesitated. Then he reached out to take her hand.

Before he could grip her fingers, the spectral struck his chest with a fistful of purple flame. And he was thrown back through the window, down to the rocks below.

Vesper's scream coincided with another strike of lightning, so loud it seemed to shatter the world.

The spectral opened his hand, and the oyster flew into it, before he and the Calavera captain vanished.

Ship in the Clouds

Time moves differently out in the sea. Days can stretch decades, years can bleed together.

It is said that out in the middle of the ocean, one can glimpse the future, or even the past. Pirate songs sing of ghosts in the night. One too many sailors claim to hear battles years after they've taken place, precisely at midnight, cannons sounding through the darkness, screams echoing across the water.

A little girl, the daughter of a rich merchant, once pointed up to the sky and smiled. "There's a ship there," she said, waving at invisible passengers.

Her parents thought her silly, perhaps too much time in the sun.

But perhaps the ocean gave the girl a glimpse of what is to come.

20

THE PEARL

Tor blinked—and Melda made a sound between a scream and a sob. She rushed toward him with wide eyes and shaking hands, as if not allowing herself to believe it.

Tor blinked again, and Melda sank to her knees, Engle beside her.

"Tor," he said, voice barely above a whisper. "Are you..."

Tor nodded, slowly sitting up. His chest burned and he winced. It felt like the skin there had been charred and cut away.

He pulled down the top of his shirt and saw something glimmering, fresh and still hot to the touch.

A new emblem.

A shield.

"That's how you survived," Melda whispered.

Engle's all-seeing vision locked in on his arm. "Look."

Right where his leadership bands used to be, wrapped around his left wrist, was a ring of purple flames.

"Another emblem?" Melda said.

He didn't know.

Blood pooled out of Captain Forecastle. Two arrows stuck out of his stomach.

"Don't take them out," Melda said, standing on shaky legs. She looked around for anything to stop the bleeding. But the room was empty. "We have to get him help, *now*."

Engle groaned as he lifted the pirate to his feet.

Tor walked toward Vesper, who stared out the lone window. Mouth parted in a silent scream, she watched the waves and rocks below. A single tear slid down her cheek. Her entire face twisted in pain.

But her eyes were angry.

She turned from the window and fled from the tower without a word.

Engle helped Captain Forecastle down the steps, the storm almost over. A light rain still fell, but the waves had settled. The pirate could still move his legs, though his eyes closed, then opened, only to close again.

"Stay awake," Engle told him, an edge to his voice. "Stairs are no place for a pirate to die."

They stumbled their way down, easier without the rain

blocking their view. Soon, they were on the sand. Vesper was already there, drawing a symbol into the base of the mountain, a marking Tor didn't recognize.

He kneeled beside her, head lowered, offering his respects. He knew words would never be enough—he didn't even know what to say.

So he said nothing and sat beside Vesper as her shoulders shook.

She had no family left. Only a grandmother, who was frozen on a Calavera ship.

Without a way out.

Without the pearl.

Vesper stood and Tor followed suit. They made their way after Engle and Melda, who were already a quarter of the way down the land bridge, sharing Captain Forecastle's weight between them.

It had all been a disaster. They had failed. The spectral and Calavera captain had gotten control of the seas, after everything.

And Vesper's brother was dead. She had watched him plummet from the tower.

His mother, his sister, his father—their entire village was moments away from being leveled by a tidal wave or attacked by hundreds of bloodthirsty pirates.

They were counting on them...

And he had failed.

They had just caught up to the rest when somewhere, far away, a roar made him go still. Tor turned, and so did Vesper.

He swallowed. A wave half as tall as the mountain raced toward it. It hit, splitting in two. Each part curved and barreled forward, right to where they stood.

High tide was rushing in.

Tor looked one way, then the other. Too much distance between the island and them. Between the docks and them. Vesper and Tor might survive—but his *friends*. They would drown.

The prophecy.

"Go!" Tor yelled, and they started to run, but the water was at their backs, curling along the sides of the mountain, charging at them at full force. Just seconds away from engulfing them.

Vesper stood very still, as if in a trance. She muttered words beneath her breath, her lips barely moving.

"Hidden in plain sight," she said quietly. Tor recognized Violet's words, from when the assassin had described surprising ways to use a magnificate's emblem. "I feel it now... There it is...hidden in plain sight."

"What are you doing?" he screamed at her back. She still hadn't moved an inch, even as the sea rushed in. Tor watched as she unclipped the sundrop salmon's scale from her bracelet and held it in her palm.

"The pearl wasn't in the oyster, Tor, the one the spectral took. The oyster was *on* the pearl."

"What?" Tor said.

Her arm shot out—

And the mountain began to shake.

The salmon scale multiplied her ability, energy emanating from her in waves. Rock crumbled away, the isle breaking into a million pieces that plunged into the sea. The stairs broke apart and toppled, one by one, off the mountain, which still stood tall and rounded. The tower at the top that had housed the oyster snapped in half, then plummeted into the waiting waters, smashing against the rocks below. Vesper cried out in effort, the scale shining bright silver in her hand.

Below the rock of the mountain was sand, and then, in half a second, it all blew away, until Tor could see that it wasn't a mountain at all.

It was smooth, glimmering white, halfway dug into the sea. Giant, like the moon.

The pearl.

Hidden in plain sight. Made large, instead of small.

Vesper put her other arm up and groaned from the pit of her stomach.

The high tide was just a breath away. Melda screamed as it rushed forward from both directions, trapping them—

With a final groan from Vesper, the pearl shrunk in a flash and propelled into her waiting palm.

She closed her hand—and the sea stopped dead, suspended in midair, lapping against an invisible wall.

● ☽ ◗ ☾

Vesper had held the pearl high until they reached the docks. When she dropped her hand, high tide had rushed forward, swallowing the land bridge, blanketing it completely, as if it had never existed.

Then, safely in the harbor, she sunk to her knees and sobbed.

Captain Forecastle was groaning.

Melda pulled something from her pocket. Her arenahora. Only a shred of sand remained.

They had gotten the pearl. Now, they just needed to get home in time to use it.

There was something else in Melda's pocket. The telecorp's coin. She gently approached Vesper, who handed over the scale, her expression never changing.

"If it amplifies power," Melda said quietly. "It might amplify the coin enough to bring us home."

Tor thanked the universe for Grimelda Alexander. His

mind was shattered into pieces he still hadn't been able to gather together.

But his family, Estrelle—they needed them.

He couldn't fall apart. Not yet.

They all stacked their palms in a tower over the coin and scale, Captain Forecastle's feeling very cold. Vesper held their ship in her other hand.

And then, they spirited away.

21

THE BOILING SEA

Tor could feel the ground beneath his feet before the rest of his body joined him. He was a shadow, then a ghost, then full and real, the weight of him slamming into place in one swift movement that left him breathless.

He opened his eyes and nearly fell to his knees.

They were in his living room, in his family's hut, built into the base of a tree. One with purple leaves, for leadership.

Melda and Engle turned to him, and he rushed to embrace them. Their last journey had started in this very room, after Tor had discovered the curse on his wrist. And now, it was where their second journey had ended.

He swallowed, taking a step back, watching as Vesper and Captain Forecastle looked around, confused.

No—it wasn't over yet. "I'll send help," Tor promised Captain Forecastle, leading him to a chair.

The pirate looked too pale, too much blood coating his clothes. Still, he managed a smile and said, "Make the sea boil."

Tor turned to Melda, Engle, and Vesper. "Come on."

He led them out the front door, into the village. Its streets were empty, just like his house. He wondered if his mother had managed to evacuate everyone in time.

Melda clutched the arenahora in her hand, watching as the final pebbles of sand fell through.

Then, the glass shattered.

"Tor!" she yelled, and he knew what it meant.

Their time was up.

The Calavera were thawing.

They reached the beach, and Tor saw his mother at the head of a small crowd gathered at the shore. He recognized them all. His neighbors, the other members of the council. His father.

All there, holding weapons. Ready to protect their home, even though they were outmatched ten to one. Even though Tor had never seen any of them fight a day in their lives.

"Mom!" he yelled and saw Chieftess Luna's back stiffen.

She turned slowly. Her bottom lip was trembling, tears gathered in her eyes. "Tor?" she whispered.

He rushed forward and threw his arms around her. "We have it, we're here," he said, just as something whipped right past his head and exploded against a palm tree.

A cannonball.

"One of them has thawed completely! The rest aren't far behind," Engle said.

"Quick, we need a healer," Tor said, finding Mrs. Herida in the crowd. He quickly explained Captain Forecastle's injury, and she rushed toward his hut.

Vesper had the pearl clutched in one hand and the scale in the other. She didn't look at Tor or anyone else. Her eyes were angry and locked on a single Calavera ship—one that held hundreds of people with hair just like hers.

Her people.

She stepped into the same water that had washed her to shore just days before, bloodied and a breath from death.

And she slipped beneath them.

Fast as a rocket, she shot through the sea, then surfaced in a breathtaking wave, the water lifting her up in a glorious spiral beneath her feet. She was right in front of the head Calavera ship.

"He's there, the captain," Engle said quietly. "And the spectral."

With a flick of her hand, she sent a wave right over the

ship that held the trapped Swordscales, and Tor watched from afar as they used it as a bridge back into the ocean, toward their home. With her other palm, she used the power of the pearl to make a wall of water, blocking the Calavera, who had started to shoot their weapons at the Swordscales as they fled.

After years of swimming in Sapphire Sea, Tor knew the bone boat was right below her. Vesper's people could use its portal to go back to their home, unharmed. When the final silver head was beneath the water, Vesper brought both of her arms high above her head—

And unleashed.

She sent giant waves crashing against each Calavera ship, forcing them together, their wood groaning and shattering as they rammed into each other. With the pearl clutched tightly in her fist, she split through two ships with slices of sea that she had honed to cut as sharply as blades. Screams pierced the air as the Calavera fell into the water, their ships falling to pieces around them.

The Calavera captain yelled orders, and the shark at the helm of his vessel broke free, then made a path for Vesper. It was five times her size, a monstrous beast that could devour her hole without a single chomp of its teeth.

But she controlled the sea. And, with a flick of her wrist, the shark turned, then launched toward its captain instead.

The mammoth creature flew out of the water, mouth opened wide to devour him.

He fell back, but the shark caught his hand—ripping it clean off before disappearing underwater.

The spectral vanished in a flash of mauve, abandoning ship.

Tor watched as Vesper shook. The ocean began to boil with her rage—her sadness. He wondered if she would drown them all with one close of her fist. If she would crush them from above with a tidal wave.

But then the sea went still.

Vesper lowered her hands. The scale burned brightly in her grip, the ocean held her in a high throne.

She lifted a single finger.

And what was left of the Calavera fleet vanished.

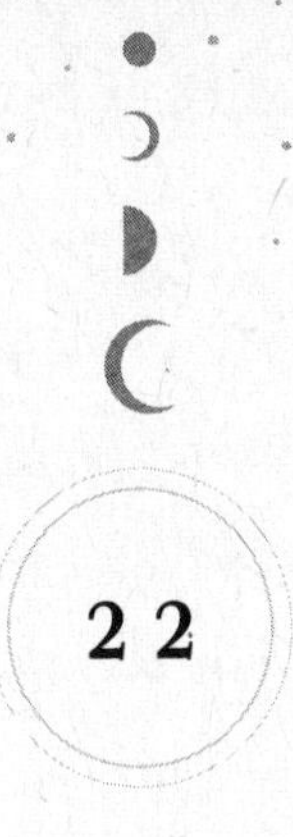

22

THE PROPHECY

No—not vanished. Vesper had made the Calavera so small, they could fit in a fishbowl.

And that was exactly where she put them. Engle watched, eye almost pressed to the glass, as the Calavera sailed the seas within the bowl, complete with tiny islands. They shot a cannon right at him—and it bounced off of the glass in a pathetic thump. Tiny yells roared from inside. Engle grinned wickedly, taunting them.

"No chance of them ever rising again," Tor said. Engle had agreed to keep the pirates at his house, locked in the orb.

The Calavera were gone.

Estrelle was safe.

Once the ice had started to crack, his mother had moved her people to the nearby Troll Tunnels—with plenty of light.

They had planned to go to the friendly Cristal Town for refuge, if the Calavera had succeeded in taking the village.

Luckily, that hadn't been necessary.

A chill slithered across Tor's shoulders as he wondered what would have happened if they had been just a few minutes late.

What would have happened if the Calavera captain and spectral had gotten the pearl? He had seen its power firsthand—wielded by a villain; it could have meant the end of Emblem Island altogether.

The pearl had been more useful than they could have imagined. After shrinking the Calavera, Vesper had used its power to shield Estrelle's coast, enchanting the waters to block danger. She had shifted the current, so it didn't lead directly to the village, and created special whirlpools just outside of its borders, that would only appear in the face of danger. Though they had stopped the deadly pirates, there were surely many more perils to be endured.

Vesper had also used the pearl and its power over the sea to cloak Swordscale once more, healing the safeguard the Calavera had destroyed.

"We'll be off then," Captain Forecastle said, wincing a bit as he stood. Mrs. Herida had healed his wound, but told him he needed bed rest for at least a week. It didn't seem as though the pirate would be following those orders, however, as he hobbled toward the door.

"Where are you going?" Engle asked, frowning.

Captain Forecastle smiled down at him. "We think we'll go try to find Bluebraid and her crew," he said. Melda blinked at him, surprised. He shrugged. "Nearly dying puts things in perspective. We'd like to take a crack at breaking her curse."

With a final nod at Engle and promise to all of them that they would meet again, the pirate left.

Vesper was standing in the center of Tor's house, staring at the tree trunk that stood in his living room. He supposed she hadn't ever seen a tree before she had washed ashore. "I'll be going as well," she said quietly.

Engle approached her first. "Thanks for the snacks," he said. "And also, for saving us...a few times. Definitely makes up for the times you almost got us killed." He tucked the Calavera fish tank under his arm, the water sloshing violently from side to side, then waved goodbye.

Melda stepped up to the waterbreather, her expression grave. "I'm sorry," she said. "For not trusting you. And...for everything else."

Vesper lifted a shoulder. "You were right not to," she said.

"Here." Melda pulled a gift from her pocket. "To match your hair." It was a silver ribbon.

Vesper blinked down at it for far too long. “Thank you,” she said softly.

Tor led her out of his house. A few people were in the streets now, only vaguely aware of how close they had been to losing everything they had known.

Like Vesper, who had lost so much.

Tor offered to see her back to the sea, and they walked to the beach in silence, each lost in their own thoughts. It had been the longest day of Tor’s life. Though Estrelle was always warm, he still felt shards of ice in his chest.

They reached sand, and Vesper turned to him. “I don’t think the prophecy was ever about you,” she said.

He hadn’t expected that. “What do you mean?”

“I’m the one who ripped the paper, and I knew what it meant when I saw the words: *Your quest will prove useless, and one of you will perish*.” Her breath was shaky. “I knew it was meant for me... *My* quest to save my brother would prove useless.” The last word cracked, and she looked to her feet, tears spilling freely. “I knew when it said one of us would die, it was either him or me.”

She took a deep breath, filling the entirety of her lungs with air. When she breathed out, her shoulders shook with a silent sob. It took a few minutes for her to meet his gaze again.

“I know it was cruel not to tell you. I could see that the

prophecy weighed heavily on you and your friends. But I just hoped it was wrong. Speaking the truth of it would have felt like fate was locked in place, like I couldn't change it..."

"That's why you took the skull," Tor said softly.

Vesper nodded. "I used up every inch of its paper tongue, hoping the prophecy would change." She turned to face the endless horizon. "But it never did."

She took Tor's hand. In it, she placed the pearl; they had agreed to hide it somewhere no one else could find. It was Tor's job to get it there. She added the anchor, attached to the Night Witch's ship, no bigger than his thumb.

Before she could hand him the sundrop salmon scale too, he stopped her. "We want you to have it," he said. "To rebuild Swordscale to what it once was."

Vesper bowed her silver head in thanks. The last of her tears fell, and Tor watched her expression transform. She held her head high. Her shoulders rolled back. Her eyes narrowed. "I told you that I came here because I had seen you before. And I knew you could help me. Thank you for proving me right." She closed his hand with her own, trapping the charms inside. "Thank you...for being a friend."

With a final nod, the silver-haired waterbreather disappeared into the sea.

Lune

One of Estrelle's original charms was a moon. She gave it to a girl named Lune, who became her closest friend.

With her moon emblem, Lune found she could control water with just her movements. She could curve it in the air in wide streaks, like a whip. She could make whirlpools, with half a thought. She could tame a storm or make it rain.

One day, far out into the sea, she created a wave as tall as a mountain, just to test her abilities, just to see how big she could make it.

Little did she know, a ship sailed not far. It tore the vessel in half, and all were dead before Lune realized what she had done.

For years, she refused her gifts, believing them a curse. She moved far into Emblem Island, and lived in isolation, tormented by the guilt of the lives lost because of her carelessness.

Then war came. And she was forced out of solitude.

Estrelle needed her.

So Lune made a promise: she would work to master her gift, to wield it with such precision that she would never make a mistake again.

Lune learned to control every inch and stitch of her abilities, practicing each day from dawn to dusk, perfecting her movements and technique. She became one of Estrelle's greatest warriors and saved thousands of innocents.

For the rest of her life, she lived on a ship, where water was always nearby.

But, ultimately, it was in the water where she died.

23

PURPLE FLAMES

Tor gripped the teleport's coin, falling forward as he landed. The wind howled in his ears as he gritted his teeth against the throbbing between his bones and stood.

Before him sat the Night Witch's castle. He took a step toward it, and all of its lights flickered on. Expecting him.

The door opened as he neared. A fire lit when he entered, warming him from the cliff's chill. He had the pearl in his pocket.

They had agreed that this place, guarded by the darkness of the Shadows and the Night Witch's enchantments, would be the only location where they could keep the Pirate's Pearl from ending up in the spectral's hands. Its power was too great to keep anywhere else; they had seen its potential first-hand, thanks to Vesper.

He climbed the staircase, and a light pattering of rain

began to thrum against the castle's glass ceiling. Just like before, a thread of power led him forward, down an empty hall, past dozens of shut doors and through an arch that led to another staircase, one that curved. He followed it until he reached the library, full of miniature enchantments.

It had felt like an eternity since the last time he had stood here with Vesper, who had been a complete stranger. A stranger who had ended up being their savior.

It was here that he had told Vesper about his powers and how much he resented them.

He still did, but things were different now. Whether or not Tor wanted the Night Witch's powers made no difference. He wished more than anything the Night Witch had chosen someone else, but his fate had been sealed, and, just like the blood queen had told him, there was no escaping it.

Tor placed the anchor, attached to the miniature *Cloudcaster*, on the shelf. He was surprised at the pang of sadness he felt, leaving it behind. The pearl went next to it.

His task completed, he left the library and turned down the corridor, ready to teleport back home.

But something made him stop.

He followed the tug down the corridor, and soon, he was in a hall with storytelling tapestries, the characters glancing at him briefly before returning to their enactments. He traveled deeper and deeper into the castle, the walls thicker than they were near its entrance, the stone older, as if the Night Witch's castle had been built over time, over and around itself, new layers added over the centuries.

It was enormous, so big that Tor thought to himself he could live in its walls for a hundred years without discovering every room. As the floor dipped, he wondered if the castle was built into the other side of the cliff or even below the rock.

He reached a door. Tall and sturdy, made from a single slab of stone. When he opened it, a fireplace in its corner lit in blue flame.

It flickered wildly, crackling and hissing. Tor knelt before it, and, without waiting to wonder if it would hurt, reached a hand inside.

His fingers grasped something solid, buried within the ashes. He pulled it from the blue flames in a flash. It was a journal.

He opened it and then nearly dropped it.

It was *her* journal. The Night Witch's.

Tor flipped through the pages, wondering why she would want him to have it, until he saw something that made him stop dead.

A drawing of purple flames, just like the ones he now wore on his wrist. With a warning.

Dread pooled in his stomach. And Tor realized there was much more to learn about the Night Witch's powers—and his.

ACKNOWLEDGMENTS

Writing the Emblem Island books is an adventure—and I'm on it, just like you, reader. Unlike any other stories I've told, these seem to unfold themselves, without much prodding from me. Soon, I'm left with characters that have minds of their own and places I desperately want to visit. But it doesn't end there. My first draft only turns into what you have read because of my incredible editor, Annie Berger, who has believed in this world from the start and always knows how to make the story better—thank you for everything. Thank you to my publisher, Sourcebooks, who delivers the most amazing covers, and has an incredible team I love to work with. A huge thank you to Heather Moore, who definitely has a marketing emblem and who I'm glad to have in my corner. Special thanks also to Cassie Gutman, Ashlyn Keil, Katie Stutz, Lizzie

Lewandowski, Caitlin Lawler, and Valerie Pierce. And to my incredible team, Eric Greenspan, Laura Bradford, Michelle Weiner, and Berni Barta.

Thank you to my family, who has put up with me on my own wild adventure. My mom, Claudy, who has always believed in me, and is the reason I've made my dreams a reality. My dad, Keith, who taught me that the harder you work, the luckier you get, and is the funniest person I know. My twin sister, Daniella, the second funniest, who read my first books, and didn't tell me they were terrible—I'm so proud of you. My love, Rron, who is unbelievably supportive, and keeps me smiling every day—I love you. My grandma, Rose, who ignited my passion for storytelling. My grandpa, who doesn't say much, but is the wisest person I know. My aunt, Angely, who has given me some of my best memories, and my uncle Carlos. JonCarlos and Luna, my star and moon—I hope you read and love these books one day, because they're for you. My early reader, Sean. My aunt Maureen and uncle Julio. Leo the poodle, for being so cute.

And thank you, reader—here's to another adventure.

ABOUT THE AUTHOR

Alex Aster is a graduate of the University of Pennsylvania, where she majored in English with a concentration in creative writing. The Emblem Island series is inspired by the Latin American myths her Colombian grandmother told her as a child before bedtime. She lives in New York. Explore the world of Emblem Island at asterverse.com.